Murder in China Red

In what little night light reached the doorway, the gun glinted like a small caliber, most likely a .22; probably a Beretta. Chinaman remembered hearing of one private detective taken out of action for over a month by a teenage girl firing "only" a .22 caliber. At close range, a well-aimed .22 caliber round was more than sufficient to take one out of action permanently.

Chinaman did his best to smile. He hoped it was a disarming one. "Evening, ma'am. I'm here to see Ms. Rita Cesar." Chinaman had always believed there were two types of people in this world: those who have had to make conversation while a gun was pointing at them and those who haven't. He was certain that those who had shared the experience would appreciate how little quaver had crept into his voice. He had smiled his best smile, he had spoken politely and he had even remembered to use the liberated form of address for a woman. Yet, despite all that, the gun still pointed exactly where it had before he'd spoken.

Also by Dean Barrett

Hangman's Point – A Novel of Hong Kong
Mistress of the East – A Novel of China
Kingdom of Make-Believe – A Novel of Thailand
Memoirs of a Bangkok Warrior – A Novel of Thailand

Dean Barrett

Murder
in
China Red

VILLAGE EAST BOOKS
NEW YORK

Published in the United States by
Village East Books, Countryside, #520, 8775 20th Street,
Vero Beach, Fl. 32966 USA

E-mail: villageeast@hotmail.com

Web site:
http://www.angelfire.com/de/YumCha/Mysteries.html

ISBN: 0-9661899-4-9

Printed in Thailand by Allied Printing

Cover and layout design:
Robert Stedman Pte. Ltd., Singapore

All of the characters in this novel are fictitious.
Any similarity to real persons, living or dead,
is purely coincidental.

Barrett, Dean.
    Murder in China Red / by Dean Barrett. -- 1st ed.
    p. cm.
    LCCN 2001096014
    ISBN 0-9661899-4-9

    1. Private investigators--New York (State)--New York
--Fiction. 2. New York (N.Y.)--Fiction. 3. Chinese
Americans--Fiction. 4. Mystery fiction.   I. Title.

PS3552.A7337R44 2002   813'.54
                QBI33-164

The coffins were beautifully varnished with the highest quality of red pigment, composed of an important ore of mercury (a sulfide of the metal known in the West as Chinese red or vermilion). It was said the one varnishing was not enough; the oftener the coffin was varnished with the pigment, the better it would preserve the corpse.

A Chinese Childhood   Chiang Yee

DAY ONE

1

THE man lay on his stomach. Snoring. Both arms raised above his head wrapped around the pillow. The hairy, trim body now dressed only in blue boxer shorts.

Judy came back out from the bathroom, wrapped herself in a fluffy gold-trimmed China red hotel robe and sat in a chair near the bed. She lit up a cigarette and observed him. His snoring grew louder. Almost rhythmic. He had been good in bed. One of the best. She should know. Since she'd first experienced sex with two brothers from Bayou Cane at 15 and taken home the dirty ten dollar bill one of them had tucked into her bra, she'd learned how to make money when she needed it.

She exhaled swirls of blue smoke and thought of the men she'd had. Only one had ever made her feel anything special and that one had even been better than this. Chinaman. Well, not better exactly. But Chinaman had a sense of humor and this one didn't. Sometimes in bed Chinaman made her laugh so much she couldn't perform. He had to get her horny all over again. But that was different. That wasn't business. Besides, Chinaman was sexy; this guy wasn't — just good in bed. Good in a technical way — like most Germans. A little rough, maybe. But that might have been the whiskey. Whatever, it hadn't affected his performance. She only hoped he'd stay asleep a while longer; she had a job to do.

She checked his shirt pocket. Even the cuffs. Nothing. In the pockets of his neatly pressed suit trousers she found six twenty-dollar bills and two fives; three quarters and a dime; and a set of keys with a round piece of plastic attached. Inside the plastic was a condom. The plastic read:

IN CASE OF EMERGENCY
BREAK GLASS

Male humor. And that was it.

She could hear a bellboy passing by in the hallway whistling "Summertime." She knew who it was because that's what he always whistled whenever she and a client took a room. Wasn't that just like a New Yorker. Whistling "Summertime" in the icy grip of winter in mid-town Manhattan. Then again maybe he'd come from some spot on the globe where it really was summertime.

Judy put out her cigarette and stared at the man on the bed. He was lost in the depths of post-sexual slumber. She reflected that she was getting good sex in a perfectly appointed room of the New York Palace hotel. And getting paid for it. Not bad. She'd come a long way from her Louisiana days as the daughter of a dirt-poor sweet potato farmer.

She reached for the suit jacket. Midnight blue. Pinstripe. Silk-and-wool blend. "F. Tripler." Nice. The breast pocket was empty. One pocket held a neatly folded tissue and a comb with a tooth missing. The other held a Waterman pen. She found a glass case in the inside pocket. Reading glasses. When she tried them on the room blurred only slightly: The gold crowns on the China red wallpaper looked more like McDonald's arches.

She took the glasses off and then hesitated while the man's snoring stopped then started again. In the pocket with the glasses was a nearly empty pack of Lucky Strike filters and a matchbook printed "Cafe Des Artistes" in gold letters. She used one of his matches to light up one of his cigarettes. Then she lay the cigarette across the hotel ashtray and lifted his leather card holder from his other inside pocket. She glanced again at the sleeping man, his form lit only by the light from the bathroom, and then silently began shuffling the plastic: Deutsche Bank A.G., American Express gold and a personal banking card from Dresdner A.G. All made out to one "Hans Schrieber."

Now the paper: A Berlin health club card. A London video club card. An international driver's license. In eight languages, no less. The man looked younger in the picture: shorter hair. No mustache. Two genuine forty-five dollar apiece tickets to "Phantom of the Opera;" Orchestra. Center. Row six.

A folded hundred dollar bill. And that was it. No photos of the little woman, the kids, the dog, the vacation house, nothing. She picked up his silk Paul Stuart power necktie with the little yellow diamonds against a blue background and checked the lining. Nothing. She even looked into his black oxfords. Still nothing. She carefully put everything back in place and walked silently on bare feet to the chair near the door.

Judy slid the man's kidskin gloves over her hands. Made her think of O.J. Anyway, no secret compartments there. She removed the gloves and turned her attention to his topcoat. Town coat, really. Navy blue, wool, double-breasted. Her search of inner and outer pockets yielded a complimentary guide to Midtown theaters, a handkerchief, a small tin of Anacin, a box of throat lozenges and a roll-on stick for chapped lips. If nothing else, Hans Schrieber was well prepared for the winter weather. But if he was worried about the freezing temperatures, he certainly wasn't worried about money: He hadn't raised an eyebrow at paying $235 plus tax for a double room for a few relaxing hours with a woman he'd just met in the hotel bar. What was it he had said: His place would be "inconvenient." Probably married. What the hell. Luxury hotel rooms were fine with her.

Judy lay the coat neatly across the chair, went into the bathroom and quietly closed the door. She stared back at the face in the mirror. She observed the lines about her mouth and eyes as she grinned. The crow's feet were definitely there but not too deep and not particularly noticeable. Not bad. Anyway, they could still be called "smile" lines, couldn't they?

Damn! Her mascara had streaked. She'd have to reapply it. She dipped a Kleenex into a jar of cleansing cream, then wiped off the makeup under her eyes. She tried to concentrate on what her contact in the bar had said: Hans Schrieber would have some documents on him. Three, maybe four. All they needed to know were the dates at the top of each one. For this they had paid her money. A lot of money. Up front. Industrial espionage for fun and profit. As American as Apple pie. Just check the documents. But there were no documents. Which meant that something had gone wrong. Or something was already wrong.

If there had been a foul-up and the man had stashed the documents somewhere, then it was all right. She would simply let them know and part company. Bad luck for them. She did all she could. They'd used her services before; they knew how good she was. If he'd had any documents she would have found them. But if they had known all along that there were no documents, then why had they paid her to sleep with him?

She turned on the cold water, and began to dab anti-wrinkle cream around her eyes. Something Chinaman had always kidded her about. Said too much of that stuff would make her frigid. What was it he had said the Chinese call 'crow's feet'? Oh, yeah, 'fish tails.' Sounded a hell of a lot better than 'crow's feet.'

Chinaman. God, she missed him. She'd already made up her mind that the time had come to let him in on her clandestine activities over a drink. What was it he liked? Black Russian. A mean drink if ever there was one. He'd make jokes about the Yellow Peril consuming Black Russians. And he could handle no more than two without getting talkative. Well, not talkative really. Just not so damned tight-lipped. How many months since she'd seen him? Months, hell, a year. That's New Yorkers for you. They live in the same city and can't bother to call each other. Well, all right, Chinaman. Prepare for a call from yours truly before the week is out.

She reapplied mascara and inspected the face in the mirror. It wouldn't launch a thousand ships but it could still get attention. That and her well exercised body was still worth $235 plus New York City and state tax plus her own tip to men like Hans Schrieber.

A noise in the bedroom. Two noises really. Like a door closing and a kind of whoosh. Or maybe a thump. Hans was up

and about. Maybe even horny again. She could fix that. She'd
been good at fixing that kind of thing for years. She often wondered
if she was so good at turning men on precisely because she herself
almost never got turned on.

She turned off the water. She drew the robe around her and
retied the sash, then opened the door and stepped into the bedroom.
At the sight of the two men, she probably let out a small scream. She
wasn't sure because, at first, it was more confusing than frightening.
It was almost like observing a carefully staged studio setting of two
doctors looking upon their bed-ridden patient with concern and
distress. Like somebody was shooting a photograph for a doctor's
calendar maybe. Or a Norman Rockwell illustration of two caring
rural doctors and their patient. A sure bet for the next *Saturday Evening
Post* cover. One man — wavy white hair over a well-sculpted, craggy
face — standing beside the bed and one — a crescent of hair away
from total baldness — at the foot of the bed. Both well-dressed.
Suit-and-tie. Respectable. Professional bedside manner.

They moved only their heads to stare at her. Body posture still
suggesting deep concern for the patient. The man on the bed — the
second greatest lay of her life — no longer snoring but still asleep.
No, not asleep. Not with that ugly, unauthorized opening at the
back of the head and the red mess splattered across the pillow. Soaking
it, really. Good thing for them Leona Helmsley had sold the damn
hotel to Arabs or somebody. Would she have been pissed.

The man nearest her, at the foot of the bed, raised his eyebrows
and gave her a kind of apologetic shrug, then raised his arm. Which
brought the barrel of his silencer-equipped semi-automatic pistol in
line with her smile lines. As she threw herself behind the chair she
heard another strange sound. Not unlike the one she'd heard when
she was in the bathroom. And now she knew. The sound of a gun's
discharge when dampened by a silencer. Whatdayaknow. Live and learn.

Another sound. Something forcefully smashing into the chair,
grazing her ear. All right, then. The chair. Throw it at the balding
man, then rush him quickly enough to grab his wrist before he can

fire again. And, whatdayaknow? It worked. Well, her robe fell open
revealing far too much but she let it go. With the other hand she even
managed to rake his face with her nails.

While she grappled with one man, the man beside the bed lifted his
own gun and pointed it at her. No shrug this time. No apology. But no
anger either. Just business. She twisted behind the man with the bleeding
face and began screaming. She was about to take a breath to scream again
when the man closest to her brought the gun down hard, cutting her nose
and smashing her collarbone. Blood spurted onto her China red robe.
She felt his wrist slip from her grasp. The room slipping from her vision.
Legs buckling. Cheek colliding against carpet. Now both men had a clear
shot. She'd been with two men at the same time before. Lots of times.
But never like this. She couldn't seem to lift her head so she rolled her body
ever-so-slowly backward until the men appeared in her line of vision. They
didn't look like doctors anymore.

The body doesn't suddenly shut down. No way. That's what a
second year med student she'd gone to bed with once told her. He liked to
talk shop even in bed. Even while he was doing the nasty. That's what he'd
called lovemaking: 'the nasty'. You'd have to blow your brains out for the
body to shut down suddenly, he'd said. Or get shot right in the head. Even
then, the heart would most likely keep pumping for a few minutes. Problem
is, it's pumping the blood *out* of the system. Like, the plug's been pulled,
and the heart's now working against itself. A brainless muscle if ever there
was one. Then the body temperature falls and the system begins shutting
down. Clinical death. Biological death. End of Story.

Judy had asked why some people die with their eyes open and some
die with their eyes shut. He had said either was acceptable. God didn't
care one way or the other. But then he'd added that the guy with his eyes
open was probably more dead than the guy with his eyes shut.

"More dead?" Judy had asked. The guy had just thrust his tongue
into her ear farther than Judy had thought humanly possible, then laughed.

Judy died with her eyes open.

★

DAY TWO

2

EXCEPT for the bodies, the narrow Beijing street was deserted. The boy was alone. Unarmed. Running. Suddenly, dozens of furious people, faces distorted with hatred, were chasing him. People who had once been his neighbors. People who had played elephant chess with his father and prepared special dumplings for his mother's birthday. The red bands on their arms read: "*Hung Wei Ping*" — Red Guards of China. Across a roof. Bright sun. Glare. A rock hit his head and he stumbled and fell. He felt hands grab him. One of those nearest him blew a loud whistle, and as the beating began, the whistle transformed itself into a ringing phone. The insistent rings pulled Chinaman out of harm's way with bovine slowness. He struggled to cradle the phone to his ear. He could feel his heart still trying to break out of his chest. His voice was thick. "Yeah."

Joseph Abrams, Manhattan's Chief of Detectives, spoke in his long perfected lion-toying-with-its-prey voice. More of a snarl: "Out of breath, are we, Chinaman?"

"Not quite, Chief. One day, maybe."

"One day, Chinaman."

The malevolent mood of the nightmare clung to him like a hangover. His hand shook. His palms were wet. "Until then?"

"Your gun permit."

"What about it?"

"I think we could have a problem with it."

Chinaman reached for a cigarette. Cops using the conditional tense always spooked him. Especially Homicide cops. Especially

Abrams. He searched for the right response. 'Too many polysyllabic words in it for you to understand, Chief?' No, Chinaman crossed that one firmly out of his mind before it could escape. He said, "Expiration date's a long way off. I got—"

"What you got is a 'full carry' permit, Chinaman. That's for private eyes who carry a full load of cases. Obviously, that doesn't pertain to you. The way I hear it your last case was over the day the Dodgers left Brooklyn."

"I tracked them to L.A.," Chinaman said. "Then the trail got cold."

"And a 'full carry' permit is for businessmen who carry bags full, you see what I mean. Every day. Suitcases full of cash. Bags full of precious gems. Somethin' like that."

Chinaman could hear ancient typewriters clacking in the background. Computers must be down again. He could almost see Abrams over the phone: Chair tilted back. Feet up on the desk. Phone stuck to his shoulder like a pirate's parrot. Ashtray overflowing. A cup of coffee in one fleshy hand. A copy of Chinaman's gun permit in the other. Chinaman had the sudden image of Abrams as a tubby child concentrating the sun's rays through a magnifying glass to fry an ant. Chinaman said nothing.

Abrams spoke into the silence. "You protecting something valuable like that, Chinaman?"

An estimated two million guns in New York City and, outside of the police department, only about 50,000 legally registered. But Chief Abrams had a problem not with the unregistered million and two-thirds. Only with his. Chinaman wondered if 'Persecute P.I. Day' should be declared a national holiday. Maybe it already was.

He threw his feet to the floor and looked about the disheveled bedroom of his East Village apartment. Dying snake plant. Broken humidifier. Wall calendar with Chinese characters beneath a drawing of the Eight Immortals. A woman's undergarments lying across a wicker laundry basket like beached mackerel. His unshaved face in a bureau mirror streaked with dust. His eyes focused on the .38 lying beside its holster. The highly polished black oxide finish glittered in the light of the early morning sun like a golden plumed bird fresh from a bath about to enter its nest. He felt a sudden inspiration. "The gun itself."

"What about it?"

"It's old. I think it might have antique value."

Abrams let four, maybe five, seconds pass. "So you're sayin' you gotta carry the gun — to protect the gun."

"Something like that."

"I think you meant that to be funny. So why ain't I laughin'?"

Because you've got the sense of humor of a war memorial, Chinaman thought. Chinaman said nothing. Outside the bedroom window, bare snow-lined branches of a ginkgo tree rapped nervously against the glass of his third-story apartment. Just inside the window, an early model radiator released intermittent hisses of steam. Rap. Hiss. Rap. Hiss. Rap. Hiss. Rap. It reminded Chinaman of John Philip Souza's marches. No. More like the heroic beat of Chairman Mao's 'Sailing the Seas depends on the Helmsman.' But a former girlfriend had complained that sleeping in his bedroom made her feel as if she were trapped inside a low budget horror movie. And, with hindsight, that's how Chinaman had felt when as a young boy he'd been trapped inside China's Great Cultural Revolution. Rap. Hiss. Rap.

"Thing is, I figure somebody — maybe even a friend of yours in License Division — must have given you a break. I won't even try to think why. But I want you to know that — irregardless of who the fuck it was — if I feel like it, if something you do or don't do pisses me off, *anything at all*, I'll have your permit revoked. Revoked so that when I'm finished you won't be able to carry a water pistol. You won't be able to point your pisser without checking in with me first. Do we understand each other now?"

Chinaman weighed the pros and cons of pointing out to the Chief of Detectives in Manhattan that there was no such word as "irregardless." That he was most likely mixing up "irrespective" with "regardless." It was an easy decision. "Perfectly, Chief." Chinaman reflected that the only thing worse than an overbearing mother-in-law was an unforgiving ex-father-in-law.

Abrams seemed to pause. Chinaman had the impression of someone aiming a .44 Magnum at him over the phone. "Meet me at the Medical Examiner's office in one hour."

As the sudden loud click burrowed its way painfully into his inner ear, Chinaman spoke to the dial tone in mandarin Chinese: "My best to the family."

★

3

THE man with the Afro slouched behind the information desk didn't quite manage to stifle a yawn as he handed Chinaman a visitor's badge. He pointed sleepily at something behind him. Chinaman glanced at a notice above the desk:

All law enforcement personnel are
required to display their shield

"I'm not with the police."

The man rubbed his eyes and opened them wider. When he realized Chinaman's confusion, he pointed to a door visible through a glass wall. "Room 106."

Chinaman glanced at the open door and the slice of sickly yellow wall visible inside the room. He passed through the inner doorway, turned right and then left, and stepped into room 106. It was a small carpeted room with two couches, several chairs, one table and a desk. As if someone couldn't decide if it should serve as a lounge or a classroom. The pale yellow of the walls was broken up by a clock, notices against smoking and eating, and an incongruous mounted poster of a dispirited looking Albert Einstein. The clock was several minutes fast and the droopy, sad, basset hound Einstein eyes stared out in sympathy with all those bereaved. Nothing in the room was out of the ordinary. Except for a large brown envelope on the table beside a lamp.

He stood briefly at a window and tilted the venetian blinds upward to watch black-bottomed clouds race each other to block out the sun. He adjusted the blinds to a horizontal position. Across 30th Street, a brick building was fronted by an imposing, prison-

like, wrought iron fence. A pair of men's trousers impaled on a
picket's spike waved limply in the wind like the tattered banner of
a defeated army.

He sat in a chair away from the envelope and, ignoring the
'No Smoking' sign, lit up a cigarette. He looked around the small
room and tried to think about other things. The trip to Taiwan
he'd been promising himself. It had been nearly a decade since
he'd been stationed in Taipei as a linguist attached to the army's
Criminal Investigation Division and he damn well missed that
island. He remembered his chagrin at having to improve his
Chinese characters when he'd first arrived — the 'short forms'
he'd learned while growing up on the mainland were seldom
employed on more traditional Taiwan. Indeed, most Taiwanese
considered 'simplified' Chinese characters an abomination. So
had his scholar father, but spies in their Beijing neighborhood
made certain his father had little chance to train him in writing
traditional characters.

He thought of Taiwan until he admitted to himself that he
was thinking of Taiwan to avoid thinking of the envelope on the
table. He forced himself to stare straight at it. Rectangular, plain
and ordinary — so why did looking at it chill his bones.

He felt as if he was in the presence of a Pandora's Box cleverly
disguised as a harmless brown envelope. Had it been left there
because Abrams thought he would open it while he was waiting?

As soon as he thought of Abrams, he heard the man's footsteps
— no-nonsense, aggressive, loud. It reminded him of the footsteps
he'd heard on his ninth birthday. When the bespectacled and
uniformed Chinese Communist Party members came to his house
in northern Beijing. The men who had once been his father's
colleagues in the university's Department of Literature. The men
who now accused his father of teaching his son the language of
the imperialist enemy — English. That was shortly before his
father had been forcibly marched away by a fanatical gang of
teenage Red Guards shouting Mao's slogans as they forced a dunce

cap upon him and pummeled and kicked him for being a "right opportunist." Before his father's ancestral shrine had been smashed, his library burned, his "bourgeois" pets destroyed and his family given notice that the house would be confiscated. Before his mother had been told to collect his father's body. Before his mother, in her grief, torment and despair, took her own life. Red China's Great Cultural Revolution. Millions dead and millions more emotionally scarred for life. Chinaman had suffered far less than his parents. But it had aged him in ways he didn't even like to think about.

Abrams walked in and, for just a second, hesitated. He ran one hand through a head of hair in an early stage of male pattern baldness, then sat heavily opposite Chinaman. His bear of a body was covered by an ill-fitting brown suit and a loud chartreuse tie which needed straightening. The outline of a 9-millimeter pistol in a shoulder holster lent his suit jacket a rumpled, wrinkled appearance, as if he'd just gotten off a long, uncomfortable flight.

His face was ruddy, rough-hewn and perpetually in need of a shave. And it reflected the same disheveled exhaustion as his apparel. A plethora of wrinkles bracketed his mouth and others bulged above his shirt collar. The winter chill had reddened his nose and imbued his cheeks with a facade of glowing health. Only the clear, green, alert eyes, ensconced beneath heavy black brows gave a clue to the man's intelligence. Over the years, Chinaman had often seen them flare at him in anger or narrow at him in menace. Sometimes unfairly. But he had learned to respect the resourceful and perceptive mind behind them.

Chinaman tried to recall if he'd ever seen Abrams smile. Certainly not at the wedding. Abrams had known with a daddy's unerring instinct that on his best day Chinaman wasn't good enough for his only daughter and, hell, didn't events prove it?

Abrams glanced at the poster of Einstein as if the scientist were an intruder; then, apparently deciding against ordering the poster out of the room, lowered his eyes. He withdrew a handkerchief from his overcoat, blew his nose loudly, and shoved it back into his coat pocket. He seemed to hesitate before speaking, as if trying to find the right words. It was the first time Chinaman had seen Abrams attempt to show consideration for another's feelings while on duty. Which only confirmed Chinaman's suspicion that the meeting in the morgue was ominous.

Abrams picked up the envelope and stared at it. Then he placed it flat on the table. He made his large hands into large fists and placed them on the envelope. "You read the *Post* this morning?"

"Nope. And I don't really give a damn how the Knicks made out at the Garden, either."

Abrams ignored the flippancy. Another ominous sign. "Listened to the radio?"

"Nope...What is it, Chief? The NYPD got you working sociological surveys, now?"

Abrams slid the envelope over to him. "I think you better take a look at these first."

"First?"

"Then we'll go downstairs...if you want to."

Chinaman slid the color Polaroids out of the envelope without quite looking at them. On normal, ordinary days, for normal, ordinary people, color Polaroids conjured up images of family get-togethers, Junior's graduation, sister's wedding, and highlights of happy vacations. Color Polaroids in room 106 meant only one thing: A corpse had been photographed. A corpse needed identification. Easier on those left behind to identify the remains of a loved one by photographs in room 106 — than by looking directly at a body lying on a metal gurney two flights down. Especially when the familiar features of their loved one had been horribly disfigured by a knife, transformed beyond recognition in a fire, or mutilated beyond belief in a traffic accident. Still, it was one step removed from the actual presence of death. And most of those left behind were wise enough to be grateful for small favors.

Chinaman let his eyes focus on the top photograph. His mind held back as a swimmer might wait to see if the water was warm enough before proceeding farther. A man's face. Chinaman inwardly breathed a sigh of relief. The man was a total stranger. Not bad looking. Mid-30s. Lots of wavy black hair. High cheek bones. Asleep. But, whoever, a total stranger. Chinaman shuffled the top photograph to the back and looked at the next photograph. Uh, oh. A rear view shot. Something had been done to the back of his head. Whatever it was it had earned him a one-way trip to the morgue.

Third photograph. Focus the eyes. So far, so good. Now focus the mind. Mind doesn't want to stay focused. Suddenly rebellious. Hey, cool it, Chinaman. Just look at the picture of the pretty lady. Asleep. He had seen her asleep many times over the years. Not lately. Before. Mainly up in Connecticut. Sexiest student any young Creative Writing instructor could ever wish for. But she didn't have that hole in her forehead then. Or the ugly crease in her nose. Aren't you forgetting something, Chinaman? Huh? Oh, right. Better start breathing again. Force your emotions to loosen their grip. Little by little. Keep your systems working. And, lest you forget, Abrams is watching. Noting every reaction. Don't give the bastard satisfaction. Slow it down. That's it. Tune out for a minute. What was it you used to tell Judy when yet another gray Connecticut winter morning had gotten to her? 'Nothing is so bad but that thinking makes it so.' O.K. So now you know. Judy's dead. The woman who may have gotten the closest to you of anyone alive. The frenzied passion, the intimate — Hey! Fella! She's asleep forever. You're a big, strong man: Deal with it.

O.K. Check the next photograph. Side view. Hey, kid, wake up — time for class. You call me 'kid' again, Chinaman, and I'll belt yah. Next. What's this? Somebody mixed in a wound chart. By mistake? Plain outline of human forms printed on a piece of plain white paper. Front and rear. Horizontal and vertical.

Almost like a kid's drawings. Unembellished outline of a face —
front view, right side view, left side view. No hair on the head or
at the crotch. Everything unisex these days; even wound charts.
But tiny eyebrows and no eyelashes gave the drawing's childlike
face a look of astonishment. Chinaman reflected that every wound
chart had exactly the same face with the same look of astonishment:
Hey, man, I was *living*! What the hell happened? Simple horizontal
dotted line across the eyebrows and a small hole drawn above it in
the forehead and a short solid line connecting them with the
notation "1/4 inches."

And that's it. O.K. Listen carefully. Three priorities: Keep
hands from shaking. No tears. Make Abrams speak first. You
can do it. If you pull yourself together. Chinaman forced himself
to slip the photographs back into the envelope, fold his hands on
the table and stare at Abrams without any visible display of
emotion.

It took everything he had.

★

4

CHINAMAN set his whiskey glass near the edge of the coffee table and unfolded the three sheets of paper. On the first page, above the double-spaced lines of type were the words:

Judy Fisher
Creative Writing
22 September 1994

A few inches to the left of her name, Chinaman had printed the letter "A" in red pencil and commented, "Excellent! You have real talent! Your writing is as lyrical and sensuous as a Tennessee William's short story."

He had found the paper a year later among some of his papers shortly after he had been fired for having an affair with a student in his Creative Writing class — Judy Fisher. Judy had always felt guilty for his dismissal. Chinaman couldn't have cared less. Based mainly on his three years in the army's CID, the college had hired Chinaman to teach courses to those majoring in Criminal Justice. His father had instilled in him a passionate love for language and literature and he had accepted the assignment to teach Creative Writing as well, but he knew he hadn't been cut out to teach it to young Connecticut yuppies. Chinaman lit another cigarette and began reading.

When I was a little girl growing up in Louisiana, my father was often out of work and we had very little money to spare for toys. I learned at an early age to amuse myself with whatever was available. And for our toy store, my father of necessity turned to nature.

In the spring my hair was covered with showy green-and-yellow, bowl-shaped flowers of the tulip tree, and in summer, red seeds of the magnolia tree decorated fruit jars glowing with lightning bugs. In the fall, the long·black pods of the catalpa tree served as weapons in unequal sword fights with my brother, and the rattle of the seeds inside the flat pods served as castanets. In late winter, my hair was decorated with the fluffy yellow balls of a sweet acacia tree.

But my most poignant memory will always be of scenes in early autumn, when my father would boost me up onto his strong shoulders, and with his huge hands firmly gripping my legs, he would carry me (laughing and excited) across a field of flowers near our house to a huge Caucasian wingnut tree. Its trunk was split and gnarled and many of its drooping branches were in easy reach of even my tiny arms.

The pendulous fruits of the tree hung nearly a foot long and looked to us children like long strings of unlit firecrackers. And, indeed, my older brother always referred to the tree as the 'firecracker tree.' The small winged nuts lining the length of the fruit were green and easily dislodged, so with my legs wrapped around my father's thickly muscled neck, and my head among the branches, I would remove the strands of fruit as carefully as if each raceme were a string of pearls, and then lower each strand into a burlap sack below held by my brother.

In the evening, my father would fill tiny jars with house-paint and I would sit on our back porch and wield a small brush to meticulously color each paired wing of each nut of each strand.

The next day, when the paint was dry, my father would expertly interweave the strands of gaudily colored fruit into a laurel for my hair, and into necklaces and bracelets. Then we would walk outside where he would pluck a rubbery, shiny, green leaf of a southern magnolia tree and stick it upright at the back of my hair as a magnificent green feather. He would then stand back and observe me as if in speechless awe. Then, with a solemnity that was rare for him, he would remind me that I was a beautiful princess and that I must never doubt that I would one day have everything I wanted. The "laurels" never lasted more than a few days; the memory will last a lifetime.

Chinaman threw the sheets of paper onto the coffee table and poured himself another large splash of Maker's Mark over his half melted ice cubes. He took a long gulp then lit another cigarette. He sat for a minute letting the Kentucky straight bourbon whiskey warm his insides and numb his grief, then picked up the college yearbook.

Raised red lettering on the white cover read, "Thames Log," and inside a circle was a representation of a lighthouse with the words, "Mitchell College, New London, Connecticut," and the Latin "scientia libertas." He opened the yearbook and flipped through the pages of graduating students, three head-and-shoulder photographs to a page, each listed alphabetically. Young, healthy faces untouched by the world stared out at him with an almost smug pride in their youth or with an easy confidence in their future.

He removed a photograph tucked between back pages of the book. He and Judy stood facing the Thames River in front of Monte Cristo cottage, Eugene O'Neill's boyhood home — the same home of unhappy memories which had provided the playwright with material for "Long Day's Journey into Night."

The day had been windy and cold, and, as he hugged her, some of Judy's long dark hair had blown across Chinaman's face. Both were laughing and clowning for the camera. Their movements had thrown them slightly out of focus.

Finally, he turned to her page: "Judith Elizabeth Fisher. 'Judy.' New Orleans, Louisiana. Liberal Arts. Our magnolia blossom from the Pelican State. Writer's Workshop, Sailing Club, Mansfield Players. Free spirit, romantic, popular, friendly, good to have around. Plans afoot to move to New York and settle down to the bohemian life of a writer. Bye, Bayou — Hello, Big Apple! Philosophy: 'The mystery of life is not a problem to be solved, but a reality to be experienced.'"

On the page facing Judy were three young men, each dressed in conservative tie and dark jacket. Above her was a woman with a winsome smile, and below her was a woman with a serious, almost solemn, stare. Each wore a string of pearls over a dark sweater. Judy had told Chinaman she thought the school "recommendation" of pearls over dark sweater for the yearbook photograph was officious and sexist. She had worn an oversized cotton turtleneck. No pearls. No winsome smile. No solemn stare.

But it wasn't simply her dress which set her apart from other women in the yearbook. Or the fact that she was a bit older. It was an intensity, an energy, a hunger for life, absolutely free of either shame or inhibition.

Chinaman turned to the back of the book to the photographs under the heading, "Spring Production — backstage: 1995." Judy stood in the wings dressed in Victorian bonnet and crinoline, about to go onstage, while an older woman frantically worked to adjust the ribbons of Judy's bonnet. Judy's face was lit up in an almost childlike grin of pure pleasure: the born actress about to give a performance.

Chinaman remembered the party after the play, and, later, the moonlit sailboat ride on the Thames River, and their passionate lovemaking on the foredeck of the boat as the mournful sounds of foghorns rolled over them.

That evening, after again making love, she had sworn to him that within three years she would get her first novel published to critical acclaim and financial success. Just three years later, almost to the day, the only book she would ever have published — a volume of short stories — hit the book stores. It was critically acclaimed, badly distributed, poorly promoted, and sank without a trace.

Over the years, Judy began to refer to the writing profession as a "sucker's bet" and her enthusiasm for spending long, solitary hours filling up blank sheets of paper in a typewriter—and then computer—began to fade.

They had both moved to New York City but kept in touch only infrequently. Chinaman was busy setting up a Private Eye business and tutoring Chinese. Judy soon met several young women — far less attractive than she — who lived extremely well by catering to the abnormal psychosexual needs of outwardly normal men. After her first "paid" date she had arrived very late at Chinaman's apartment and gotten very drunk. She'd laughed and cried, slapped him, swore at him, cursed herself, and then fell asleep in his arms. Judy's evolution from committed writer in love with literature to high class whore making love for money was complete.

The next morning when Chinaman woke up, she was gone. Her note read:

> I am what I am what I am.
> Let's just call it a smart career move.
> Please don't hate me, Chinaman.
> Love, Judy

Chinaman had met someone shortly after that and in just under a year had married her. Since then, he had seen Judy only a few times. And, with one exception, never in a bedroom. But that one exception had cost him his marriage. Judy felt both his dismissal in

Connecticut and his divorce in New York were her fault; Chinaman simply saw it as karma.

He got up and walked to the window. The temperature had risen from the early 30's to nearly 40 and the much-predicted snowstorm had very quickly turned to light rain. He looked at his watch. 4:55. It was already nearly dark. Thick streaks of pink clouds burrowed their way across a darkening blue sky. Several water tanks on top of distant roofs were silhouetted against the sky and from somewhere below great puffs of dirty-white steam billowed upward into the cold.

Chinaman thought of the woman he had first met in his class: A woman so full of lust for life and inexhaustible energy that she had overcome his carefully constructed defenses and reawakened something in him that he thought he'd lost forever. Lost to a nation gone mad with hate and fear and self-inflicted terror. But even his well-guarded emotional sanctuary had been quickly breached by Judy's vivacity and by her refusal to allow him to withdraw into himself.

Then he remembered what he had seen lying in the morgue. The warm, curvaceous body that had so often stimulated his passion lay cold, death-white, naked and, yes, repulsive. The forehead he had covered with tender kisses had been shattered, exposing skull and tissue and blood. Judy's sentient existence had been violently ended. Her personality effaced. Her spirit stilled. All neatly and clinically demonstrated by the pathologist's "wound chart."

Probably Abrams had been right. He shouldn't have gone downstairs to see her. He remembered it as if he'd been walking through a nightmare. He had just passed a tiny room crammed with stacks of plain wooden coffins when the smell hit him — the overpowering stench of formaldehyde and decomposing bodies; the partly dressed corpses lying on gurneys beneath fluorescent lighting like snowbound sun worshippers in a tanning room; the rectangular white identification tag fastened to Judy's toe by a piece of string; the metallic click when the black man in a green mask and protective clothing wheeled her back into her compartment and closed the door. The four-page autopsy report on the body of an "unknown white female" concluding death by homicide. They'd discovered Judy's identity soon enough; but, for Chinaman, the autopsy could be summed up in six words: One live round. One dead woman.

He thought for a moment of Abrams's warning not to get involved in what was a police matter. Chinaman almost smiled at that. Then he threw on a neckscarf and a long, wool coat. The coat had been a Christmas present from his ex-wife; the scarf had been a birthday present from Judy. He turned on his message machine, turned out the lights and left the apartment.

★

5

CHINAMAN stopped the cab on Madison Avenue between 50th and 51st. The driver had somehow managed to lose his way in midtown trying to find the New York Palace Hotel, a mistake which increased the fare, but Chinaman tipped him well and wished him a "Merry Christmas." The man grunted and sped off.

He turned up the collar of his coat and faced the hotel. Just above the locked gate of the courtyard dozens of yellow bulbs had been arranged to form the shape of a large crown. Inside the courtyard the branches of linden trees had been draped with orange bulbs. The courtyard itself as well as the sidewalks along Madison were deserted, and the crown and empty courtyard imbued the scene with the forlorn and slightly unreal mood of a hastily abandoned palace just before the arrival of armed and angry peasants. Chinaman reflected that with the hotel's once proud "queen" now long since departed, the mood was appropriate.

With his head down and his shoulders hunched forward against the icy wind, Chinaman rounded the corner to 50th. He quickly passed the doorman and entered the building with the determined step of a man late for an appointment. Once he reached the foyer, he sat on a cushioned circular couch not far from the glittering Baccarat chandelier and glanced at his surroundings. He'd been inside the hotel only once before to meet a friend from his army days in Taiwan. The friend had done extremely well in some kind of slightly illegal, off-shore, import-export company based in Hong Kong. They were to meet in the lobby bar but it had been after five o'clock and Chinaman had been told in no uncertain terms that he "lacked the proper attire" to enter the bar. He had suppressed his anger and they had done their drinking in his friend's room.

Chinaman glanced impatiently at his watch and continued to imitate the manner of one waiting for a tardy friend, while mentally noting the movements of bellboys and hotel security personnel. For a hotel which went to great lengths to present itself as the last word in luxury, he was surprised to see that the two hotel security men he spotted were informally dressed, one in jeans and turtleneck and the other in slacks and flannel shirt.

They stood near a wall decorated with Christmas wreaths, a display of azaleas and an armorial coat of arms the size of a wading pool. Both men leisurely gripped the walkie-talkies fastened to their belts; whatever they were discussing threatened to widen the grins on their faces into leers. They stood beneath yet another crown and their well-muscled bodies partly blocked the motto, "*Dieu et mon droit.*"

The man wearing the slacks was tall and dark and stood before a unicorn, and the man wearing jeans was heavier, sported a goatee and partly blocked a lion. Each man had unwittingly stood beside the animal he resembled, as if they too were part of the shield's escutcheon.

Women dressed in lustrous coats made from the skins of dead foxes and men dressed in overcoats of camel hair ascended the wide marble staircase and made their way to the restaurants on the floor above.

Chinaman caught the security man by the unicorn eyeing him suspiciously. No doubt had him pegged for an illegal immigrant fresh off the boat from Fujian province who needed a place to keep warm in between working two jobs to pay back the thirty thousand dollar smuggling fee. He seemed about to approach him when his walkie-talkie suddenly crackled to life. The man spoke quickly into it and the two security men walked off toward the front entrance.

Chinaman decided he'd have to do his waiting upstairs. He got up and walked to the elevator. He stepped back as two middle-aged women in black leather coats stepped out, then entered the elevator and pressed "12." He wasn't certain which aspect of the elevator was more disconcerting: The red-and-gold color scheme or the overpowering residue of expensive perfume.

He stepped out onto the 12th floor. Not far from a portrait of a Prussian grand duke in military uniform the number "12" appeared on a mirror surrounded by a laurel motif and topped by a crown. Chinaman followed the red carpet down the hallway until he reached 1204. Like the other rooms along the corridor, it had its own crown on the door. Chinaman had never slept behind a door with a crown. He wondered what Judy had thought of it.

The door also had a "Do Not Enter" sign and a police "crime scene" notice. It didn't matter. Chinaman had no intention of trying to enter the room. Abrams had placed his own homicide unit in charge of the investigation and he was satisfied that if there was anything to learn about the murder from the room itself they would have found it. He'd have to find a way to get that information later. But if Abrams was right, and the killers were professional hit men, there would be no clues in room 1204, anyway. What he had to do was to learn what anyone in the hotel had seen. If they'd talk about it.

He continued on down the hallway. He stopped before the only set of doors without imperial regalia and pushed. He had found what he was looking for. A small room most likely used by employees for their cigarette breaks. Several chairs had been piled beside a laundry chute and three vacuum cleaners lined a wall like dispirited prisoners waiting to be interrogated. Dishes with remnants of food had been removed from guests' rooms and placed beside freight elevators ready for pickup. Three wine glasses — two of them cracked — surrounded an empty bottle of Romanee-Conti. A *menage a trois* had enjoyed a passionate escapade accompanied by the best red burgundy money could buy. Some people had all the luck.

Chinaman removed a chair from the stack and placed it behind the others so that anyone entering the room wouldn't immediately spot him. He sat in the chair facing the elevator, lit a cigarette and waited. He wanted to keep his mind clear of personal emotion but memories of Judy kept crowding in. Judy clad in sexy underwear exercising to rock music inside the bedroom of his New London, Connecticut apartment; Judy strapped in her skis, sprawled helplessly against a snow-covered hillock on a New Hampshire mountain; Judy dressed in halter top and shorts bicycling through the streets of Greenwich Village. Judy laughing, crying, flirting, fighting — alive.

Fifteen minutes later, Chinaman heard voices in the hallway. Someone with a Hispanic accent was explaining something to guests checking in. Chinaman dropped his cigarette into the wine bottle and stood by the door to the hallway. When he heard the bellboy returning he opened the door and stepped out.

The boy came toward him wheeling an empty luggage rack. He glanced at Chinaman in confusion, trying to decide if he was a guest to be acknowledged or an intruder to be challenged. Finally, training overcame suspicion and he greeted Chinaman with a "Good evening, sir."

Chinaman returned the greeting and blocked his path. He held out his leather folder with his badge and photograph. "I'm a New York-licensed special investigator assigned to the double homicide in 1204. I'd like to talk to you for a few minutes if I may." As usual, Chinaman had carefully avoided saying exactly who it was who had assigned him to an investigation. Nor had he said he was a police officer. Merely implied it. He had enough problems without facing a third degree felony charge.

The boy stared blankly at Chinaman's identification. He seemed neither suspicious nor impressed, merely confused. Chinaman felt as if he was showing his identification to an inexperienced border guard who didn't know whether to salute or to shoot. The boy wore a maroon jacket with gold epaulets and the usual crown motif, well-pressed slacks and slip-on shoes. His nametag read "Francisco Sanchez." Chinaman pegged him at about 21 or 22. Sanchez spoke with a pleasant lilt and a heavy accent. "Mister, I wou' like to 'elp you but the police 'ave sealed up that room. There's no way I–"

Chinaman returned his identification to his jacket's inner pocket. "That's all right. I'm not interested in gaining access to 1204. I'm interested in speaking with anyone who might have seen the couple the night of the murder. Possibly a bellboy escorted them up or maybe they ordered something from room service."

"Freddie. He's the man you want. He tol' me the lady ordered some dessert. But I didn't escort them up. I would have if they're on this floor. But I didn't."

"You're saying they weren't on this floor."

"No. I'm saying they had no luggage."

"Is Freddie on tonight?"

"Yes, sir. Until midnight."

Chinaman pulled out a twenty dollar bill, folded it lengthwise with Andrew Jackson's face on the crease, and held it out. "I'd very much like to speak to Freddie for a few minutes, if I could. I can wait in here. He can use the freight elevator if necessary. Do you think you could arrange that? Quietly?"

The gaze of the boy held on the twenty dollar bill then glanced away. "I guess I could."

Chinaman held the bill closer to the boy. "Take it. It's yours."

Sanchez pocketed the twenty and smiled broadly. "Sure. No problem."

"One more thing. Any chance you could help me get a copy of their check-in slip and bill?"

The boy stared at the convoluted patterns of the carpet before speaking. "That would be kind of difficul'. It's on the computer or in Angela's files. But maybe I cou' do something for you. Angela's a good friend of mine."

Chinaman handed him another twenty and his card. "You can reach me at this number. But I need this information as soon as possible."

This time the boy took the twenty without looking at it and pocketed it with the card. "Ok. I understand. I'll try to get it later tonight. You wait in there, right? And I'll get Freddie." Forty dollars richer than he was five minutes before, the boy turned and wheeled his luggage rack with a new spring in his step, whistling snatches of 'Summertime.'

Chinaman sat again in the chair facing the elevators. He gathered from the newspaper accounts of the murders that no one at the hotel had seen the killers or remembered seeing them. It didn't surprise him. Unlike some of the grand hotels of the Third World where wages were low, New York hotels could never afford to hire a clerk on each floor or a boy for each elevator. But he wanted to talk to someone who had been inside that room.

Nearly ten minutes passed before he heard the sound of a freight elevator being operated. An extremely handsome, well-built man in his mid-twenties stepped out. He was dressed in white tunic and trousers. His name tag read, "Fred Garrett." Beneath his wavy blond hair, he stared at Chinaman with suspicious blue eyes and unsmiling thin lips. Chinaman had the odd feeling that the boy looked familiar. He stood up and held out his hand. "You Freddy?"

The man gave the hand a hard stare and took it briefly in his before releasing it. "I'm Fred. Sanchez says you're asking questions about what went down in 1204."

"That's right. I understand you brought them something from room service." Chinaman held out his pack of Marlboro. Fred Garrett shook his head and made a slight face suggesting repugnance. Obviously a body-building man who frowned upon anyone polluting his air. Chinaman returned the pack to his pocket.

Fred leaned against the wall and folded his thick arms. "The woman ordered ice cream and fruit for one and coffee for two."

"About what time was that?"

The hard glint of suspicion deepened in Garrett's eyes. "I already told you."

Chinaman straddled a chair and wrinkled his brow. "You did? I must have missed it."

"If you're the police, I did. Sanchez said you're some kind of cop."

"Private. Is that a problem?"

Garrett stared at him for several seconds, then visibly relaxed. "No. I guess not. But I don't want any trouble. I need this job."

"There won't be any trouble. I'm just trying to find out what happened."

"You don't think the police will find out?"

"They might. But the police are busy people. And they can't put everything else on hold to concentrate on one homicide; I can. And the lady was a very good friend of mine. More than a friend."

Garrett ran a comb through his hair and returned it to his pocket. It struck Chinaman as more of a nervous tic than an act of vanity. "So it's personal."

"Very."

Garrett stared at him for a few moments. Maybe trying to imagine the two of them together. His slight sigh suggested there was just no accounting for the taste some women had in men. "OK. It was about half an hour before I got off work. Say, eleven-thirty."

"Did the woman seem frightened or nervous in any way?"

"No. In fact...."

"Go ahead."

"She kind of smiled at me the whole time I was setting up the tray, you know what I mean?"

Chinaman nodded. He knew exactly what he meant. He knew the smile well. The one reserved for interesting men, especially for good looking body builders with wavy blond hair and clear blue eyes. She would have favored him with her Judy Special, full of more promise than a politician's platform. But he also knew it was all a tease. He knew Judy valued men for little else than money. And he knew why.

"She was dressed in the hotel robe and she, uh...."

"Go ahead."

"Well, she showed a lot of leg."

"The man didn't seem to mind?"

"Oh, no. Well, anyway, he was on the phone the whole time I was in the room. He never said a word to me. And he was kind of facing away, toward the wall."

"Did you hear anything he said on the phone?"

Fred Garrett's personality suddenly slipped into automatic; a tone of surprise overlaid with a hint of disapproval. "Mister, I'm sorry about the lady but at this hotel room service personnel don't–"

Chinaman held out the folded twenty. The boy took the bill without looking at it and immediately pocketed it. He continued without missing a beat. "Something about how he didn't think he'd like it there."

"Where was 'there,' do you know?"

"No. He never said. At least not while I was in the room."

Chinaman pulled out a notebook and pen. "Anything else he said you can remember?"

"It was like he was complaining, but kind of in a joking way. Something about the place not being right for his lifestyle and, oh, yeah, something about it being dry."

"He said, 'dry'?"

"I think so."

"Anything else?"

"Not really. I wasn't in the room very long. And whoever the man was talking to must have been doing most of the talking."

"Do you remember anything at all unusual in the room?"

Garrett shook his head thoughtfully. He smoothed back a dislodged lock of hair. Chinaman studied his long wavy hair, his heavy eyebrows, thin face, prominent nose, thin lips and intense expression. Suddenly he knew why he had thought he looked familiar. With a professional makeup artist to help age him, Garrett could have passed for Andrew Jackson. "I remember they were both in hotel robes. The man was lying on the bed talking on the phone and the lady was telling me where to put the tray. And giving me the eye. I kept making small talk about the weather — how cold it was, how slippery it was — but she just kept smiling at me."

Chinaman handed him a card. "If you think of anything else, anything at all, call me. OK?"

Garrett took the card and put it in his pocket without looking at it. "OK. I'll do that."

He pushed the button for the freight elevator. The door opened and Garrett stepped inside. Then, holding the door open, he stuck his head out. "The guy on the bed."

"Yeah?"

"He spoke with a real heavy accent. Maybe Russian or German or some Eastern European country. Something like that."

"Thanks."

He grew thoughtful for a few seconds before speaking again. "Jesus, why would anybody want to kill a woman like that?"

Chinaman lit up a Marlboro and leaned back before exhaling so that the smoke swirled upward, keeping Garrett out of harm's way. "That's exactly what I intend to find out."

★

6

THE bartender slid his horn-rimmed glasses with their thick lenses farther down the bridge of his thick nose and squinted. First at Chinaman's shield and then at the photograph of Judy. He handed them back and grunted. "Yeah. I remember her."

"You sure? That's an old photograph."

"Doesn't matter. She's been in here before. Three or four times. Maybe more." He pushed his glasses back up his nose. The back of his hand was an exotic landscape of black hair and brown liver spots. "So she's the one who bought it in 1204, huh?"

"She's the one."

The bartender walked down the length of the bar to serve another customer. Bar lights reflected from between strands of hair on his nearly bald head. Chinaman finished his Black Russian and turned to watch the pianist with the bow tie and bright smile at the end of the bar wrap himself around a melancholy version of "White Christmas." Chinaman looked at himself in the mirror behind the bar. His head and shoulders appeared between the bottles of Boodle's British Gin and Remy Martin XO. Thick mane of jet-black hair, yellow skin over high cheek bones and eyes shaped by epicanthic folds. Judy had always said he had the face of a mood ring: Extreme intellectual one moment, "almond-eyed assassin" the next.

He studied the coat his ex-wife had given him. She had taste. Good quality and a style that was just classic enough to always be in fashion but, wouldn't you know, without a tie and jacket, Chinaman once again wasn't properly attired. But he kept the coat buttoned up and his scarf in place, and no one in Harry's New York Bar cared to know what lay underneath.

When the bartender came back, he ran a hairy hand over his balding head and pointed to a booth across the room. "That's where they were sitting."

Chinaman glanced at the empty booth and back to the bartender. "You mean the man she picked up?"

"No. He came in and sat at the bar. Alone. She picked him up later."

"So, who's 'they'?"

The bartender shrugged. "How should I know? A guy in the booth with her. Then the other guy comes in, sits at the bar and within five minutes the woman is sitting at the bar with one between."

"One between?"

"Two stools away from the guy. The proper distance for a pickup, you know?"

"Not too close as to be embarrassingly obvious, but not so distant as to be hard to talk to?"

"You got it."

"What about the guy in the booth?"

"When I looked over, he was on his way outta here. I guess he didn't want her company. Or else she was outta his price range. Who knows?"

Chinaman looked toward the booth, trying to conjure up an image of the two of them, then turned back to the bartender. "Had you seen the guy at the bar before?"

"Nah. Not him. But the guy in the booth. I'm not real sure, but I think he's been in here before." He pointed to his eyes. "I may not read so good anymore, but I see across a barroom just fine."

"Have the police asked you any questions about this?"

"Nobody asked me nothing."

Chinaman kept his hands out of sight and took out yet

another Jackson and folded it. Andrew Jackson — the private investigator's memory refresher and thank you note. He placed it under one of his namecards and handed it to the bartender. "If you ever see him again, the man in the booth, I'd really appreciate a call."

The bartender pocketed the card and bill without looking at them. Almost no one at the New York Palace Hotel looked directly at anything — certainly not money. He leaned on his side against the bar and looked toward the booth. "I'm sorry about the girl. She was a real looker. Can't say I'm sorry the guy got it though."

"I thought you said you didn't know who he was."

"I didn't know him. But I lost an older brother because of them. During the war. The real war, I mean. And, believe me, if you think those people have learned a damn thing about democracy you got your head screwed on wrong. And now the damn fools let them unite, so we'll be fighting them again. Mark my words."

"You're saying the man at the bar had a German accent."

"You got it."

★

DAY THREE

7

"PLOW the park?"
Chinaman struggled through a dreamlike series of
images, rearranging words, searching for meanings.
Nothing. Because the question made no sense. He'd heard it
wrong. He lifted his head from the pillow and waited.

"How's my arc, damnit?"

Chinaman opened his eyes and saw a dull yellow blur passing
inches in front of his nose. Like a tiny rainbow had attached itself
to him. He shook his head, closed and opened his eyes. The blur
was still there. Behind it was a see-thru bra and behind that a
woman's well-formed breasts. Chinaman relaxed. At least
*some*thing was in focus.

"Watch! A reverse throw!" The blur changed shape slightly,
reversed itself, accelerated into a streak, then disappeared altogether.
"So what do you think?" The young woman standing beside the
bed held one yellow ball in her left hand and two in her right. She
knelt on the bed beside him. Black bra, black-and-red panties,
yellow balls. Chinaman could smell bacon and coffee.

"Damnit, Chinaman, I've never done a reverse throw before
today. Say something!"

Chinaman reached out and with one hand behind her head
brought her face close to his. Her long fine black hair spilled onto
his neck and chest. The smell of bacon and coffee was replaced by
the odors of perfume and perspiration. "You are the world's sexiest
juggler. That much I can tell you."

She pulled away from his kiss. "When are you going to start
juggling? You said you'd let me teach you."

Chinaman studied her glossy hair, oval face, dark black eyes, generous mouth. She was Chinese-American; born and raised in Flushing. The western epitome of a beautiful "China doll" — until she opened her mouth and revealed her New York accent and American mindset. She often echoed the complaints of Chinese born in America of being lost between two cultures, but Chinaman envied her. He had been born in one culture and caught up in the trauma and horror of that culture feeding on itself in waves of mass self-destruction, and his outlook and mindset was as different from hers as a FOB (Fresh-off-the-boat Chinese) was from an ABC (American-born Chinese). He rested his hand on her thigh. Cool. Smooth. Familiar. "You know I'm not mechanically inclined."

"Oh, bullshit. Juggling isn't 'mechanics'; it's...it's an art form."

He stroked her thigh. From her red-edged black nylon panties to her knee and back again. "So are you, Mary Anne. Believe me, so are you." Chinaman sat up and stretched. "But how many times have I asked you not to wake me before *I* wake me. If you see what I mean."

"Not as many times as I've told you I'm not Mary Anne. I'm *Jo* Anne. Mary Anne is your wife's name. If you see what *I* mean."

"Ex-wife."

Jo Anne Lee stared at him, then slid off the bed and walked to the door. Suddenly she turned and threw all three balls at him, one after the other. Hard.

Chinaman ducked two and caught one. "Sorry, doll. I think I got it straight now. Mary Anne was the ball breaker. Jo Anne is the ball juggler."

She moved on her bare feet to his bureau drawer, removed three rolled pairs of socks and began juggling them; then juggled two with one hand, then threw one at him. "Hey, no problem, Chinaman. I've only been sleeping with you several nights a week for three months. Don't try to cram too much information into your fat head all at once." She threw him a pair of jockey

underwear. A damn-the-expense Calvin Klein she had bought
for his birthday. His 35th. She had said the black with specks of
grey matched his eyes. She had called it 'Chinaman grey'.
Chinaman wondered how much longer before it matched his hair.

Jo Anne spoke while looking at herself in a wall mirror, hands
locked behind her head, breasts uplifted. "Three guys tried to
pick me up in the bar last night, Chinaman. One of them said I
was the most naturally seductive woman he'd ever seen."

"He must have been drinking old Irish Whiskey."

"Ha, ha, laugh. But you won't think it's so funny when you
walk in one day only to find that I've run away with a guy who
knows how to treat a lady."

"Most men who know how to treat a lady are dead broke."

Jo Anne gave forth with a long-suffering sigh and walked to
the window to open the blinds. Chinaman turned his head from
the light. "Sydney called. Said to give you a message something
like, if you don't come in by tomorrow at the latest to finish copy-
editing he's going to erase your computer tapes."

"Sydney takes his magazine deadlines seriously."

"You really shouldn't copy-edit pornography, Chinaman. It's
bad for your detective image."

"So's starvation; and I just can't seem to kick the eating habit."

Jo Anne had also told him his copy-editing pornography was
bad for the image of "our people." Chinaman always flinched
when someone spoke of "our people." It usually meant they had
an agenda of their own; an agenda so flaky that they had to appeal
to the emotions rather than to reason; and Chinaman had quite
enough of people's emotions. Not to mention their perspective:
While Chinese dissidents and Tibetans were being illegally arrested
and abused in Chinese prisons, Judy and her Chinese-American
friends debated over whether or not the word "Oriental" was
derogatory to Asians. The gap between Chinaman and Chinese-
Americans was too great to close. Before she walked out,
Chinaman's ex-wife had told him the gap between him and *anyone*

was too great to close; and that his experience growing up in China had scarred him too deeply for him to be emotionally involved with someone. Chinaman knew she was right when she said he never let down his guard. Only Judy had somehow found the right combination to get inside the defense perimeters he'd set in place. And Judy was dead.

Jo Anne picked up a catalog from the dresser and flipped the pages. "Your mail's on the bed."

Chinaman reached for the opened envelopes. "Anything interesting?"

"Mostly bills. Your bank statement. And another great catalog from L.A. with state-of-the-art electronic equipment for guys like you."

"Not like me. You have to be electronically inclined to operate that stuff. I'm not."

"And letters from Save the Whales, Save the Elephants, Save the Children and the Greenpeace Foundation — all asking for money. And one from the Little Sisters of Mercy in Holy Seclusion. Or Total Seclusion. I forget which. Anyway, it's there on the bed."

"Also asking for money?"

"No. Asking for support."

Chinaman glanced at the contents of the envelopes and tossed them into a wastebasket. "I must be on somebody's list."

"Just think, Chinaman, all those people paid something to buy your name."

"Serves them right, then."

Chinaman opened his bank statement and began shuffling through the canceled checks. Jo Anne sat on the dresser, engrossed in the glossy color photographs of overpriced electronic penetration products. "Wow! Look at this catalog! It's got every eavesdropping and debugging device ever made. All kinds of neat things. Oh, wow, a voice changer! Hey, Chinaman, can we get a voice changer?"

Chinaman continued shuffling through the checks and spoke

in falsetto. "What for? We've got one."

"No, I mean, really. It says here you just connect it to the phone and it can change your voice to female."

"Just what I need — a transvestite telephone. And how much will it cost?"

"Two hundred dollars. But it's on sale."

"I'll tell you what. If I take a case and I need to speak with a woman's voice over the phone, I'll pay you five dollars to speak for me and save the other one hundred and ninety-five."

"Oh, come on, Chinaman. Detective work should be fun."

"Detective work should be profitable. Then I wouldn't have to copy edit Sydney's books and magazines."

"Look, this model has a special button on it. When you press it a dog starts barking in the background."

"What kind of dog?"

"What kind? It doesn't say. What's the difference?"

"All the difference in the world. If it's a German Shepard or a Doberman, then the person I'm calling might respect me for living in a tough neighborhood. But what if it's a chihuahua or a basset hound? They'll think I'm a wimp. You'd better write the manufacturer and ask him if his dog-"

"Jesus, Chinaman. You are the most frustrating–"

Chinaman propped himself up on an elbow and stared at the back of a canceled check. "Aha! Presto! Mrs. Van Orden will throw herself at me for this."

"She already has, I'm sure. But why would your horny client throw herself at you because of a canceled check?"

"Because this canceled check is from the Manhattan Oriental Antiques House on Fifth Avenue."

"Where you bought my silver bracelet?"

"The very same. Owned and operated by Mrs. Van Orden's ex-husband, Mr. Van Orden."

Jo Anne held up her wrist. "You bought me this bracelet from a store owned by the ex-husband of your horny client?"

"Yep."

"Why?"

"Because my horny client would like nothing better than to slap a levy on her ex-husband's company bank account which he recently moved. But now thanks to this canceled check we know his bank is Chase Manhattan on University and 9th Street and we know his account number." Chinaman handed it to her. "On the back."

"That's dirty, Chinaman."

"Dirty? He owes her alimony and support for—"

Jo Anne threw the check onto the bed. "You didn't buy me the bracelet because you were feeling romantic like you said. You bought it to get information." She slid the bracelet off as she walked to the door, then turned and threw it at his head. Chinaman caught it before it could hit his face. Jo Anne exited and slammed the door. Chinaman barked — like a hungry St. Bernard which had just lost its breakfast.

★

8

CHINAMAN took a last drag on the last cigarette from his pack and glanced about the bar. Ceiling lamps in the shape of ship lanterns added to the unsettled melancholy of the bar's early afternoon gloom. A gloom beyond depressing. Almost funereal. That was it. Chinaman decided that whoever designed lighting for Harlem bars must be the same guy contracted to light up morgues and funeral parlors. Outside, trees were bare and a thickly layered steel-gray sky threatened to unleash another few inches of snow. A deflated Mylar balloon swung from a branch of a sugar maple like a broken metronome.

Chinaman turned back to stare at the man sitting across from him. The man sat just below the poster of a curvaceous young black woman in a red bikini squeezing a bottle of beer between her legs. The man's deep-set, street-wise eyes were as black as his skin. His curly hair was tinged with white, especially along the sides. The well-shaped face might have presented an almost distinguished air had it not been for the gaunt, used-up, sickly appearance of a drug addict. Chinaman watched the man's bony shoulders bounce nervously, erratically, not quite keeping time with a jukebox jazz beat. He wondered which of the many pockets of his denim jacket had the pills, powders, vials and crystals. Probably all of them. Two years ago, Chinaman thought, Stiggy still had his act together. But, then, two years ago, so did he. Chinaman put out his cigarette and folded the pack in half. "All right, Stiggy."

"All right, what?"

"I'll bite. What makes you think I'm on a case?"

The tinge of yellow in Stiggy's eyes seemed deeper and more bilious each time Chinaman saw him. Chinaman wondered if Abrams was still using him as an informer. "'Cause when you on a case you diffrunt from when you ain't on a case. You ain't a caterpillar no more. You hatch out into a bat and you flies off into the sky. Takin' shit from *no*body. The mild-mannered English teacher becomes a don't-fuck-with-me detective."

While Stiggy took another hit on his drink, Chinaman tried to figure out what he'd taken to get high. If he could figure that out, then he'd know if there was any purpose in talking to him now or if he should come back another day. The shiny eyes, dilated pupils and hyperactivity suggested stimulants. Nothing like popping a few jolly beans to deal with whatever might present itself. If the world doesn't have a happy face, help it along. Basic Addiction 101. ""Creative Writing teacher, Stiggy. Not 'English' teacher. And that's ancient history, anyway."

Stiggy shrugged.

"And bats don't come out of caterpillars. Butterflies do. Caterpillars become—"

Stiggy waved the remark away as of no consequence. "Whatever. Butterflies don't take no shit either. I seen 'em on TV."

Chinaman decided Stiggy was up on amphetamines. New York Speed locked in a wrestling match with Tennessee Whiskey. Best two out of three falls. That might still be okay. He could still listen. And reason. And remember. As long as he hadn't been smoking or injecting as well. That would be a tag team match even Stiggy couldn't handle. Then he would be too wired to think straight. With Stiggy it was hard to tell. His motor was always overheated.

Chinaman took another hit from his Black Russian and leaned back against the cheap vinyl booth. The first jazz set wouldn't begin for another six hours but that didn't stop the diehard drunks from getting good seats at the bar. What's a six-hour wait when you're having fun? Young lovers held hands across the table of another booth and exchanged knowing stares. Chinaman had done that with Mary Anne before they were married. Later he learned that there are many kinds of knowing stares. Pre-marital. Marital. Divorsal. He refolded the cigarette pack still smaller. Mary Anne had told him the way he folded and refolded empty cigarette packs smaller and smaller indicated underlying hostility. He had told her to shut up. She had said, "See?"

"In fact, Chinaman, when you on a case, you remind me of one of them flowers."

"What flowers are those, Stiggy?"

"You know, man. The ones I just seen on TV. Late last night. Or night before. Channel 13."

"I didn't know you were into watching public television, Stiggy."

"Yeah. Like when I got me a little something to get high on, I mellow out in front of the set. And I loves to watch them monkeys swingin' from trees and lions tearin' the flesh off their dinner. But the flowers is the best. The colors, Chinaman. You wouldn't believe! And last night it was the flowers what always tempt the bees. By pretending to *be* a bee!"

Stiggy waited for an appropriate response from Chinaman. Chinaman said, "No shit?"

"Yeah! But all the time the flower's really trying to get something. Something it wants bad." Stiggy grew thoughtful. Chinaman recognized another of Stiggy's talking jags coming on. Nothing to do but wait it out.

"Wait a minute, now. The bees I thinkin' of is diffrunt."

When Stiggy's eyes remained focused on his glass for nearly a minute, Chinaman decided it was safe to conclude that he'd lost his concentration. "What *about* bees, Stiggy?"

Stiggy looked up abruptly as if he'd been slapped. "What?"

"You said the bees you're thinking of are different."

"The hell I did."

Chinaman hoped Stiggy wasn't entering a paranoid phase. He could see people passing by the bar fighting the wind for their open umbrellas. The tree-trapped balloon swung around the branch like a demented possum. A perfect day for paranoia. Crack-induced, or otherwise. "Sorry. I might have heard wrong."

"What I said was bees *is* diffrunt. You start playing English teacher on me and I could just clam up tighter'n a virgin's vagina at Riker's."

"So how do I remind you of a bee-tempting flower?"

"Actually, I remember now it's *wasps*. That's what I was doin'. Just now. Concentratin'. When I do that I remember." Stiggy drained his glass. Chinaman waved to the waiter for another round. Rain spattered against the window. Horns honked angrily at a stalled car.

"So these flowers I'm talking about swell up their abdomen like it was a female wasp ready and willing." Stiggy thrust his emaciated stomach out and gripped it. "With whatever lucky dude comes around. And the poor wasp, horny as hell, not knowing that he being suckered by a flower, unzips his pants or whatever wasps do, and he buzzes left, and he buzzes right, lookin' to do the deed, right? He thinks he goan slap the wood to somebody. But there ain't nothing there. Not what he thought was there. No woman wasp. All the goddamn flower wants is to get...."

"Pollinated?"

"That's it! Pollinated! So in the end the wasp gets nothing. While the flower gets what it wants."

"So you're saying the flower never did give a damn for what the wasp wanted."

"That's it! The wasp was jus' bein' used — like you usin' me."

Chinaman glanced at the check and threw some bills down

on the table. "All right, Stiggy. I apologize for trying to use you. I should have known that wasn't the Christian thing to do with a God-fearing man like Stiggy Freeman. What would a big-time drug dealer like you have done with a few crisp, twenty-dollar bills, anyway?" Chinaman started to get up.

Stiggy reached over and put his hand on Chinaman's shoulder. "Hey, don't be so sensitive, my man. Old Stiggy just spoofin' you a bit. Makin' conversation. Sit. Relax. Have a drink. Just tell Ole' Stiggy what you need. You want stimulating ladies or the latest stimulants, superior fire power or the news of the hour. Whatever: Ole' Stiggy is here for you."

"All I want, Ole' Stiggy, is the money your friend Weaverton owes me."

Stiggy gave a slight nod of the head. He seemed about to say something, then stopped.

"Look, Stiggy, you approached me to take the guy's case. I took it, I located his ex-partner. The guy who supposedly owed him a lot of money. Now, whether Weaverton got paid or not, he owes me money. Serious money. I want it."

"No sweat, my man. No sweat. Weaverton got paid and he didn't exactly skip. He's just holed up for a while with some pretty ladies. You want me to find him, I'll find him."

"That's exactly what I want."

"OK. Somebody owe you money, Chinaman, it's the same as he owe me money. And if he's dumb enough to show his black ass in Harlem, Ole' Stiggy will make sure he be payin' his debt. And then some."

"I just want the money promised." Chinaman wondered if Weaverton's disappearance wasn't the result of a deal between Stiggy and Weaverton to cut a percentage for Stiggy. Since he'd become a detective, Chinaman often found himself looking for the worst in people; and finding it. "Stiggy, I get paid, you get...ten per cent."

Stiggy leaned back and stared at Chinaman with an expression combining equal amounts of suspicion and amusement. "It don't figure."

"What?"

"You being so anxious about money. That's not the Chinaman I been dealing with all these years."

"I'm putting my cases on hold to take care of something else."

Stiggy raised his thin eyebrows. Somehow the action made him look older. "Something personal?"

"The New York Palace...used to be the Helmsley."

Stiggy stared at Chinaman in silence and took a long drag on his cigarette. "Oh, yeah. I heard about that one, all right. Heavy stuff went down. A dude and his lady got wasted."

"I don't know if she was his lady or not. She used to be mine."

Stiggy now gave Chinaman his full attention. "Damn. Sorry, Chinaman."

Chinaman could almost see Stiggy's mind working its way to its happy conclusion: If she had been Chinaman's woman, any information should be worth a pretty penny. Chinaman knew just how sorry Stiggy was.

When the two men entered the bar the open door sent a sudden draft of wet, cold air over to Chinaman's booth. Water dripped from their shiny black rain hats and shiny black raincoats. The first was well into his forties and well over six feet. Even his large-size raincoat was inadequate to accommodate his enormous bulk. His muscular neck could have been mistaken for Mike Tyson's. His companion was younger by at least two decades, less into body building, and his tough guy mien was borrowed from his older, more professional friend. Who had plenty to spare.

Chinaman watched them out of the corner of his eye as they looked about the bar and then walked toward his booth. They stood beside Stiggy, the thick-necked giant closest to the table; his companion behind. Both men glanced briefly at Chinaman, then at the sex symbol with the beer bottle still squeezed between her legs. Then their full attention shifted to Stiggy.

Stiggy looked up and his shoulders immediately came to life, jerking and jumping. His eyes joined in the dance. The alignment he forced his lips into wasn't much of a smile. It was too nervous and uneven for that. But it was a smile. "Hey, bro'! What's goin' down?" Stiggy's voice had developed a sudden raspy quality, as if something had lodged in his windpipe.

The man's stare never left Stiggy's eyes. "We'll be talking outside."

The grating quality of Stiggy's voice grew more pronounced. The thought flickered through Chinaman's mind that if he closed his eyes, he might think he was listening to the late Miles Davis. "Yeah, hey, I was gonna call you, you know? Thing is—"

"We'll be talking outside."

Chinaman took a drink with his right hand then placed his hand underneath his jacket on the seat beside him. "My friend and I are having a meeting."

A patch of skin on Stiggy's cheek developed a sudden twitch. The man's stare held Stiggy's eyes the way headlight beams freeze a deer. He looked straight at Stiggy. Chinaman looked straight at Stiggy. But their full attention was now on each other. "Your friend and you had your meeting." He seemed to consider Chinaman's new hand position out of the corner of his eye, then spoke again to Stiggy. "I don't want to have to tell you again."

Chinaman moved his jacket-covered hand onto the table. "I don't want to have to tell *you* again."

The man now stared directly at Chinaman. Now all three men were staring at Chinaman. The man spoke beneath his dripping rain hat. "Didn't you' mama never tell you a Chinaman shouldn't be tryin' to throw his weight around a Harlem bar?"

Chinaman was impressed. He didn't normally tolerate being referred to as "Chinaman" by anyone other than his closest friends, but at least the man hadn't assumed he was Japanese. He leaned forward and moved the jacket several inches toward the man. His hand under the jacket was now just off the table. "I was an orphan. I missed a lot."

During a long silence, drops of rain slid from the man's hat and spattered onto Chinaman's jacket. Steam rose from his raincoat. "You' not the Man."

"You got that right."

The man looked at the jacket and back to Chinaman's eyes. "You think you the only one in this bar got a gun?"

"Nope...."

"What then?"

"I think I'm the only one in this bar who at this moment in time has the barrel of a fully loaded Smith and Wesson .38 Special pointing right at your pecker. And if I cough, sneeze or twitch, or for whatever reason apply 13 pounds of pressure on this trigger, what once provided your lady love with hours of rapturous joy is going to sail across Amsterdam Avenue like an unlit cigar."

The man's thick neck began pulsating. Part of his eyes disappeared beneath their lids. Anger seemed to puff him up even larger, threatening to burst his raincoat. His companion had grown completely still also, but Chinaman knew that was from fear. But the big man's stillness was of another kind: an experienced hit man's calculation of the odds. And he was a hit man, no question about that: No one would ever confuse him with Mother Teresa. But he looked like that rare breed of hit man who didn't kill anyone he didn't have to, who didn't cause any more pain to anyone than absolutely necessary, and who probably even policed up his brass before he left the scene of the kill — not simply to avoid detection, but because his mama didn't raise him to be a litterbug. What more could anyone ask of a hit man?

Three more drops of rain slid from his hat onto Chinaman's jacket before he spoke again. "You're bluffin'."

Chinaman took a drink with his left hand and set the glass down noiselessly. "Well, it's your pecker; so it's your call."

The man's eyes glanced over at Stiggy. Stiggy's twitch threatened to explode his cheek but his shoulders were now perfectly still. His wide eyes stared out of an ashen face into a remote distance, far from the vicissitudes of human conflict. The man turned to Chinaman. "It's not over. We be back."

Chinaman nodded in acknowledgment of unfinished business between them. The man turned to Stiggy. "And for sure we be seein' you again, nigger."

The men walked out of the bar and into the rain.

Stiggy exhaled his long-held breath. "Chinaman, they are bad dudes!" His shoulders started their dance again. "Oh, man. You don't want to be threatenin' dudes like that with a gun! If I told you what I seen that guy do to–"

"It's okay."

Stiggy's lips peeled back to reveal several nicotine-stained teeth. "Okay!?"

Chinaman threw his jacket onto the table. "I didn't threaten them with a gun. Just a fist. I left the gun home."

Stiggy squeezed the jacket as a drowning man might squeeze a deflated life preserver, then threw it back on the table. "You got no *gun*? Are you crazy?! They know that, they — oh, man!" Stiggy drained the whiskey from his glass. The hand holding the glass started shaking. Ice tinkled. He reached into his jacket to bring out a small glassine packet of wedge-shaped blue tablets, diamond-shaped pink tablets, white pills slightly smaller than aspirin, and black-and-green capsules.

Chinaman's hand gripped Stiggy's bony wrist even as he inwardly assessed the drugs. Amphetamine, phenmetrazine, cocaine tablets and an amphetamine-barbiturate combination. All stimulants.

He tightened his grip. "Stiggy. Until you locate Weaverton for me, you stay off this shit. You understand? I mean it." Chinaman stuck some twenties into the open pocket of Stiggy's jacket. "This is a downpayment on your ten per cent."

The whiskey and the money seemed to have a calming effect. Stiggy looked at the twenties and shoved the packet back into his pocket. "OK. You'll have Weaverton's bread by the end of the week. In fact, I'll do the collecting personally. You'll have all he owes you...minus my...fifteen per cent — by Friday or my name's not Stiggy Freeman."

Chinaman sighed his acceptance of Stiggy's increased percentage. Stiggy looked toward the door. "But I don't know if you gonna' be around long enough to get it."

"I'll be around," Chinaman said.

"Good. 'Cause I gonna help you with that other thing, too."

Chinaman gave him a quizzical look.

"That hotel thing."

Chinaman took a moment to speculate on the possibility that Stiggy might be of any help with Judy's murder. Despite his drug habit, Stiggy was still one of the best info men in the business. He had never failed to add at least something to any puzzle Chinaman had been working on. But up to now he had only hit up Stiggy for information about cases connected in some way to Harlem. He doubted that Stiggy's expertise extended below 110th Street. But what did he have to lose?

Chinaman slipped into his jacket and stood up. He looked at Stiggy's eyes. The pupils looked all right — almost normal. Still, with Stiggy, you never knew. "You know what hotel I'm talking about, right?"

Stiggy waved to the waiter for another whiskey. "Twelve-oh-four."

"You know the *room* number?"

Stiggy's shoulders again twitched to another jukebox selection. "Oh, yeah. When I heard the news, I was workin' on my Lotto slip, and I worked the room number into my system. For luck."

Chinaman had passed several booths before he heard Stiggy call to him. When he turned, he saw that Stiggy actually had a smile on his face. "You see what I said about you, Chinaman?"

"What's that, Stiggy?"

"When you on a case, you peel off your caterpillar outfit and become a don't-fuck-with-me bat. A yellow bat out of hell."

★

9

AS the icy wind effortlessly penetrated his black leather jacket, Chinaman leaned into the pedimented doorway of the West Village apartment building. The door had a metal hook and a small length of red ribbon — remnants of a Christmas wreath or other holiday decoration which had probably been stolen five minutes after it was put up. He was about to buzz again when a voice crackled through the intercom with the metallic delivery of a computerized mouthpiece. "Whatever you're selling, we don't want any."

Chinaman stared into the camera's eye, its activated lens flushed with a sickly yellow glow. "Are you Cindy Mae?"

"Cindy Mae moved out. I'm the Easter bunny."

"I'm a private investigator. I'd like to talk to you about Judy Fisher."

The alcohol-slurred voice sped through the intercom system with the hint of an echo. "The Easter Buddy told the police all she knows. She doesn't want to talk to anyone else about anyone else."

"Cindy Mae, I was a friend of Judy's." Chinaman spoke quickly into the silence. "She used to be in my class at Mitchell College in Connecticut."

So many seconds passed that Chinaman thought he had lost her. "Are you Chinaman?"

"Yes."

The door buzzed and Chinaman pushed it open. He stepped into the dark, faded elegance of the hallway. Its decorative moldings needed cleaning and some of the stair's balusters were chipped but, in its day, the building must have been one classy lady. He glanced at himself in a gilt-framed wall mirror. The figure who stared back at him looked more like the stereotype of a burglar than a detective. Chinaman wondered if he had missed his true calling.

A string quartet's maudlin version of Christmas carols wafted inoffensively through ceiling speakers. Reggae lyrics, heavily laden with social comment, blared through a closed door somewhere down the corridor. The red-and-gold runner lining the stairs was wet from the recent tread of snow-covered footwear. He walked to the end of the second floor hallway to apartment 2-F.

When he knocked, Cindy Mae opened the door wide and let him in. Strands of curly blond hair framed her bitchy-beautiful face prettified with hastily applied makeup. Her eyes were a flirtatious shade of blue, her nose was pert and cute, and her mouth was small and heart-shaped. She wore a black halter top, a short white skirt over black leotards, and ankle boots. Her hand held a tumbler of liquid layered in beautiful shades of red and gold. Her long fingernails matched the deepest red band at the bottom of the glass.

She shut the door after him and led him through a short hallway to the living room. She pointed to an arrangement of white metal tubes twisted into a sculpted form, slightly resembling a chair. Chinaman sat on it and found it to be as uncomfortable as it looked.

The latest in polished chrome light systems hung from the ceiling, suspended over a modern beveled-glass-and-gleaming-brass dining table. The walls and ceiling were a heroine shade of white, and the wall-to-wall carpet just a shade darker than a nickel-plated pistol snuggled inside a prostitute's purse.

Chinaman wasn't certain what statement the room was supposed to be making, but whoever designed it must have used terms like innovative, contemporary and architecturally interesting. To Chinaman it looked like a surgeon's operating theater of the future. Or a Palm Beach morgue.

In a black frame on the wall above a couch, Charlie Chaplin, dressed in character as the Little Tramp, looked down at the room with sad eyes. Cindy Mae quickly moved dishes, glasses and newspapers off a layered and looped stainless steel coffee table. She flashed him a perfect smile. "Sorry about the mess, Chinaman. I entertained a gentleman-caller last night and I didn't feel well enough to clean up."

As Cindy Mae straightened the newspapers, Chinaman noticed that the pattern of her gold earrings matched the gold bangles lining her soft, delicate arm. He reflected that Cindy Mae might not be feeling well but she was certainly doing well. Very well indeed.

Cindy Mae bent over to toss floor pillows into a corner, then reached up to place a stack of CD's onto a high shelf. When she bent over, her halter top ballooned out to reveal an immodest amount of her unencumbered breasts; when she reached, the halter top rose along the curve of her waist, displaying a generous amount of smooth white mid-riff. Chinaman hadn't seen such carefully calculated female artifice since Scarlett O'Hara flirted with her flustered beaus in "Gone With the Wind."

He decided that no one had to give Cindy Mae lessons on how to dress for success. As he watched her he thought of a companion volume: *Dress for Success; Move to Entice.*

Once the show was over, Cindy Mae sat down on the red-and-white chintz-covered loveseat facing him, placed the rim of her tequila sunrise tumbler between her parted red lips, and stared at him appraisingly. "Judy used to talk about you a lot."

"I hope she said I was a good teacher."

Cindy Mae picked up a large stuffed bunny with sad round eyes and placed it on her lap. She cradled its nose against her breasts and hugged it with both hands. "She said you were a great lay."

Chinaman took out a notebook and a pen. "Judy always did exaggerate," he said.

Cindy Mae suddenly flung the bunny aside as if it had peed in her lap and jumped up. "Oh, dear, I *am* forgetting my manners.

What can I get you to drink, Mr. Chinaman?"

"Just call me Chinaman. And a beer would be great."

Cindy Mae crossed the carpet with a self-consciously seductive stride and disappeared into the kitchen. On the wall opposite the doleful eyes of Charlie Chaplin was a large poster advertising an Hispanic Art Exhibition at the Brooklyn Museum. The painting featured on the poster was of a Mexican village transformed by eerie colors and elongated shapes into a beautiful but unsettling dream-fantasy.

A spotlight over a liquor cabinet faced a Chinese fan plant centered on a chrome end table. The spotlighted plant would have presented a dramatic form — had the light been turned on. As it was off, Chinaman decided that Cindy Mae didn't cotton to competition of *any* kind.

He heard the sound of a refrigerator being opened and then the sound of Cindy Mae's voice. "Damn. Chinaman, I forgot to get beer. I'm all out of — no, wait! I found a Dos Equis. Is Mexican beer all right?"

"Perfect." Goes with the painting, Chinaman thought.

Cindy Mae gave him the beer and a glass and sat down again on the loveseat. "Cheers, Chinaman. To getting the bastards who took Judy from us."

Chinaman removed his jacket and took a drink. He wrote the date, time and place into his notebook. He decided to ask his questions and get the hell out before Cindy Mae was back in the mood to put the make on him again. He wasn't certain he would resist if she did, and he didn't need any vague but persistent after-sex guilt from having gone to bed with Judy's roommate while he was supposed to be searching for her killers. "When did you come to New York, Cindy Mae?"

Cindy Mae leaned into the loveseat. "I left Charleston for New York a couple of years back. You remember that terrible Hurricane back then?"

Chinaman nodded. He remembered it well. That was the

week Mary Anne found out about Chinaman and Judy. Or rather found Chinaman and Judy—in bed. Whatever, in his mind, that was The Week That Was.

"Well, I had a ladies' clothing store before the storm came. And just a pile of rubble after it left. I was mostly insured, of course, but I made up my mind then and there not to let some ill-bred gust of wind with the manners of a carpetbagger make a fool of me again."

Chinaman jotted down something about Cindy Mae arriving in New York in the fall of 1999. His mind was still on his breakup with Mary Anne. The accusations. The arguments. The sound. The silence. The separation. "That was some rain storm," he said.

The slight southern drawl of Cindy Mae's speech suddenly deepened and blossomed into that of an antebellum southern belle. Chinaman began to fall in love with Scarlett O'Hara all over again. "Well, that little ole rain storm ripped up telephone poles and sent them cartwheelin' all ovah the streets of Charleston like soldiers of the Union Army. When I got back to look ovah mah store, I couldn't believe my eyes: A telephone pole had thrust itself right through the glass front door." Cindy Mae's body seemed to tense as she spoke. Tense in an inviting way. She sipped her tequila sunrise and fluttered her eyelashes. Chinaman started to speak but Cindy Mae wasn't one to leave a Freudian image unembellished. "All the ladies' unmentionables — the panties, the brahs, the stockins — just everything was wet and soiled and full of glass. Ah swear, Mr. Chinaman, I felt as if ah mahself had been personally violated."

Chinaman offered Cindy Mae a cigarette and lit it for her. Then he lit his own. The thought occurred to him that it would take far more than a telephone pole forcing its entry through her glass front door for Cindy Mae to feel violated. "How long did you live with Judy?"

Cindy Mae's voice returned more or less to normal. "Almost two years. The lease is up in three months and I am *not* renewing.

I can tell you that."

"You mean because of what happened to Judy?"

"Sure. We don't even have a doorman here. Anyway, it was Judy's idea to live in the Village, not mine. She wanted to be around artists and writers and all that. Every artist I ever met in the Village was as queer as a three dollar bill. And broke. I'm lining up a place in the Upper East Side."

"With a doorman?"

"Damn right, Chinaman."

"I suppose the police asked for Judy's appointment book, address book, anything like that."

"They did. She had an appointment book with lots of telephone numbers in the back. All men, of course. The police went through all her possessions and took away everything they wanted." Cindy Mae took a drink and sighed. "Her only family's a brother in Louisiana. In prison for manslaughter and some other things Judy didn't want to talk about. I'm packing everything of hers that's left and sending it to him."

"You knew most of Judy's boyfriends?"

Cindy Mae ran her drink-free hand through her hair and formed her lips into a knowing smile. "You mean 'boyfriends' or gentlemen-of-substance who know how to treat a lady?"

Holly Golightly you'll never be, Chinaman thought. "I mean, did she have any special boyfriend she was meeting? One who wasn't paying for her favors?"

"Judy?! No way. It was always cash up front. I don't think she ever met anybody she really cared about...anybody like you."

Chinaman ignored the baited compliment. "How about the others? Her clients. Did you know any of them?"

"I knew all of them. At least, I think I did. Unless she hid a few from me."

"Can you think of any one of them who was ever violent? Maybe got his kicks giving pain to women? Or who might have had any specific reason to hurt Judy?"

"You really think that's what this is all about? A sadist went after Judy?"

"No, I don't. Whoever hit Judy or ordered the hit did it coolly and professionally. It wasn't the sudden twisted passion of a nut case. I think Judy was just in the wrong place at the wrong time. But I have to cover all bases."

"No violent customers that I can think of." Cindy Mae's voice edged Southern again. Chinaman could almost smell the chicory coffee and beignet. "I mean, one or two of our gentleman-callers might have gotten a little drunk and stuck his groping fingers where they didn't rightly belong. And more than one well-known gentleman about town enjoyed dressing up a lady as a little girl and putting her over his knee and lifting up her dress and pulling her panties down to her ankles and while she was in that completely helpless position, giving her a good spanking, until the exposed white cheeks of her behind turned a deep shade of crimson. Is that the kind of man you mean...Mr. Chinaman?"

Cindy Mae spoke the last part of her teasing discourse almost in a breathless whisper. Chinaman felt unmistakable stirrings in his own lap. He decided an undiluted dose of brutality was called for. He spoke in a matter-of-fact tone: "Not really, Cindy Mae. What I'm talking about is the kind of man who would point a silencer-equipped semi-automatic pistol into a beautiful woman's face and fire a soft-point bullet, a kind of round with a portion of its lead core exposed to allow for maximum expansion inside human flesh, and blow bits of skin and skull and muscle and brain and lots of blood all over a luxury hotel room, from drapes to doorknobs. Not to mention cranial fluid on the carpet."

Chinaman saw the tears brim in Cindy Mae's eyes. They quivered along the lower lashes, then spilled out and streamed down her cheeks. Her voice had a sudden scratchy quality. "You're a real–"

"Yeah, I know. I'm a real bastard. My ex-wife never failed to point that out. But murder's only fun on TV and in the movies. In real life it's obscene. Now what about it?"

"Nobody I ever saw her with would have...done that to her."
She wiped her eyes with a napkin and took a long drink. "I don't
think I put enough Vodka in this." She stared into her glass but made
no move to add the missing Vodka.

"You said the police were here. Do you remember if one of
them was named Abrams?"

Cindy Mae's pert nose wrinkled in disgust. "Him! He acted
like *I* had been involved in Judy's death. I'm scared enough as it is
without police harassment. He demanded that I give him her
appointment book and he searched every inch of her room and
went through everything in the boxes. *Everything!*" Cindy Mae
stretched out her fingers and looked at her nails. "The two with
him were all right but that one needs a refresher course on how to
treat a lady." She looked up at Chinaman, remembering
something. "Judy said something about you being married once
to the daughter of a—"

Chinaman stood up. "If it's all right with you, I'd like to
take a look at Judy's bedroom."

She gave him a hard stare. "I don't think you're the kind of
man who worries too much whether something is all right with a
lady or not."

She got up by moving through a series of titillating feminine
movements calculated to seem natural, but rehearsed to perfection.
The thought occurred to Chinaman that if Cindy Mae had put as
much effort into studying karate as she had in being sexy, she
could probably have destroyed both Chuck Norris and Jackie Chan
on the same night. "Her belongings are all packed, but if it'll
help, you can see it."

A seriograph of Andy Warhol's "Marilyn Six-Pack" on the
wall over the bed provided the only decoration. Where pictures
had been, bare rectangles lined a wall. The bed was queen-size
and its mattress had been stripped of sheets and covers. Carton
boxes labeled "clothes," "books" and "Misc." were piled on the
bedboard and on the floor against a wall. All were addressed to

"Edward L. Fisher, Louisiana State Penitentiary, Angola, Louisiana, 70712."

Cindy Mae put her glass down on the bureau. "She sure did love to read, Chinaman. I guess you were responsible for that, huh?"

Chinaman opened and closed the drawers of an oak bureau inlaid with bits of sky blue porcelain, then opened the drawer of a vanity table with the same design. He looked at his image in the swing mirror surrounded by light bars and thought of Judy sitting before it looking at hers. Something about the empty drawers made him angry. Judy had been picked up and packed away. Boxed up and ready for shipment. The residue of a woman's life: a few containers addressed to a state penitentiary and a few rectangle imprints on a wall. He slammed the drawer shut and fought to control his voice. "Nope. Judy was a natural. A born reader. And one of the best writers I had in any class anywhere."

Chinaman watched the mirror image of Cindy Mae sit on the mattress. Cindy Mae and a mattress seemed as natural together as Willy Mays and a baseball glove. She pointed to the boxes. "Everything's packed. You can unpack what you like but please put it all back in the boxes when you're finished. I broke three nails closing all these boxes."

Chinaman opened the closet door. Shoes and a few dresses. He closed it and walked into the hall. "If the police were here, there's not much point."

"Burt Reynolds always finds something important the police overlook."

Chinaman thought of Judy's corpse and of Cindy Mae's nail problem. "Bully for Burt. Maybe you should call him in."

Cindy Mae followed behind him, drink in hand. "Maybe I will! Maybe he follows police procedures better than you."

"Maybe he follows a shooting script and wouldn't know a police procedure if it peed on his pants leg."

"Well, there's no reason to become vulgar."

"No reason at all." Chinaman looked around the living room. "Would you happen to have a recent picture of Judy?"

"In my bedroom." In her pique, Cindy Mae reverted to a normal, uncontrived style of walking. She left the living room leaving Chinaman to deal with his sudden bout of anger. Maybe the beer. Maybe Cindy Mae. Maybe the weather. Maybe the senseless death of the only person he could ever open up to. He looked through the bay windows onto a row of bare ginkgo branches and another row of brownstones across the street. Snow perched prettily on pediments and window ledges and fire escapes, like something out of an idyllic Christmas card print of Greenwich Village.

He sat on the loveseat. Cindy Mae handed him the photograph and walked to the bar to refresh her drink. "It was taken at a party at the Union Square Cafe. A few weeks ago."

Judy in a charcoal gray turtleneck dress. A bright green drink in her hand. At the center of a crowd of well-dressed older men and younger women. Everyone smiling. Judy clowning for the camera. The flash had given her red-eye but she was as beautiful as ever. Cindy Mae stood next to her looking every bit the image of a runner-up.

"I'd like to keep this."

Cindy Mae turned to face him. "Did you love her, Chinaman? Is that why you're mad?"

"Maybe that's it, Cindy Mae. Or maybe it's just that I don't like people robbing the dead."

Cindy Mae's eyes flashed in indignation. "What the hell do you mean by that?"

Chinaman tapped the photograph. "I mean the jewelry Judy was wearing in this picture is now on you. How much of her stuff did you keep for yourself?"

Cindy Mae seemed about to angrily deny the charge, then changed her mind. "What am I supposed to do, Chinaman? Send all her best jewelry and her best dresses to her country-bumpkin

brother in a prison cell?" She stared into her drink. "Anyway, I
am sending most of it."

Chinaman placed Judy's picture in his pocket, finished his
beer, and stood up. "Well, you've been very helpful. Judy's killer
won't rest easy tonight; that's for sure."

Cindy Mae gave him a speculative look as if about to make a
decision. Then she rose and walked to a shelf of paperback books.
She pulled out something behind a row of romance novels. She
walked toward him holding a small leather notebook. She handed
it to Chinaman and with her other hand brushed his cheek. " I
want this back, Chinaman. I mean it."

Chinaman read the cover. "Daily Appointments 2001
Property of Judy Fisher." He flipped through its pages. They
were full of men's names, times of appointments, restaurants
and bars. In the back was a list of men's names, along with
their ages, professions, income rating and 'sexual preference.'
"I thought you said the police took this."

"I said they asked for it."

"You really should have given it to them, you know."

Cindy Mae's eyes widened theatrically and she favored him
with a perfect southern belle pout. "And lose the phone
numbers and addresses of all those gorgeous, well-heeled men,
maybe forever? Not on your life, Chinaman. Judy and I
exchanged men sometimes. When we got bored, I mean. But
she always had a lot more than me." A dull anger appeared in
Cindy Mae's eyes. For just a moment, their clear shade of
flirtatious blue clouded over. "Sometimes she'd even take men
I didn't want to exchange with anybody." She pointed to the
book. "Some of them I want back. And I intend to get them
back!"

"You mean Judy stole some of your dates."

"I mean...she sure did! Some of my best! Sometimes, she
made me so mad, I could have-" Cindy Mae locked her hands
behind her back like a little girl or rather like a voluptuous

woman who knows how appealing she looks with her hands locked behind her back and gave Chinaman her most disarming smile. "Well, I mean, sometimes even best friends have quarrels."

Chinaman handed her a card. "If you can think of anything else that might be helpful. Anything at all — call me."

Cindy Mae took the card and studied it. "English *and* Chinese. I like that. Let's see, Judy said your name meant 'Braveheart' or something like that."

"Not quite. It means *a mind as sharp as a sword.*"

"Wow! Could you give me a Chinese name, Chinaman?"

"Sure. I'll work on one for you. Just don't forget to call me if you think of anything."

Cindy Mae bit the card as if testing a suspicious coin. "Sure, Chinaman. I'm a very helpful kind of girl. But you know what?"

"What, Cindy Mae?"

"I think you're suppressing it."

"What am I suppressing, Cindy Mae?"

Cindy Mae draped her arms around his shoulders and kissed him on the mouth. Her tongue darted in and out of his own mouth like a child playing hide-and-seek. Chinaman wasn't sure what perfume she was wearing, but he suspected that it was a far more expensive brand than Jo Anne wore. She spoke with her lips inches from his own. "The acute case of sexual dynamics between us. And it's not good to suppress something like that."

Chinaman doubted that Cindy Mae had ever suppressed *anything* like that. He pushed her gently out to arm's length. "What about a rain check?"

Cindy Mae gave him a pout of disappointment, then replaced it with a perfect smile. "Oh, all right, Chinaman. But one of these nights you'll be in the mood to hippety-hop down the bunny tail, whoops, I mean, trail. And won't you be sorry if I'm not in the mood."

"I'll be sorry," Chinaman said. You were born in the mood, Chinaman thought.

★

10

AT the sound of the scream Chinaman picked up his glass of Southern Comfort and coke and walked unhurriedly to the window of his one-bedroom apartment. The green letters of his video clock flashed 1:15 a.m. Except for the angry, probably drug-induced, obscenities of the hooker arguing with her pimp, East Eleventh Street was quiet.

When the nearby dormitories of New York University had been occupied, Chinaman had assumed that hordes of pink-cheeked coeds would soon crowd out the hookers from the area, as inevitably as supermarkets were eclipsing bodegas. But after midnight, a few emaciated, shop-worn prostitutes continued to stand their ground peering and leering into slowly passing cars hoping to entice any john too dumb or too horny to worry about AIDS.

From his window, Chinaman could see several four-story tenement buildings across the street, their deserted, snow-covered fire escapes eerily outlined by the golden glow of a street lamp. The incessant yelps of an unhappy dog drifted in from the east, from somewhere inside the depths of the East Village.

He returned to his desk and moved the lamp closer to Judy Fisher's daily appointment book. Judy had decorated the cover and several pages of the book with sketches of faces, flowers and cats in various poses. According to her entries, she had met her clients in some of the city's most prestigious and most expensive restaurants, and danced the night away in the latest and most chic clubs and nightspots. On several occasions, she had marked a date with an "in" or "out," presumably indicating a rendezvous at her apartment or at the man's apartment — no dinner, no dancing, no preliminaries.

Of the more than 60 names of men listed at the back of the book only two were known to Chinaman: A flamboyant trial lawyer and the editorial director of a mid-town publishing firm. Most of Judy's clients were in their 40's although three were in their 30's and four were in their 50's. The only two in their 60's had question marks after their ages.

Their professions ranged from hotelier to politician, from businessman to artist, from restaurateur to judge. About half had their phone numbers jotted down as well. The prefixes were almost all "212" but those would be their business numbers; men cheating on their wives would know better than to give out their home phone numbers to women they dallied with.

In the sexual preference column, Judy had written "norm" after about ten names, "norm plus" after most and "weird" after two. The first "weird big creep" was a Michael Steiner, 53, "architect," and the second was a Richard McGovern, 47, "antiques store owner." Under the last column headed by a dollar sign, each entry had been allotted one, two or three exclamation points. Both Steiner and McGovern had rated all three.

Chinaman turned back to the date Judy was killed and read the entry written in blue-black ink: "Peacock Alley - R. McGovern. 8:00." Below it in slightly bluer ink was the hastily scribbled entry: "Harry's — 10:00." Judy had presumably met McGovern in a lobby bar of the Waldorf-Astoria and then met someone in the lobby bar of the New York Palace.

The toetag on the man in the morgue, the last man Judy Fisher had ever slept with, had read "Hans Schrieber." Chinaman checked Judy's book, and compared the names of everyone she had met for an appointment with those listed at the back. There was no "Hans Schrieber." But there was a name written into the diary section on three different dates; a name not listed at the back: "Julio Cesar." Chinaman would have to check if the name meant anything to Cindy Mae.

He closed the diary and inserted it inside the jacket cover of a large-sized trade paperback on the life and times of Edgar Allen Poe, then placed it in the non-fiction section of a corner bookshelf. He stared out the window for several minutes while finishing his drink and then went to bed. Within minutes, escorted by the familiar wails of nearby car alarms and distant sirens, he was asleep.

Chinaman dreamed of raging winds and heavy rain and flying debris and from somewhere inside a house being blown apart — a house the hurricane-force winds prevented him from reaching — Judy Fisher cried out for help.

DAY FOUR

11

A late morning shaft of light streamed across the crowded interior of "Southeast Asian Antiquities" and bathed selected shelves and their wares in a warm yellow glow. Sandstone Buddhas with full lips and enigmatic smiles meditated beside bronze Buddhas with elaborate decoration and haughty mien. A Buddha head with a tall flame-like skull protuberance peered at Chinaman through half-closed eyes and gave him a look bordering on a sneer.

As Chinaman opened the door, a bell rang and a well-coifed woman about forty emerged from inside the inner office. She also boasted elaborate decoration and a haughty mien. The tone of her "May I help you?" suggested that, in all honesty, she'd rather not.

Chinaman flashed his folder with its badge and handed her a namecard. "I'd like to speak with Richard McGovern."

As she stared at the namecard her very red lips curled in distaste. "So, am I to understand that you are a kind of police officer?"

"Private."

She repeated the word "private" as if she had bitten into a bad apple, then suddenly remembered what she'd learned in Dealing with Tradesmen Strategies 101: "Do you have an appointment?"

Chinaman favored her with the most enigmatic smile he could muster. The woman in turn gave him a smile both fixed and forced, iced a "One moment, please," and re-entered the office.

Chinaman stared back at the Buddhas, straining inwardly to

block out the memory of savage young men in blue peasant clothes and red armbands smashing his father's porcelain Buddhas and burning the wooden ones on their living room floor. All the while beating his "revisionist" father even after he was bloody and unconscious.

He spent the next several minutes watching mid-town traffic crawl its way down Second Avenue and calming his inner turmoil with well-practiced breathing meditation. When the inner door opened again, a grossly overweight man with beady eyes, thin lips and an aquiline nose waddled his way toward Chinaman. His bulk quickly reclaimed most of what little shop space his collection of Buddha images had left available. His right hand held the namecard while his left hand adjusted his paisley tie. The understated blue of the tie picked up the nearly invisible blue lines of the plaid suit. Neat, Chinaman thought. "Good morning," Chinaman said.

Richard McGovern stared at Chinaman for several moments as if trying to decide which of his many personalities the situation called for, then finally stuck out his hand and spoke with a British accent. "Sorry to keep you waiting; I was on a long-distance call." He glanced again at the card. "Mr...Chinaman. An interesting name. You are American-Chinese?"

Chinaman shook the man's fleshy, clammy hand. The expression, 'Tis time to fear when tyrants seem to kiss' flashed through his mind with the force of a slug from a bull-barreled Ruger. "Born in Beijing."

The man slipped the card into his vest pocket and folded his hands over his paunch. A perfect fit. "I used to deal in *Chinese* religious wares as well; especially Ming. Then the Communists suddenly released hundreds of Ming Buddhas onto the market and I lost a fortune." Chinaman tried to look sympathetic at the fat man's misfortune. "Now what is it I can do for you, sir?"

Well, for openers, fatso, you can drop the phony British accent, Chinaman thought. "I'm investigating the death of a Miss

Judy Fisher," Chinaman said.

The man's eyes remained fixed on Chinaman. His expression revealed nothing. His hands were immobile. Only slight lines of puzzlement creased his forehead. You're good, Chinaman thought.

Chinaman continued. "The young woman was murdered in the New York Palace Hotel a few days ago. You may have read about it."

"The New — Oh! Sorry. Leona Helmsley once bought a few items here to decorate her office, and I still think of it as the Helmsley. Yes, sir, I certainly did read about that ghastly murder. I dare say it sent shudders down my spine. But I fail to see how I might help you."

"You did know the girl, did you not?"

McGovern's eyes widened in surprise, then he allowed himself something between a chuckle and a chortle. His right hand again found itself tinkering with his tie. "Mr. Chinaman, I don't know what gave you that idea, and, while I would genuinely like to help, I'm afraid I–"

"McGovern — that's an interesting name too, but I don't really have time for your pretentious bullshit so why don't you stop pawing the paisley, lose the phony accent and we'll take it from there. It'll save us both a lot of time."

The man's hands attempted to regroup on their fleshy perch then dropped precipitously as if they'd been kicked off. McGovern drew himself up to his full height and out to his full width. "How dare you! You will kindly leave immediately or I'll be forced to call the police." He turned and began his waddling shuffle cum shuffling waddle back toward the sanctity of his inner office.

"That'll make two of us."

McGovern stopped in mid-waddle.

"Calling the police, I mean. You see, I haven't turned Judy's appointment book over to them yet and, well, sweetheart of a guy that I am, I was hoping I wouldn't have to. The way I see it, a man's sexual proclivities are his own business. Even the fact that he was

with a woman on the night she was murdered might not mean a
thing. But, if you insist, we'll make it official rather than private."
Chinaman turned and walked to the door.

"Mr. Chinaman." McGovern's British accent had faded with
the shaft of sunlight. Chinaman took his hand off the doorknob and
turned. McGovern briefly fingered the paisley then reached out to
nervously rub the shoulder of a large standing bronze Buddha. "You
understand, I have a wife and two children. I can't–"

"McGovern, your moral lapses interest me about as much as
your fake antiques. On the other hand, if you killed Judy..."

"*Killed* her? My God!" McGovern glanced toward his office
and lowered his voice. "Look, we had a dinner appointment on the
night she was killed. We met at the Waldorf for a drink, but when
she got there she said something urgent had come up and she couldn't
have dinner with me."

"Or take you to her apartment later."

"All right — or take me to her apartment later. I was upset but
she insisted; so after one drink, maybe 20 minutes, she left the bar."

"And what did you do?"

"I had one more drink, then went on home."

To your beloved family, Chinaman thought. "Did Judy appear
nervous?" he asked.

"No, not at all. Just in a rush."

"Did she say anything about whom she was meeting?"

"No. That's what upset me. She just kept repeating it was
something unexpected and something she couldn't get out of, and
that she'd make it up to me."

Chinaman stared at the man's fleshy face. "I don't know why,
McGovern, but somehow I believe you." Chinaman turned to
go. "I might be in touch."

"Mr. Chinaman. About that appointment book. I wouldn't
want to be involved in a police investigation. I would in fact be
willing to make it worth your while to let me have the book. You
see, any scandal could ruin me."

"Well, then, McGovern, you'd better hope that I catch the sons-of-bitches who did this. Because if I do, that appointment book is history."

Chinaman gestured toward the rows of Buddhas as he opened the door. "On the other hand, if I find out you *were* involved in Judy's death, you'd better find Enlightenment before I find you."

★

12

The older of the two girls was about 19 — a voluptuous Scandinavian with hazel eyes and the longest, most curvaceous, legs Danton had ever seen. She lay across the bed sheet in lace panties and see-thru bra flicking her moist, pink tongue along the head and shaft of his manhood with abandon. The second girl was a nubile Oriental — slim body, golden-brown skin, ample breasts and long, shiny, black hair. She was completely naked. She seemed even more at ease out of her clothes than in — almost as if she'd been born that way. She began licking and kissing his nipples and then moved to blow gently into his right ear. Just as Danton was about to explode with passion, the door crashed open and several well-armed and leather-clad women-warriors of the Amazon Annihilators raced into the room and surrounded the bed. While his two sex kittens fled in panic, the Amazons pointed their semi-automatics at him. Several of them knelt on the pink sheet and pinned his arms and legs to the bed and held him down until the leader of the group — a sultry redhead with green eyes blazing fiery hatred — placed the cold steel barrel of her Uzi 9 mm Parabellum against his now shriveled manhood and laughed. "You shouldn't have interfered in my operation, Danton. For that, I promise you'll get a bang out of this. Now say 'bye bye' to your joy stick."

THE AMAZING ADVENTURES OF
DANTON VS. THE AMAZON ANNIHILATORS
WILL BE CONTINUED NEXT ISSUE!

Chinaman studied the pages for several seconds then picked up his copy pencil and drew a heavy line through the sentence: "She seemed even more at ease out of her clothes than in — almost as if she'd been born that way." He added the squiggly proofreader's mark for "deletion" in the margin and allowed himself a sigh of regret. Sydney Goldstein didn't appreciate Chinaman's irreverent humor inserted into the company's lavishly illustrated, pornographic comic books, or, rather, as Sydney defended them to all comers, "avant-garde graphic novels, art books for the connoisseur."

And Chinaman's tiny glassed-in office as well as his desk and computer, were, after all, property of Sydney's Family Values Publishing Company — a company for which Chinaman supplied part-time copy editing and proofreading in exchange for the full-time use of an office, desk and phone; secretarial services, computer, fax and coffee were extra. Included in the arrangement were the embossed letters on the outer door well below the name of Goldstein's publishing company and one-fifth its size: *Chinaman Investigations*

He placed the pages of computer printout in his out basket then retrieved them as he noticed Goldstein's secretary walking by, her more-than-ample behind making impossible demands on her just-below-the-knee flannel skirt. He opened his office door and held out the sheets of paper. "Audrey, here's the last of it."

Audrey Lieberman had just unhappily celebrated her 30th birthday and, according to office gossip, was unhappily involved in an affair with Sydney, about 30 years her senior. Another five pounds and Audrey would be shopping for her hip-hugging office outfits in a "Big is Beautiful" store.

In the three years Chinaman had been working out of the magazine office, Audrey's disdain for the (porno)graphic novels Sydney published had intensified. She seemed to hold a personal grudge against the magazine for being filled each issue with expertly drawn, young, well-endowed, lascivious women; especially evil in her eyes was the luscious leader of the Amazon Annihilators. Chinaman had come to realize that Audrey was a woman who harbored more jealous anger toward a fictional character than toward the flesh-and-blood women in the office — Chinaman had tucked the observation away in his mental file as an important footnote on feminine psychology.

Audrey took the papers from his hand with a scowl and a sigh and, at arms length, carried them to her desk, as one might handle a decomposing, malodorous rat.

Chinaman leaned forward in his chair, turned on the computer, and began hitting keys. From the corner of his eye he spotted Sydney waddling up to his cubicle embalmed, as usual, in his own swirling wreaths of cigar smoke. His red-and-gold tie with flamingos profiled against a Florida sunset easily overpowered his blue-and-white checkered shirt. His large brown eyes and the enormous bags under them gave him the appearance of a credulous, cigar-smoking comedian; people who had failed to deal carefully with him in business soon learned just how shrewd a businessman Sydney Goldstein really was. He entered Chinaman's room and stood beside the desk with his paunch thrust out and one meaty hand gripping his hand-braided leather belt in the position of a happy Jewish Buddha and exhaled a stream of smoke past Chinaman's ear. "So, how's it look?"

"All set. Ready at deadline as promised. But I have to tell you, Sydney, it looks like Danton's finally finished this time."

Goldstein allowed himself a guffaw vaguely resembling a chuckle. "Don't kid yourself. That shmuck's got more lives than a pussy. And does that stuff sell magazines! I'll cash out long before Danton does."

Chinaman swiveled in his chair to a position just out of reach of spiraling eddies of blue smoke. "You keep chain-smoking cigars, you may be right."

Goldstein gave his cigar a look of incomprehension. "What? This? It's only my ninth this morning. I'm cutting back." He pointed the cigar in the direction of the computer. "You got any female clients like Danton got?"

Only one, Chinaman thought. Now deceased. "Not a one, Sydney. Not even close."

"Sam Spade always gets there first, huh?" Goldstein followed up his remark with a guttural sound somewhere between a laugh and a grunt and strode off abruptly to scream a string of epithets at a package-laden office boy about to enter the hallway.

Chinaman stared at the computer just as it announced:

Scan completed; press to see your results

Chinaman pressed the return button:

No record found.

He cursed the cursor and shut down the machine. As he'd expected, there was no record of a Hans Schrieber from any source he had access to — and that included sources whose coverage supposedly extended to Western Europe. Of course, with an avalanche of new data bases coming online every month, the chances of his having the latest one or the perfect one for a particular task were increasingly remote. The time involved in analyzing which data base was essential and which was dispensable was enormous, and as Chinaman couldn't afford any new ones anyway, it was a moot point. But he did feel some empathy for harassed doctors desperately trying to keep up with new medicines flooding the market.

It was true that data bases had sometimes proved useful in pointing him in the right direction but as his mentor, the late police detective Jimmy (the Tiger) Sterling, had solemnly warned at the beginning of Chinaman's career, "Data bases don't solve cases."

A few months after his father had been killed and his mother committed suicide, Chinaman had been smuggled to Hong Kong. A year later, thanks to the political pull of an NYU professor—a close friend of his late father's—Chinaman had arrived in New York. He had been befriended by the professor's brother, Detective

James Sterling, and had practically grown up with his two sons, one now a Manhattan cop and one with the CIA in Bangkok.

If Chinaman's data bases were to be believed, the last man Judy had ever slept with never went to college, never entered the military, never applied for a driver's license, and never opened a bank account. He'd also never been born, married, divorced, arrested (or, at least, not convicted), or felt the need to own a credit card. Close to one hundred dollars worth of data base time wasted on a man who didn't exist. At least, who didn't exist under that name.

Chinaman leaned back in his chair and looked at the framed covers of past erotic adventures hanging on the wall of a passageway just outside his office. He had wanted to meet the reclusive illustrator of Sydney's graphic novels for years. "Nymphet and the Nightstalker," "Amazon Annihilators," "The Legacy of Lolita," "Comrades and Concubines," and "Vindictive Virgins of Venus" might all be correctly described as soft porn but the beautifully colored illustrations and precisely drawn linework was erotic art at its best.

Whoever "Y.S. Lin" was, he or she often drew the required sensual human and mythical figures against a landscape resembling a traditional Chinese painting. Voluptuous, sexily clad female warriors in skimpy Western dress or in cheongsams slit to the waist fought to the death against a background drawn with an economy of strokes favored by Chinese masters.

Glimpses of willow branches hung heavy with snow, bamboo beneath desolate overhanging cliffs and plum blossoms beside waterfalls were often worked in between dialogue balloons and thought balloons. Even simple sound effects were often drawn with powerful calligraphic brushstrokes. Chinaman had the feeling that an extremely talented Chinese artist was slumming.

A sharp rap on his door woke him from his reverie. He looked up to see Audrey standing beside a plump, middle-aged, over-dressed woman with owlish eyes. Chinaman stood up and waved for them to come in although he knew that Audrey would open the door for a client but seldom ventured in herself. She had once told him that his office gave off bad vibes. He would have to ask McGovern to lend him a particularly auspicious Buddha.

The woman entered and sat down primly in the chair facing Chinaman. Chinaman sat down, only now remembering Audrey had said something when he came in about an appointment she had made for a caller when he was out. As he smiled at her, he tried to recall the name.

The woman's lips and fingernails were bright red, her eyes blue and her fleshy fingers were covered with gaudy rings. She had draped several strands of pearls around her neck, applied heavy eye shadow, heavier mascara and enough foundation powder to supply a good many of New York's actresses for several performances. Her hat was of the tight-fitting cloche variety but was adorned with a green feather and glittering sequins. The long, colorful dress over her dumpy figure may have been fashionable during the time of the Czar. For all Chinaman knew of women's fashions, Czarist dress was now all the rage. He suddenly remembered reading of yet another woman who had claimed to be one of the Czar's daughters. Maybe this was the one. Chinaman couldn't remember her name either.

The woman sat back in the chair and looked around his office without expression. Her deep blue eyes took in the blue-bordered New York State detective license, course training certificates and detective association certificates without expression.

Her eyes then moved on to the rubber plant, Dictaphone, corner book case and steel grey filing cabinets. She glanced briefly out the window at the cast iron building across the street, then returned her attention to his detective license as if checking to ensure that it wasn't outdated or forged.

Chinaman leaned forward and offered her a namecard. He tried unsuccessfully to keep the sarcasm out of his voice. "The

license says that 'Chinaman Investigations' has been duly licensed
to transact business as a private investigator and I just renewed it
a few months ago. You can verify that with the Department of
Licensing Services."

The woman took his card and smiled mysteriously. Her voice
was low and husky. "I am not a fan of the Department of Licensing
Services, Mr. Chinaman. Sometimes they fail to appreciate our
business."

Through the glass behind her, Chinaman could see Sydney
at a desk with a phone at each ear. "Oh, are you also in the
investigation field, Mrs...?"

The woman opened her purse and took out a robin's-egg
blue namecard. She handed it to him with a graceful motion.
"Not exactly, but much the same business; if one looks beneath
the surface."

Chinaman looked at the card. Beside the phone number
and address was an embossed illustration of a crystal ball and tarot
cards:

MADAME ROSHA
PSYCHIC ADVISOR
IN TOUCH WITH THE SPIRITS

Chinaman silently acknowledged that she probably looked
the part of a psychic far more than he looked the role of a detective.
"And how may I help you, Madame Rosha?"

"This is merely a courtesy call, Mr. Chinaman. To let you
know that *I* am available to help *you*. I only recently moved to the
Tribeca area of Manhattan and I am making people in certain
professions aware of my ability to aid them in their line of work.
Sometimes an investigation into the affairs of this world needs a
bit of assistance from those of another world." Each time she
enumerated one of her talents, Madame Rosha held up a pudgy
finger and tapped it with a pudgy forefinger of her other hand:
"Locating missing persons, telepathy, seances, psychometry — all

this I can do. And much more. I am often able to reveal a person's past, present and future without asking a single question. Why should time or distance stand in the way of success?"

One of the things about the P.I. business that had intrigued Chinaman early in his career was the number of weirdos, kooks, space captains, airheads, bimbos, moonstruck sunworshippers, the loony and the lonely, the cracked and the crazed there were who seek out the services of private detectives. He sometimes wondered what exactly that said about the profession he had chosen.

He held his smile in place. "Well, Madame Rosha, I do appreciate your dropping by to let me know about this. The next time I run into a dead end I'll certainly–"

Madame Rosha placed Chinaman's namecard to her forehead and held it in place with both hands. She began humming in a low, flat monotone while rocking slightly back and forth. Chinaman wondered if a donation of some kind might be necessary before he could get her to leave his office. It wouldn't be the first time he had paid someone to leave. Suddenly she stopped humming, stopped rocking, and opened her purse. She dropped the card inside as if it were too hot to the touch and snapped it shut. More than a touch of concern showed through her smile. "Mr. Chinaman, do you drink coffee?"

Chinaman pointed to the cup on his desk. ' "Tea at night. Coffee on the job." ' Something much stronger when the memories hit.

Madame Rosha allowed herself a theatrical sigh. "I do not always understand the messages I receive, but I see that coffee is not good for you. I see that it is somehow connected with danger. Mr. Chinaman, please avoid coffee for the next week or two if you can. Please."

Chinaman stood up, hoping Madame Rosha would also. She did. "Well, Madame Rosha, I thank you kindly for that warning and I can assure you I intend to heed it."

She smiled at him and shook her head slightly. "No. You are not one who believes that my methods of investigating are as sound as your own. But I think one day you will. Please remember my warning." With that, Madame Rosha gave him a kind of curtsy, turned and left his office. Chinaman sat down heavily, wondering if what had taken place had taken place or if Madame Rosha was a figment of his imagination.

He drained his coffee cup just as Audrey's voice streaked through the air like the agitated whine of a car alarm. "Chinaman! Line three!"

Chinaman picked up the phone and pulled his notebook out from under a stack of books written to aid copy editors and proofreaders. He reached for a pen as he spoke into the phone. "Chinaman Investigations."

The voice was heavy with a Spanish accent. "Mr. Chinaman. This is Sanchez. You remember me from the hotel?"

"Sure, Francisco, how you doing?"

"I'm doing OK. Look, Mr. Chinaman, Angela...she's a little mad at me. I don' think I can get anything from the file righ' now."

"That's too bad, Francisco. I was hoping to get a lead."

"Well, I did manage to get a look at the check-in card and bill. On the computer. You got a pencil?"

"Sure. Shoot."

"OK. The room cost $235 plus tax and she paid with a Diner's Club card."

"Who did?"

"The girl. Judy Fisher."

"Freddy, who was the bill made out to?"

"Judy Fisher."

"Judy is listed as the check-in guest on the card?"

"Right, Mr. Chinaman. Judy Fisher. Seventy-six Charles Street. Apartment 2-B. Manhattan."

Chinaman's mind began racing. If Judy billed the room, somebody must have made it worth her while. And that means the john wasn't staying in the hotel. Or else he did but wanted to avoid bringing Judy back to his own room. But that was the least likely and Abrams would have covered that angle; so it meant the john just went to the hotel to drink at the bar and Judy picked him up. But then how did the hit men know where to—"

"Mr. Chinaman, you still there?"

"Yeah, Francisco. Sorry."

"That's OK. Well, the number in the party was listed as 'two' and, like I said, the rate was $235 plus tax. There was only the restaurant charge on the bill. The food Freddy brought them, I mean."

Chinaman sighed. "That's it, then."

"And the phone calls."

Chinaman sat up in his chair. "Phone calls?"

"Yeah. You want me to give you the numbers?"

"Does Jesse Jackson want to be president?"

"Does Jesse Jack- Oh! You're making a joke. OK. The local one is Six. Eight. Six. Four. Seven. Eight. Eight."

Chinaman repeated the number.

"And the bill for the phone call is three dollars."

"That much for a local call?"

"Yeah. The guy spoke for 23 minutes. And the other one is an overseas call."

"Where to?"

"Well, the country code is 218. City Code is 21. The number if Four. Three. Five. One. Seven. He spoke for eleven minutes."

"OK, I'll check that. Freddy, you did a great job."

"Well, thanks, Mr. Chinaman. Sorry I couldn't get you the bill."

"Forget it. You got me what I needed. Good luck with Angela. And, thanks!"

Chinaman hung up the phone and turned to page 35 in the Manhattan phone book, "International Country and City Codes." He found "218" and "21" third from the top in the fourth column. Two-one-eight was the country code for Libya. Twenty-one was the city code for Tripoli. He lifted a volume from his bookshelf

— Coles Cross Reference Directory Manhattan 2000 Issue. He turned
to the section listed as the "Numerical Telephone Directory" —
names of telephone subscribers arranged in sequence by their
telephone numbers. Coles was on-line now but Chinaman found
checking the book a bit faster. "686 exchange area code 212."
"4788 Walter Hauptmann 410 E. 32nd Street." In *Coles* a phone
number would get him a name and address but not an apartment
number. He turned to the section labeled "street address directory."
Walter Hauptmann had first been listed in the directory in 1998.

Chinaman closed the book, grabbed his jacket from the back
of his chair and left the office.

★

13

THE superintendent leaned several rolls of his abundant fat against the bedroom doorway of what, until about 30 hours before, had been Walter Hauptmann's apartment. A study in sloth, the man was dressed in a food-stained undershirt, naturally faded jeans and mismatched sandals. His sole expenditure of energy was concentrated in maneuvering a toothpick between yellowed teeth and sending forth an occasional belch.

With minimum interest, his deep-set eyes followed Chinaman's movements as Chinaman opened and closed drawers and doors, ran his hand under tables and shelves, and stood on chairs to examine light fixtures and the backs of pictures.

"Like I told yah, the cops missed the guy by about three hours; you missed him by thirty. They combed the place up and down and came up empty. And you–"

"You said somebody" — Chinaman sneezed three times before he could finish his question — "in the building spotted him leaving?"

"Mrs. Armentrout. In 5-B. She's retired. Likes to sit by the window and watch the street. She don't miss a thing. She saw the guy taking off with luggage. Moving like a bat outta hell. And she says he was looking over his shoulder like he was afraid of something. So, she stopped by to tell me; thought I should know in case the guy's a serious scumbag trying to beat the rent or something."

He waited for Chinaman to finish sneezing before continuing. "So I checked it out and, sure enough, the place was just like you see it now — empty." He shrugged — a slight movement which inexplicably released another rumbling belch. "OK by me. He's paid up till the end of the month. And he didn't bother to collect his deposit."

So the landlord's got his deposit and you've got the twenty I gave you to let me in here, Chinaman thought. 'God's in his heaven and all's right with the world.' "How do you know the cops came up empty?" Chinaman asked. The man again waited for Chinaman to finish another fit of sneezing.

"How do I know? 'Cause I checked the place over before they arrived. Still beats the hell outta me how they knew he was gone in the first place. Or why they were so interested in him. He and his buddy were probably the quietest guys I had in the building."

"His buddy?"

"Yeah. Another guy's been staying with him for about a week. So quiet you wouldn't even know he was here."

"Mid-thirties, dark hair, clean-shaven, handsome?"

"Yeah, that's him. Good-looking like a movie star. A little like Rock Hudson before he stepped into the shit. I never got more out of him than a smile and a nod. Well, man wants to keep his affairs to himself, that's fine with me. And, like I said, the cops came up with nothing."

Which is exactly what I'll most likely come up with when I check out Walter Hauptmann's name in computer data bases, Chinaman thought. First, Hans Schrieber. Then, Walter Hauptmann. Two Germans. One living in New York City under a phony name. One staying in his apartment, also under a phony name. One gets killed, one runs away. It was beginning to sound like a Brothers Grimm fairy tale. Why was one killed? Why was one running scared? And how close is Abrams to finding out?

Chinaman examined the fine-grained black dust on the back of a white metal chair. When he began sneezing again, he moved to the door. He blew his nose in the hallway while the super closed and locked the apartment door. "That's a nasty cold you got."

"Yeah. I always get one this time of year," Chinaman said. Especially when I'm in a room with carbon-based fingerprint powder sprinkled all over, Chinaman thought.

★

14

CHINAMAN placed his muff-type protectors over his ears and opened the door to the indoor firing range. He walked to a firing position and placed several bullseye targets and a box of .38 police special cartridges on the shelf before him. He clipped a target onto the line and wheeled it out to about 20 yards, then loaded five one hundred grain wadcutter rounds into his revolver.

On either side of him several positions were occupied and the sound of gunfire was clearly audible despite the ear protectors and the sound-proof dividers. He fired off the rounds slowly and deliberately, then wheeled the target back in to check his group.

As he did so, he felt the presence of someone behind him. He turned to see Cathy Farmer, an athletic, almost muscular, woman in her late 20s, whose expertise with guns was among the best of anyone at the range. Chinaman could often tell from the sound of a gun's report what weapon was being fired; it was rumored that Cathy Farmer could identify the weapon *and* the type of ammunition being used.

When he had first begun to practice at the range, Chinaman had spurned her sexual advances. After that, for a brief period, she completely ignored him. Then she began making it a point to come on to him whenever he went to the range to practice, her conversation laced with sexual remarks and innuendoes and *double entendres*. Chinaman was more concerned with her barely suppressed anger than with her lewd speech: A woman with a loaded gun who knew how to use it and who was angry at him always made Chinaman nervous.

She looked out at him through the tinted glass of her impact-resistant lenses. The blue of her ear protectors nearly matched the blue of her tight sweater and even tighter jeans. A red-white-and-blue button on her sweater spelled out Cathy Farmer's succinct philosophy:

The more people I meet
The more bullets I need

Her left hand held a target known as a "bad guy" and her right hand held a Smith & Wesson model 4506, a "new generation" .45 autoloader. No longer the latest; but one of the best. She gave Chinaman a smile bordering on a leer. "Hey, Chinaman, how ya doin'?"

"Chinaman is doin' just fine, Cathy. How you doin'?"

She gave his revolver a look of disdain. "You still using a 'wheelie', Chinaman?"

"Yeah, I finally traded in my Flintlock."

Cathy Farmer was one of the breed of gun-lovers who had decided that anyone not using a semi-automatic pistol was still ensconced in the Stone Age. "I hear wheelgunners drink only near-beer, that right, Chinaman?"

"Milk, mostly. Sometimes, close to bedtime, only near-milk."

Cathy held up her still unmarked 'bad guy' target. The 'bad guy,' a heavy-set, beefy, repulsive hoodlum armed with a deadly weapon, epitomized the fears of all New Yorkers. He sighted at Chinaman through his right eye down the rear sight of a revolver held in his right hand. His left eye was closed in a squint and his left hand was held across his chest. The backs of both hands and fingers were covered with curly hair. He had a full head of greasy hair over a fleshy face fixed in a nasty scowl. His trousers were rumpled, especially near the crotch. Chinaman had long ago decided that the illustrator must have modeled the 'bad guy' after a photograph of his ex-father-in-law.

Cathy slipped a nine-shot clip out of her belt pouch and slammed it into the butt of her stainless steel pistol. "This next group is for you, Chinaman." She blew him a kiss then disappeared behind the divider.

Chinaman cranked a new target back out to twenty yards just as Cathy wheeled hers out to ten yards. Chinaman wasn't certain if, like Annie Oakley, Cathy Farmer had learned that "You cain't get a man with a gun." He felt some comfort in the knowledge that inside the green acoustical tiles and soundproof board of each firing position's divider was a metal plate. Or so he'd been told.

He tried to concentrate on his own firing. Then he heard the sound of Cathy's carefully spaced rounds and he glanced over at her target. She was squeezing off her nine shots to encircle the "bad guy's" crotch — in the shape of a heart. Chinaman fired off a round at his target. And missed.

★

15

JOANNE walked to his table and slammed the beer bottle onto the table's checkered red-and-white cloth, crushing Chinaman's cigarette and missing the fingers of his right hand by about an eighth of an inch. She threw her head back and stalked off to the bar without a word.

Larry Sterling ogled her exposed midriff and shapely backside and turned back to Chinaman. "If I didn't know better, amigo, I'd say your lady is anxious to do you bodily harm."

Chinaman lit another cigarette. "Who isn't? She'll just have to take her place in line and wait her turn like everybody else. And guess who's right at the head of that line?"

Sterling chuckled and spoke through a mouthful of beef — medium to well done. "Abrams still on your case, is he?"

"He seems to think I done his daughter wrong."

"Did you?"

"Like Gary Hart said, 'I don't have to answer that.' Or was it Bill Clinton?"

"I suppose the old boy has warned you not to fuck with his case, right?"

Chinaman nodded. "But he knows damn well I'm on it full throttle. I just arrived at Schrieber's apartment a day after Abrams did. It was covered with fingerprint powder."

"So? The Homicide boys always–"

Chinaman held out his thumb and forefinger indicating an inch in thickness. "It was this thick. And I'm allergic to that goddamn stuff. And Abrams knows it."

Sterling spoke while laughing and chewing. It sounded like

a man choking. Chinaman wondered how many things he could do at the same time. "Anybody ever tell you, Chinaman, old friend, that you private eye types sometimes get more than a bit paranoid?"

"All the time."

"Maybe he just didn't like Mr. Moto marrying his daughter."

Chinaman smiled at the memory of Larry and his brother Scott, both about 13-years-old, assisting a 12-year-old Chinaman in fights against Lower Eastside kids who constantly called him a "Jap." As they grew older, the brothers had good-naturedly labeled him 'Mr. Moto'. And how's Scott doing in Bangkok?"

"Loves it. Maybe I'll leave New York's Finest and join him one fine day." Sterling hurriedly picked up his napkin, dipped it in his water glass and energetically rubbed it over a fresh food stain on a cuff of his long-sleeved shirt. He was the type of heavy eater whose face, arms and legs remained thin even as his abdomen spread ever larger and completely out of proportion. Chinaman suspected that, in the buff, Larry Sterling resembled not so much a man as a garden spider. It was the first time he'd seen him since his father's funeral. If he felt any regret at not living up to the image of his famous detective father, he didn't show it.

Chinaman timed his next remark in between Sterling's forkfuls of beef. "Not to change the subject, but speaking of what happened in a hotel room in mid-town. And speaking of the New York Palace Hotel...."

Sterling took a swig from his own beer bottle. Chinaman could almost picture bits of partly chewed meat cascading and rollicking on rivulets of beer as they spun and rolled and tumbled their way into the man's cavernous stomach. Chinaman had once seen the plaque on his desk which announced that one Larry Sterling had set a department record for gulping down the most pizza at a police picnic.

Sterling lowered his voice. "The papers had it almost right for once." For a moment he stared at the slice of beef on the end of his fork as if it was revealing to him what went down in room 1204. "It was a two-man hit team. The guy on the bed took a slug from a silenced .22 Beretta automatic pistol. The girl got it with the same caliber. Different gun. Two more slugs in the walls. Same caliber. Same weapons. Anyway, you know most of what we know from your chat with Abrams at the morgue, right?"

Chinaman thought of the slugs in the walls and of Judy trying desperately to escape the inevitable. "Oh, yeah. Abrams volunteered the information that the blood under Judy's nails proved conclusively that her assailant was human."

"That narrows it."

"And that he has blood type O."

"Great."

"Yeah, great. That narrows it to four out of every ten people in the country."

"At least you can eliminate runaway apes and Bigfoot as suspects."

"How do you figure it?" Chinaman asked.

"I figure it was her bad luck to pick up the wrong john just when he'd been marked for a hit."

"Fingerprints?"

"Nah. As they say on TV, these guys were pros. Credit cards and cash all there. And nobody in the hotel remembers seeing two men together on that floor. They were careful, these bastards. But from the slugs and whatever else the homicide people came up with, the lab boys say there were two. No more, no less."

"So how'd they get in?"

"Looks like the guy never knew what hit him. So either the girl fell for some kind of room service scam or else they used some kind of pick. These guys — they probably know how to open locks with picks faster than we open them with keys."

"I doubt that they picked the locks. The hotel's got card slots. Then again card slots aren't that new. Maybe some bright criminal mind came up with a counter."

"Yeah. Probably some guy doing twenty to life had nothing better to do. So he applied himself. Probably took out a patent."

"What about Hans Schrieber?"

"Lots of I.D. on him. Money too. The dough's legit; the I.D.'s as phoney as a three-dollar bill. We're running the usual checks. But if Abrams has come up with anything I'm not likely to hear about it. He's clamped down hard on this one."

"What about Schrieber's fingerprints?"

"No match yet. But, like I said, Abrams doesn't rush downstairs to share his information with those of us in License Division."

"What about the information they filled in when they checked into the hotel? Credit card receipt."

"Abrams is sitting on it."

"Can't you do better than 'Abrams is sitting on it'?"

Sterling reached across the table and with both hands pinched Chinaman's cheeks. "Hey! Chinaman! I got my secretary to have lunch with Abrams's secretary to pump her for info. For you! And now I got to buy *my* secretary lunch for doing it. And if Abrams suspects I'm your stoolie in the department, I could have some very rough days ahead."

Chinaman called for the bill. "I know. I do appreciate it, Sterling. That's why this lunch is on me."

"Yeah. I'm touched." Sterling's belch was loud enough to turn a few heads. Sterling didn't seem to notice. "So, you got any leads?"

"A hotel bartender who might recognize one of the men Judy had been with in the bar. If the guy comes in again. Says the guy was in a booth with her, then left; and he's been in the bar before." Chinaman rubbed his hand across his chin. He had forgotten to shave. He wondered if that was a sign of aging. "And Judy's appointment book."

Sterling raised his bushy eyebrows and gave him a conspiratorial grin. "Abrams know you got her appointment book?"

"Appointment book? What appointment book? You must have heard me wrong."

"I hope so. I ran into a gumshoe once; the guy had withheld information from Abrams and Abrams found out." Sterling gave him a histrionic shudder. "I don't even want to think about it."

The two men suddenly turned in the direction of a waiter raising his voice to three well-dressed men in their late twenties. Men with club ties and vulgar faces about to walk away from their table. The waiter held a tray in one hand and his other hand on his hip. His posture and voice were effeminate. "Sir, you can tip as you like, but waiters have to give 10 per cent to the bus boys, 5 per cent to the bartender, one per cent to the food runners and one per cent to the hostess. When you leave a three dollar tip on a sixty dollar check, it means I'm paying money so you can sit here."

The man he addressed his remarks to had an almost square head which was far too large for his body. His face was red with liquor or anger and his eyes narrowed as he spoke. "Tough shit, honey. Sometimes life is a real *drag,* right?" The man beamed with cleverness. His two friends joined in his laughter.

Chinaman called out to the man. "No need for vulgarity."

The men turned to him. The one who had commented on life spoke again. "You talking to me?"

"Indeed. I said there was no need for vulgarity." He laid a hand on Sterling's shoulder. "My friend here is allergic to it."

The man's eyes narrowed even more. Chinaman wondered if he was in danger of losing them altogether. The man theatrically cradled his right fist in his left hand. Chinaman tried to decide if it was a failed attempt at muscle flexing or if he was warming his knuckles in preparation for The Big Fight. He spaced out his words dramatically. "You want to play his hand for him?"

Chinaman looked at Sterling. "Did you hear what he said?"

"Yeah."

Chinaman spoke the line slowly and carefully. "'Do I

want...to play...his hand...for him.' A great line! Wasn't that one
of Edward G. Robinson's in 'Little Caesar'?"

"Nah! I think it was Bogey in 'To Have and Have Not.'"

"I think somebody said it to Charlie Chan once."

"I think I remember Amos saying it to Andy."

"I remember somebody saying it to Spiderman once."

"I remember hearing it on 'Gunsmoke.'"

"'I remember Mama'. Remember that?"

"I remember. They don't make programs like that, anymore."

"That's for sure."

Chinaman and Sterling turned back to the man. The man
seemed confused, then ventured a tentative step in Chinaman's
direction. One of his companions placed a hand on his recently
flexed arm and whispered something. The square-faced, muscle-
flexed man listened, released his left hand from his right and
allowed himself to be led to the door. As he walked he gave
Chinaman a wave of dismissal — there would be no Big Fight
after all; Chinaman had been deemed an unworthy opponent.

The waiter passed by Chinaman's table. "Thanks, guys."

"Anytime," Chinaman said.

Chinaman glanced toward the bar. Jo Anne was being hustled
by a yuppie type in a pin stripe. She had positioned herself in
such a way as to watch Chinaman's reaction. Chinaman made an
attempt to give her the show of jealousy he knew she wanted then
turned back to stare at the two X's on his beer bottle. He took a
long drag on his cigarette and spoke softly. "A .22 Beretta automatic
pistol, huh?"

"Yeah. Strange weapon of choice for a hit man, huh?" Sterling
positioned the thumb and forefinger of his left hand as a hammer
and barrel. When he let the "hammer" drop, he belched loudly.
"Who the hell uses a silenced .22 to make a hit?"

"Beats the hell out of me," Chinaman said. The
Israelis, Chinaman thought.

★

DAY FIVE

16

DESPITE his efforts to keep the man on the line, Chinaman could feel he was about to lose him. "Mr. Chinaman, let me again suggest that you direct your questions to Dr. Eliot. He is the forensic odontologist with the office of Chief Medical Examiner. And I really can't–"

"Dr. Martin, I appreciate that, but Dr. Eliot is a very difficult man to get hold of," Chinaman said. A very difficult man period, Chinaman thought. "And, according to his office, he did consult with you on this autopsy. The deceased's fingerprints didn't appear in police computers so I just wondered if you could tell anything from his teeth. You know, any fillings or crowns he might have had. Anything at all. I am a duly-licensed New York State detective." For whatever that's worth, Chinaman thought.

A sigh of surrender — music to Chinaman's ears. "All right. The man had two stainless steel crowns and a porcelain crown. Stainless steel simply isn't used in the United States."

"Would you have any idea where–"

"Communist countries. Or rather ex-Communist countries. They all use stainless steel crowns. Go to any New York Russian community like Brighton Beach and, if you can make anyone smile, you can see plenty of them. But the porcelain crown looks typical of Western dental work and it looks very professionally done."

The door to his office opened and Audrey Lieberman, chewing gum with her mouth open, placed a note in front of him and stood with arms folded across her chest waiting for an answer. Chinaman tried to read the note while concentrating on his telephone conversation.

The Medical Examiner's office called. It's been approved: You can call a mortuary and arrange to take care of the body. Should I call one? If yes, read below:

1. Do you want me to shop around for the best price or just do it?
2. Do you want any kind of service?
3. Marker or tombstone?
4. What religion was she?

Chinaman picked up a pen and circled the word "yes," circled "just do it" to one, "no" to two, circled "marker" and wrote "Catholic." At the bottom he scribbled, "Thanks, you're a rare treasure!"

Audrey loudly popped a gum bubble, cast him a glance balanced between boredom and cynicism and strolled out.

Chinaman pressed the phone closer to his ear and continued making notes. "If I had to guess I'd say your man was born in one world and moved to the other. Most likely he was born in a Communist country and, perhaps as a young man, moved to a Western country. Something like that. But I dislike guessing games. Now, I'm sorry, but my patients–"

"Doctor, you've been very helpful. May I ask, if you had to guess, which country you would say the man was from? Based entirely on what you saw in his mouth, I mean."

"Mr. Chinaman, you are the detective, not me. And I'd rather *not* make any more guesses. As I've told you, Dr. Eliot is a prosthodontist; I am an oral surgeon. If you want that kind of speculation–"

"Off the top of your head, doctor. If you had to guess."

"I told you — I have patients waiting! Now, goodbye, Mr. Chinaman!"

"Dr. Martin, I'm trying to find a murderer!"

A long sigh of resignation. "The deceased had bridgework

which Dr. Eliot is checking further. But from its shape and contours, again, as you say, off the top of my head, I would say the work was done in West Germany. And since you enjoy pure speculation, I will speculate further that the man was born in what was East Germany and moved to what was West Germany but, for whatever reason, didn't get around to replacing his stainless steel crowns with porcelain crowns. Now, off the top of my head, I have patients waiting and I have no more patience with your questions."

"Doctor, did anyone ever tell you you're a modern Sherlock Holmes?"

"Mr. Chinaman, did anyone ever tell you are a persistent pain in the ass?"

"Most people who meet me," Chinaman said. Including your friend, Dr. Eliot, Chinaman thought.

★

17

CHINAMAN sat at his desk and opened the mail: A card from his younger sister and her Caucasian husband in L.A. wished him a Happy Birthday and many returns. They'd gotten the day right, just the month wrong. The card included a square color print of the two of them sitting on a couch cuddling their Eurasian baby and a cocker spaniel. Domestic bliss. The kind of bliss that simultaneously fascinates and repulses wary bachelors. At least she'd been too young during China's years of madness to have been persecuted; or — unlike Chinaman — deeply traumatized.

A Con Edison bill which had been put into his box by mistake, a "We've Moved" notice from a clothing store he'd never heard of, a special offer on overpriced sunglasses stamped "For Your Eyes Only," and a credit card notice with a late payment charge that resembled a lotto jackpot. A catalogue of bullet-proof articles, including 'Kevlar Klothes for the Kids,' displayed happy children bundled up in colorful winter clothes designed to stop anything less powerful than a Scud missile. The catalogue blurb explained how the ultimate in protection against bullets would favorably impact their feeling of safety. Chinaman always wished people who used "impact" as a verb could be legally blown away. He wondered if all ex-Creative Writing teachers felt the same way.

He fumbled inside a desk drawer and pulled out a small personal address book. He thumbed through it as he picked up the phone. Chinaman was just about to hang up when Sam Richards finally picked up. "Richards, here."

"Sam. It's Chinaman."

"Chinaman! How the hell are you? Long time no nothin'
from you. I wasn't sure if you were still among the living."

"Sometimes I'm not sure."

"Ah, that's just the New York blues. Why don't you come
down to D.C. for a while? The winter's whiter here. And the
change'll do you good."

"Thanks, anyway. Better the blues you know then the blues
you don't."

"You got that right. Hang on one second. I'll turn the stereo
down."

Chinaman waited for the Pilgrim's Chorus of the Tannhauser
Overture to drop several decibels. In all the years Chinaman had
known him, opera had been Sam Richard's love. Opera and the
multi-layered, deceptively arranged world of intelligence agencies.

"OK. So you're calling to tell me you've decided to get out
of the gumshoe racket and join the Agency."

"No, Sam. I'm calling to tell you that Judy's dead."

"Judy? Judy Fisher? How? When?"

Chinaman filled Sam Richards in on what he knew. After a
short silence, Sam spoke softly. "Judy. I can't believe it. I only
met her a few times with you, but she seemed so...."

"Alive?"

"Yeah...alive. You got any leads?"

"I got a bartender in the hotel bar who might recognize a
guy Judy was with the night she was killed. Assuming the guy
ever shows up again. I got a psychic that says coffee could be
dangerous for my health. I got an ex-father-in-law crowding me
off the case."

"That's not much."

"Yeah. Sam, you might be able to help me on this one."

"*I* can? I'd love to. But how?"

"I smell something."

"Give it to me."

"I'm not sure yet. But the dead man was a German. All I.D.

was fake. The weapon the hit man used was a silenced .22 Beretta. That ring any bells for you?"

Wagner's music filled in several seconds of silence before Sam Richards spoke again. "Can you hold a minute?"

"Sure."

Chinaman waited. In the background he could hear Tannhauser play his harp and sing of love. Chinaman took a drink of his Scotch and shuffled again through a pile of color prints. Sam Richards and Chinaman watching the skaters at Rockefeller Center. Judy striking a silly-sexy pose beside the Center's 60-foot balsam fir. Judy and Sam Richards eating hot dogs in Central Park. Sam Richards and Chinaman on the steps of the Met. The three of them together standing beside a horse-and-carriage on 59th Street.

"Chinaman."

"Yeah."

"OK, look. I've got Company business in New York this week, anyway. So, here's the deal. You book us a nice place for lunch in mid-town. I can make it tomorrow, if you like. Something with a little class, but not too expensive because this one's on you. As soon as I hang up, I'm going to do some checking. I can't promise anything but I'll call in a few favors on this one. If it was what it sounds like, I'll find out why."

"I want names."

"Chinaman! I'll do what I can. I'll make some phone calls. See what turns up. You just sit tight. I'll be at the skating rink at Rockefeller Center. Where we met last year. One o'clock."

"Thanks, Sam."

"Chinaman, I'm sorry about Judy but take my advice and sit tight until I get there. You want to avenge Judy's death? Fine. Just remember what the Sicilians say about vengeance. And, believe me, they're experts on the subject."

"What do they say, Sam?"

"'Revenge is a dish best served cold.'"

"I want justice, Sam, not revenge. And justice is a dish best served steaming hot."

"Chinaman. Wait."

"Sure."

"I mean it."

"Right, Sam," Chinaman said. No way, Sam, Chinaman thought.

★

18

THERE were days when Chinaman felt the texture of life hardening, congealing into a tight band clamped around his skull. If he could, he would rent a car and drive out to Long Island, up into the Catskills, or around rural New Jersey, especially Amish country. Usually, he couldn't.

On those occasions he would sit at his desk and turn to the inside back cover of his appointment book where he had taped a newspaper article which consisted entirely of 13 short lines. The article had turned yellow with age and he had forgotten to write down the year. But it was an AP story about a 52-year-old real estate broker in Little Rock, Arkansas, who loaded his .32-caliber pistol, walked out onto a remote jetty on the Arkansas river, and shot himself in the chest. According to police, the man was attempting to make a suicide look like homicide: his pistol had two balloons attached and would have floated away, but the man's hand became entangled in the strings.

And that was it. Or, as Chinaman's Vietnam vet friends sometimes said, even after all these years, "There it is."

A man desperate enough to end his own life. Yet a man still concerned enough to try to make it look like murder. Why? Insurance money for a loved one? A means of throwing suspicion on a known enemy? A sly attempt to present an unsolved mystery to the citizens of Little Rock and the world? A *beau geste*?

This real estate broker: Did he see before he died that the balloons had gotten entangled? And did he struggle with his last ounce of strength to pull his hand from the strings? Or did he enjoy the irony and laugh his way into eternity?

Balloons were for festivals and gatherings; jugglers and clowns; parades and parties. Birthday parties. Garden parties. Coming-out parties. Balloons tied to prevent a suicide gun from drifting away were balloons for another kind of party: A Going Away party.

The article was only one short paragraph but it had started Chinaman writing again. Intermittently. With long weeks, even months, in between sessions. But something in the final act of an Arkansas real estate broker had done the job; primed the pump. Something in both the man's attempt and in the result screamed out a message that exploded inside Chinaman's brain like a stun-grenade:

THERE IT IS!!!

Chinaman closed his appointment book and dialed Cindy Mae's number. Cindy Mae picked up on the sixth ring. Her greeting sounded rushed. Chinaman wondered if he was interrupting something. "Hello, yes?"

"Cindy Mae? This is Chinaman."

"Chinaman! I bet you're calling to tell me you're on your way over."

"I wish I were, Cindy Mae. I'm calling because I've been looking through Judy's appointment book and I need to ask you a question. I'm not interrupting anything, am I?"

"Nothing that can't wait. And helping you on a case makes me all warm inside; makes me feel satisfied. Like scratching an itch, or fulfilling a sexual ache. So you ask away, Chinaman; don't you worry about little 'ole me."

"OK. Judy wrote the name "Julio" or "Julio Cesar" three times in her diary. Twice in late October and once in early November. The name is the only one in the appointment section that isn't also listed at the back of the book. She also didn't write down where they met."

"I know."

"You do?"

"Well, I glanced through it once or twice after Judy's...death."

With a fine-tooth comb, Chinaman thought. "Did Judy ever mention him to you?"

"Never. But I remember I took a call once from a man with a Spanish accent asking for Judy. He wouldn't leave his name. When I mentioned it to her she just thanked me and kept quiet. It wasn't like her; usually we talked about men. Swapped gossip, you know?"

"When was that?"

"Hmmm, early November, I think."

"All right, Cindy Mae. Many thanks."

"Any leads in Judy's murder, Chinaman?"

"Nothing very promising. But I'll keep on it until something turns up. I can promise you that."

"Didn't the police even find a murder weapon? Burt Reynolds—"

Yeah, maybe Burt Reynolds did it, Chinaman thought. "They won't find any weapon," Chinaman said.

Cindy Mae sounded disappointed. "They won't?"

"Amateurs are attached to their guns, but professionals throw their weapons away after a kill. They don't want a weapon that's been 'compromised,' one that might lead the law to them. The gun that killed Judy is most likely in the East River."

"I bet it is!"

"You do?"

"Sure! The TV news always has something on guns and bodies being found in the East River. They ought to close that river down and make it into a big superhighway!"

Chinaman wasn't certain if Cindy Mae was drinking or was just naturally spaced out. "Thanks, Cindy Mae."

"Sure, Chinaman, any time. And, remember, when you get tired of fighting what's between us, just give me a call."

"Between us? Oh! Sexual dynamics, you mean?"

"You got it."

"Cindy Mae, I can feel my guard dropping every time I talk to you." As he hung up, Chinaman realized there might be more truth in that then he'd wanted to admit.

★

19

AN hour later Chinaman sat back in the chair peeling a banana. He cradled the phone's receiver between his shoulder and ear. As the lawyer's anger increased and his voice rose with indignation, Chinaman let his shoulder down a few inches. The man's voice seemed to rise in volume to compensate. The last thing Chinaman wanted to discuss was a case that had nothing to do with Judy's death. Especially one he had successfully completed but for which he hadn't been paid. "And it's the sloppiest document I've ever seen. Do you know how many misspellings I counted? If your secretary can't type, then for God's sake-"

Chinaman placed his lips close to the mouthpiece and shouted. "Hey!"

He scrutinized the banana's mushy spots and spoke softly and patiently into the sudden silence. "What do you see near each of those misspelled words? What...do...you...see?"

"Initials. I see initials."

"Good! Very good. Now beside my initials you also see the initials of the witness. Is that right or wrong?"

"Yeah. So–"

"Right! So that later on down the road, if the man does what accident witnesses are wont to do and changes his story and says he didn't know what the document he signed was all about, you have proof that he and I read it over *carefully* together. That we even corrected and initialed any and all misspellings together. Now what that is is standard procedure to insure that a witness can't claim later that he didn't read the document or didn't understand what he read. In other words, my secretary is professional enough and *experienced* enough to misspell words *intentionally* in documents such as this one."

"I see."

Chinaman took a bite of a banana. "Do you see? Good. Now see this: I don't ever again want some wet-behind-the-ears lawyer calling me on my home number during the evening especially during the news simply to demonstrate his amateurism. That quality being something I already noted as soon as we met."

"Hey, you get a lot of work from me, fella. You can't—"

"Can't I?" Chinaman hung up and pressed the remote control to turn up the volume. A leathery faced Dan Rather informed Chinaman that the events he'd just missed were "part of our world tonight." The news was over. Chinaman finished the banana and threw the peel in the general direction of a rattan wastebasket. The phone rang again.

Chinaman picked up the phone and spoke into the mouthpiece. His voice was just short of a scream. "Yeah! Chinaman!"

Silence. He listened for breathing. Still more silence. He used the remote to turn the TV down. Then he heard it. Almost inaudible. "Chinaman?" A female voice in pain. A lot of pain.

"Yeah. Who is this?"

"...Cindy Mae."

"Cindy Mae. What is it? Are you all right?"

"Chinaman...He hurt me...."

"Who hurt you, Cindy Mae?"

"Oh, God. He hurt me bad." Chinaman had heard it before. The moan of a human being pushed beyond human limits.

He snapped off the TV. "Cindy Mae, where are you? And who hurt you?"

Her words were distorted by a mixture of anguish and pain. "He hurt me. I begged him not to. He didn't have to. He could've had the money back. Chinaman, help me."

"Cindy Mae, where are you?"

"Home. I'm home." Cindy Mae's voice suddenly choked on spittle or blood. Her sobs rose and fell and trailed off to become a long, low whimper.

"Cindy Mae, I'll call an ambulance. Just wait by–"

"No. No ambulance. Just you."

Chinaman calculated the length of time it would take him to get there. If he could get a cab right away.... "All right. I'll be there in ten minutes. Do you understand?" Chinaman thought he heard the sound of the receiver hitting the floor. "Cindy Mae, do you understand me?" Silence.

He threw on a sweater and slid a holster onto the left side of his belt into a cross-hand draw position. He loaded his Smith and Wesson with Winchester 158-gr. lead HP +P rounds, snapped the cylinder shut, and slid it, butt forward, into the holster. He paused just long enough to make one quick phone call, then threw on an outer vest and a leather jacket and headed for the door.

★

20

CHINAMAN pounded harder on Cindy Mae's apartment door. He could hear the tinny, mechanical, sound of "Love Me Tender" repeating itself over and over from inside the apartment somewhere near the door. The wooden door was thick and sturdy — but if it hadn't been locked from the inside, merely shut, he might be able to get it open.

He took out a small leather card case and selected his American Express card. Never enter a home without it. It was nearly expired and if the card were ruined in the process of serving as a key, it might as well be that one. He inserted the card between the door and the doorjamb just above the knob and just below the lock — and pushed. The card bent around the door and Chinaman worked to slip it past the latch bolt. Half a minute passed without success. He swore out loud and pushed on the door with his body to allow maximum space for the card. He jiggled the card and pressed on it until his wrist was sore. Finally, he heard the sound of the card snapping the latch back. He pushed the door open.

A dancing sunflower lay on the floor near the door. The plastic flower writhed as it turned, the motion of its stem and leaves rolling its attached pot first one way and then another. It moved as something alive and in agony. Chinaman reached down and shut it off. Its writhing stopped, its tiny light went out and its hideous version of "Love Me Tender" ceased. He unzipped his jacket and slipped his .38 out of its holster. He passed through the dimly lit hallway into a brightly lit living room. A coffee cup lay on the floor and several magazines were scattered about: The result of a struggle or simply signs of a careless housekeeper. He was about to call out when he heard the groan from the bedroom. Cindy Mae lay on the floor beside the bed. The receiver was off the hook and had fallen to the floor next to her. She was completely naked. Chinaman knelt beside her and spoke softly. "Cindy Mae. It's Chinaman."

There was massive swelling of tissue above and below her left eye, a superficial but lengthy gash on her forehead, and blood on her swollen lower lip. A spot of blood had dried at the entrance to one of her nostrils and an ugly reddish blue bruise was spreading over one cheek.

The contents of a soft drink bottle had spilled near the bed. The bottle itself lay on its side, its blood-stained rim almost touching the receiver. Chinaman placed his fingers on her neck just below her jaw and felt her pulse while he listened to her breathing. Both were regular. She had been badly beaten but as far as he could tell there was no internal damage. But the swelling and discoloration gave her face the appearance of a grotesque mask and Chinaman could feel his stomach beginning to churn. He'd always found the sight of a bashed-in, still living, human being far more gut-wrenching than that of a corpse. And Cindy Mae's once attractive face had been beaten into something not quite human.

Cindy Mae stared at him through her one unblocked eye and spoke in a whisper. "Chinaman. Get me up to the bed." Her raspy voice sounded as if it came from the parched throat of a withered old woman.

As Chinaman gently lifted her onto the bed, he saw the crisscross pattern of welts across her buttocks and the dried blood on her inner thighs. She grimaced as he lay her on the bed and covered her with a sheet. She coughed and cleared her throat. Phlegm passed from her mouth and dribbled onto the sheet. Chinaman quickly placed several tissues in her hand, then went to the bathroom, wet a face cloth with hot water and returned to wipe her face. The open eye stared into his own. The swollen lips opened slightly. "He shoved the bottle into me, Chinaman. He shoved—" Her voice rose and cracked and Chinaman interrupted before she could get hysterical. "Relax, Cindy Mae. Just relax. If you feel you're able, tell me who did this to you and where I can find him.

Through obvious pain and barely moving lips, Cindy Mae managed to give him the man's name and address. And then she insisted on telling him the whole story.

"All right, tell me what happened." He placed her thumb and forefinger on her nose. "But pinch your nose, don't blow it."

She followed his instructions and held the bridge of her nose. "He came here before. Maybe four times. He's a Wall Street bigshot. He likes to dress me up in pinafores and frilly dresses and bows and bobby socks. Then he speaks to me like I'm a wayward daughter. He spanks me over his knee and makes me promise my "daddy" that I'll be a good girl. He always, I mean, usually, after spanking me with his hand or a brush, he'd enter me. Briefly. And that would be it."

"So, once his paid-for power trip was over, he'd get dressed?"

Cindy Mae nodded. "He even gave me tips on stocks and bonds while he got dressed. Judy and I both made money on them."

"OK. But tonight it was different."

"Yes. It started out the same but after the spanking he stood up and took his belt off. He told me I had been such a naughty girl I needed a whipping. When I resisted, he beat me and then whipped me with his belt. When he stopped he demanded that I thank him...thank my "daddy" for disciplining me. But he said I didn't thank him respectfully enough and he called me a fucking cunt and a treacherous slut who deserved to die. He demanded fellatio, and when I wouldn't he forced the bottle between my legs, again and again. And the whole time he did it with the bottle...he was singing a child's lullaby. He kept...."

Cindy Mae wept softly and then uncontrollably and finally

began screaming loudly. Chinaman decided to let her get some of it out of her system before stopping her. He wiped her forehead and held her hand. "Cindy Mae, I've called a friend of mine. He's a doctor. He's on his way here. When he arrives, he'll take care of you. But I want you to promise me that if he says you've been hurt inside, you'll go to a hospital. Promise me."

Cindy Mae's voice came out as a broken whisper. "All right. I promise. But I hate hospitals. My sister almost died in one when they gave her the wrong—"

Chinaman told her to calm down. She wasn't going to die in any hospital. He replaced the receiver and stared at the empty bottle. 'Black Cherry Soda. All Natural.' He went to the kitchen, filled a face cloth with ice cubes and returned to the bedroom. He placed it gently over Cindy Mae's eye. When she winced he squeezed her hand. He sat with her in silence for several minutes until the doorbell rang.

Frank Wynne was a burly, bearded, dark-complexioned, bear of a man who took birth, death and everything in between in stride. His bedside manner was relaxed enough to lead dying patients to believe they'd star in the next Macy's Parade along Fifth Avenue. He could so quickly put people at ease and get them talking about themselves that Chinaman always thought Wynne would have made the perfect detective.

During the three years he'd been with a large New York detective agency, Chinaman had investigated a former patient of Wynne's who was suing him for malpractice. The agency said it was most likely a lost cause and told him to advise Wynne to settle. But Chinaman had smelled greed and deception and had kept at it, even on his own time. And, sure enough, the alleged victim had run the same scam in three states before moving to New York. Over the course of the investigation, Wynne had changed from Chinaman's drinking buddy into Chinaman's friend.

Chinaman filled him in as he led him into the bedroom. Frank Wynne greeted Cindy Mae as if she were an old friend who'd had an accident and sat beside her on the bed. He named each instrument as he pulled it from his bag. "First the eyescope; then the stethoscope; then the blood pressure gauge. Nothing I take out of this bag will cause you any pain or discomfort. OK?" Cindy Mae nodded.

While he examined her he kept up a humorous monologue about his problems with his wife and mother-in-law. Chinaman knew he had never been married, but he saw Cindy Mae's swollen lips part in a smile.

Wynne held up one finger. "How many do you see — one or two?"

Cindy Mae's swollen lips formed to indicate "one."

"You haven't vomited, have you?"

She blinked her one good eye and shook her head.

"Good. Now as soon as the voyeur-detective leaves the room, I'll be able to remove the sheet and examine you further." Wynne turned to Chinaman. Chinaman took the hint and left the room. He picked up the cup and magazines and straightened the throw rugs. Wynn's reassuring bedside monologue drifted into the living room like the well-modulated voice of an early morning radio announcer.

Chinaman stared at the swirling snowflakes outside the window trying to ignore the unmistakable stirrings of vengeance inside him. He wished he had left his .38 in the apartment. Poorly proportioned snowflakes as large as bits of paper floated gracefully by the window, rose effortlessly, and disappeared. December — the month for traditions: jingle bells, sleigh rides, Christmas cheer, good will toward men. Also, as every cop knows, traditionally the most violent month of the year.

After a few minutes, Wynne stood next to him. Chinaman spoke without looking at him. "She looks like hell."

"She looks worse than she is."

"What about the abrasion on her forehead?"

"Laceration."

"All right, goddamn it. Laceration."

"It'll heal on its own. No stitches needed. No scar."

"Well, what about—"

"Look, Chinaman. The guy punched her on the nose and ruptured some blood vessels. So she's going to have a bloody nose for a while. He punched her in the eye causing still more ruptured blood vessels. Lots of tiny ones. And the skin is most transparent there, so she's going to have a black eye. She's got an accumulation of fluid in the tissues around the eye. So she's got a *swollen* black eye. All of that will heal. Her face will be fine. Most important, she's got no vision problems."

Chinaman turned to look at him. "Are you her doctor or the guy's attorney?"

Wynne glared at him. "How'd you like a few ruptured blood vessels on *your* face?"

"Sorry. Behavior displacement. It's not you I'm angry at."

"The only serious problem she might have is her vagina. I don't think there's anything to worry about, but if it'll make you feel better, I'll sleep on the couch tonight and check her over thoroughly tomorrow. I'll also talk her into getting some X-rays at my office. And some counseling."

"Thanks, Frank."

"Yeah, thanks, Frank. Now, unless you're a registered nurse, or trained to help rape victims get back their self-respect, get the fuck out of here."

"Fine. I'll just say goodbye."

As they entered the room, Wynne sat on the bed. "Our girl's going to be sore, and she won't be nightclubbing on New Year's Eve. But, for now, I can fix her up right here." He looked at Cindy Mae and winked conspiratorially. "I don't like hospitals much either." He reached into his black bag and removed a hypodermic syringe. "Tomorrow, I'll have her give me the name of a girlfriend who can come over and stay with her for a day or two; tonight, what she'll get is a good, uninterrupted sleep. You, Chinaman, can piss off and tend to whatever nefarious gumshoe business awaits you. Just call my office late in the morning for a progress report."

Chinaman squeezed Cindy Mae's hand. He knew she was trying to convey gratitude but something about her contorted one-eyed stare made him feel naked and ashamed. He crossed the bedroom to the door. "Thanks, doc."

Wynne turned toward him and lowered his voice. "You want to thank me? Get the bastard."

"Consider it done."

As Chinaman left the apartment, he could hear Frank Wynne detailing some fanciful adventure about Chinaman and a nurse and he heard a noise from Cindy Mae. Painful, cracked, raucous and barely recognizable — but it was a laugh.

★

21

"YOU'RE supposed to put the goddamn thing under the windshield wiper! Not *glue* it onto the *windshield*, asshole!"

Chinaman walked carefully over long stretches of ice frozen to the circular sidewalk of Battery Park City's luxury condominium while keeping his eye on the uniformed doorman. The man stood near the entrance of the building stoically weathering the abuse of an outraged motorist, a furious, middle-aged man holding a windshield scraper and pointing toward a Mercedes almost totally enveloped by the late afternoon's snowfall. Stuck fast to the windshield was a large Day-Glo green sticker:

> This vehicle is parked here illegally.
> Your license number has been recorded
> and repeat offenders will be reported
> to the traffic bureau for towing.
> The management

Off to his left, a crane roared into life, and Chinaman turned to see the huge orange cranes working on the rubble of what until recently had been the World Trade Center Complex of buildings. Powerful lights infused his view of the scene with an eerie glow, a macabre set for a horror movie. Cranes, grapplers and a wrecking ball lined up in such a way as to suggest the Chinese character for "heaven." The night was just cold enough to conceal the unpleasant odors which continued to haunt lower Manhattan.

He shifted his attention back to the outraged motorist and

the doorman. Just above the men, a few snowflakes spun aimlessly about in the light of a street lamp before being blown inland by a cold breeze off the Hudson. Chinaman listened to the high-powered, Mercedes owner scream abuse at the doorman. Wealthy WASP vs. blue-collar black.

Knowing how to manipulate people into giving him what he needed often meant the difference between success or failure on a case. Chinaman knew he had gotten good at it. But he had wondered about his chances of actually getting past a doorman and inside the apartment of someone living in a well-guarded building of a luxury condominium. Now, he had his answer.

The doorman kept his gloved hands folded in front of his chest. "Sir, I already told you before: You can't park in front of this building for more than twenty minutes."

Chinaman approached the doorman and briefly flashed his leather folder with its detective shield, then replaced it inside his jacket pocket. "Is there a problem here?"

The motorist pointed his scraper at the watchman. "He pasted the fucking sticker on my windshield! How am I supposed to see to drive? He's supposed to place it under the wiper, not glue it to the windshield! And I told him I'd be out in half an hour."

The watchman turned to Chinaman as the acknowledged arbitrator. "Half an hour? Officer, that car's been here since early this morning. And this isn't the first time. It's about the tenth time."

"Bullshit! I only ran in to change clothes."

Chinaman had guessed right. No one involved in a heated argument would check his identity closely. If he represented authority, they didn't want the specifics of his identity; they wanted his approval — his support. Chinaman stared at the car for several seconds, then turned to the motorist. "Those icicles along the bumper didn't form in half an hour."

The man shrugged and held his palms out. "OK, so maybe I–"

"You broke the rules so you paid a price. If I see that car here when I come back downstairs, it'll be in a police pound. Now clean off the windshield as best you can and move it!"

The man muttered and swore under his breath but did as Chinaman ordered.

The watchman's face lit up with pleasure. "Thanks, officer. I'm sorry about the glue. But that guy uses this place like it's his own personal parking lot."

"No problem. I know the type." Chinaman gestured toward the building. "I'm here to see a Ronald Hillman in 9-D and I want to make sure that, if he's in, he stays in until I reach the apartment. I'd appreciate it if you call him *after* I'm in the elevator?"

The watchman led him out of the wind into the hallway. "You got it. But if you could just sign in so I can cover my ass if he complains...."

"Sure. But I'll make sure he doesn't make any trouble."

Chinaman signed in the log as Sgt. Kuan Yu, the name of a hero from the Chinese novel, *Romance of the Three Kingdoms*, who eventually became worshipped as Kuan Kung, God of War. He scribbled a precinct number so that it was illegible, then headed for the elevator.

Even before he knocked, Chinaman could tell from the darkened peephole that he was being watched. The voice inside was gruff and low-pitched. Even impatient. Ronald Hillman had obviously decided his best play would be to show the cop how tough he was. "Yeah?"

"Police officer," Chinaman said. He briefly opened his leather folder to flash his detective shield near the peephole. "Would you open the door please, Mr. Hillman?"

The voice lost a bit of its defiance but the door remained as it was. "What's the trouble, officer?"

Chinaman slipped the folder inside his jacket pocket. "Someone has filed a four-fifty-one. I'm here to check it out."

"What the hell is a four-fifty-one?"

It's the temperature at which paper burns, Chinaman thought. Which even a scumbag like Ronald Hillman would know had he read Ray Bradbury's novel, *Fahrenheit 451*. Sounded nice and official though, so what the hell? "A young woman has filed a complaint against you charging assault and battery."

"Against *me*?!" Innocence. Disbelief. Indignation. An innocent citizen unjustly accused.

"Against a Ronald Hillman of this address. Could you open the door, sir?"

Chinaman heard a lock turn. And another one. As he listened to the sounds, he could feel something inside him stirring. He took a deep breath to calm himself. The door opened a few inches. The chain lock remained in place. The tone of the voice was poised somewhere between defiance and fear. "You got a warrant or something?"

"Look, Mr. Hillman, the lady will probably change her mind by tomorrow morning and withdraw the charge. Believe me, her type often does. I just need to ask you a few questions. I'm off duty in ten minutes — until then I've got to go through the motions. Now could we talk inside?"

Chinaman heard the chain being slid along the groove of its door plate. It seemed like minutes. He tried unsuccessfully to avoid thinking of Cindy Mae's hideously distorted face. His ex-wife had been right: There *was* something out of control lurking inside him. Something behind a barrier just waiting for a chance to escape. Something, as she had put it, "Poised to wreak havoc. To smite the foe." And despite all the padlocks, and chainlocks, and dead bolt locks and combination locks Chinaman had installed over the years, that something was always there. Sometimes she had referred to it as the Mr. Hyde inside Dr. Jekyll; Chinaman had denied it, sometimes angrily, sometimes with a dismissive laugh. But she had been right. And she knew it. Chinaman hated her for being right. And she knew that too.

Chinaman took another deep breath. The door opened.

Ronald Hillman wore a burgundy designer robe with an initialed crest and a yellow tennis racquet motif over flannel pajamas. A thick blue towel was draped over his broad shoulders. Not the kind of bathrobe or pajamas or towel sold on 14th Street. His hair dripped water onto his leather slippers. His fleshy face wore the expression of a busy man annoyed by an unnecessary interruption. He was a couple inches over six feet, almost exactly Chinaman's height, but he was several years younger and must have been 20 pounds heavier. Hillman carried it well enough but the good life of a Wall Street securities analyst was quickly catching up with him.

He motioned impatiently for Chinaman to walk inside and then he closed and locked the door. He passed Chinaman and entered the living room ahead of him. He spoke with the arrogance of a man used to having his orders obeyed. "Look, I just took a shower. So make yourself comfortable while I put some clothes on. I'll be out in five minutes, OK? That'll still leave us with five minutes to laugh this off before you go off duty and out of my life. And, Jesus Christ, wipe your feet, will you? It cost me a fortune to get the ash out of that carpet!" Hillman glanced around the apartment, his eyes narrowed in an almost murderous rage. "Every goddamn thing in here had to be replaced."

"You weren't here when the planes hit the towers?"

"Nah, Paris."

Chinaman thought of his writer friend who had run from her apartment in the next building screaming hysterically, her arms swollen with bits of iron and glass from the collapsed towers; of her harrowing escape to New Jersey; of her constant headaches, depression and nightmares. "You were lucky."

"Lucky? The towers were across the fucking street! It still looks like a war zone out there. Property values here have collapsed."

"I mean you're alive."

Hillman gave Chinaman a look suggesting Chinaman would

obviously never understand the importance of coming out ahead on an investment, and then disappeared into an inner hallway. Chinaman looked down at his slush-covered shoes. Sure enough, they needed wiping. But that could wait. The wall above the couch was almost completely covered by an enormous oil painting consisting of nothing but blue squares, black rectangles and gray circles overlapping black squares, gray rectangles and blue circles.

An aquarium lined the entire length of the wall opposite. The tank had been placed just outside the range of track lighting and was bathed in a subdued blue glow from recessed lighting underneath. Inside the glass barriers every color of the rainbow was in motion. For a minute, Chinaman watched the hypnotic display: Elaborate and impossibly graceful dorsal fins, caudal fins, pelvic fins, pectoral fins, and anal fins swayed languorously back and forth while slim bodies enclosed in magnificently colored scales of perfectly symmetrical designs were propelled by fantails, sword tails, round tails and flagtails. Chinaman stared at the yellow eyes, green eyes, black eyes and orange eyes which returned his stare without expression.

On the coffee table an art deco halogen lamp cast a dim glow over a neatly arranged pile of investment newsletters and stock market reports. Bound volumes of Value Line ratings and reports lined the room's only bookshelf. A work table was set up with a computer no doubt directly linked to a stock market or a brokerage house.

The only other printed matter in the room was a stack of *Power and Motor-yacht* magazines. Ronald Hillman didn't seem to have much time for literature. Between beating up women and keeping track of the commodity and stock markets, the man probably had his hands full.

Chinaman thought of the makeshift shrine two blocks away near the Hudson River. The hundreds of teddy bears with photographs of those killed in the attacks; the poignant letters from family members left for their lost loved ones. Chinaman was quite certain that if Ronald Hillman had been killed in the attack, no one would have left a teddy bear for him.

Over the purr of Hillman's hair dryer, the soft sounds of Kitaro drifted innocuously from Bose speakers bathing the room in New Age music. The dreamlike melodies and saccharine harmonies made Chinaman feel as if he were being asphyxiated by a slow leak of odorless gas. He crossed the thick cream carpet to the window and looked out at the choppy black water of the Hudson and across the wind-blown waves to the lights of New Jersey.

His eye was drawn to a well-lighted railway station and on to the huge Colgate clock. The hands of the clock read 11:03. Chinaman stared at the river and thought of Cindy Mae. He pushed up the window and let the cold air rush into the room.

Hillman had entered the room without a sound but Chinaman turned at the powerful scent of men's cologne. Hillman was dressed in a crewneck sweater, pleated trousers and tasseled loafers. On panel after panel of his sweater a carefree yuppie couple was frozen in the act of hitting a tennis ball to one another over a net. He looked at the open window. "Jesus Christ! Are you crazy? It's freezing in here. Shut that window!"

Chinaman closed the window and walked a few steps toward the center of the room. With the window closed, the man's perfumed scent grew stronger, almost overpowering. Something about Ronald Hillman's face puzzled him. Then he realized the man had no character in his face. No depth. It was like looking at a re-run of 'Leave it to Beaver.' The man would be a natural to act as one of the blind date disasters on 'Sex and the City.'

Hillman spoke with his hands tucked imperiously into his pockets. "Now, what is all this absurd nonsense?" Hillman delivered the word 'nonsense' with a British accent. Yet another obnoxious Anglophile. Chinaman remembered reading an article about Americans being overawed by an upper-class British accent.

Hillman must have read the same article.

Chinaman unzipped his jacket and took out a notebook. He looked at it as if reading. "A Miss Cindy Mae Gardner domiciled at seventy-six Charles Street, apartment 2-B, Manhattan, has filed charges against you of assault and battery in that between the hours of nine and ten this evening you threatened her and then carried out those threats physically, causing her extensive bodily harm." Chinaman closed the notebook. "Are the lady's charges correct, Mr. Hillman?"

"Lady?!" Hillman gave Chinaman a smirk and took a cigarette from a silver case on the table. Lettering on the case said something about a sailing club. He lit his cigarette with a silver lighter, exhaled histrionically and sat on the sofa. "Look, officer, I think I'd like to speak with my solicitor before answering any questions."

"Solicitor" instead of "lawyer." Another nice British touch. Strange. Chinaman was under the impression that at least that first war — the one with the British — Americans had won. He'd have to check. He sat on the edge of a leather ottoman, his head beneath the level of Hillman's; his body posture suggesting his own awareness of Hillman's superior position in life. He tried to inject a hint of a whine into his voice. "Look, Mr. Hillman, we haven't officially filed the lady's complaint yet. We're not certain we're even going to have to. Four-fifty-one's are a pain in the butt. And I've got enough paperwork on my desk without this. If you could simply tell me your side of the story, we can probably drop this right here. Especially if the woman in question was, as I suspect, a...professional."

Chinaman watched Hillman's thick lips break into a smile. The fish had taken the bait. Chinaman was more than ready to give him all the line he needed. If only Chinaman could avoid thinking of Cindy Mae's face. It reminded him of his father's face; what had been left of it.

Hillman leaned back comfortably into the sofa, arms

stretched, legs crossed. "Yeah, you could say she was a professional."
He rose, walked to the stereo system, restarted the CD, then sat
back down on the couch. "What did you say your name was?"
"Kuan Yu. Sergeant. Investigative Division. One Police
Plaza."

"Well, sergeant, you hit the nail on the head. The *lady* was
no lady. She's a hooker. Oh, she's good at it. Damn good. She
doesn't have to freeze her ass off walking the streets or hanging
around Lincoln Tunnel servicing the schmucks from Jersey. She
just lies on her backside in a fancy Greenwich Village apartment,
you know what I mean? And she rakes in the loot faster than half
the guys on Wall Street." Hillman paused to stare at the window
noisily banging in a sudden gust of wind. He had obviously
decided he didn't need the phony accent. Chinaman was one of
the boys. A locker room buddy. Chinaman glanced at the fish
tank. Flashes of reddish gold darted through the water. The chase
was on.

"But the broad has had it too good for too long. She forgets
she's supposed to give some *service* — especially for the kind of
money *she's* charging. So, tonight, I asked her for a few favors. I
mean, hookers and innovative sex acts go together like a horse
and carriage. Right? For them it's all an act anyway."

Chinaman stared into the plush expanse of carpet and allowed
furrows of complexity to crease his forehead. "Well, Mr. Hillman,
the woman claims that when she refused to provide you with
certain services, you physically assaulted her."

Hillman spoke while putting out one cigarette and lighting
another. "Hey, come on, sergeant, I may have slapped her or
something. I mean, I was sore. Who wouldn't be? Two-hundred-
and-fifty bucks is for a good time. A guy doesn't get it, he gets
bitchy, but, hell, she'll get over it. She doesn't want to provide
service, she shouldn't be in a service industry." Hillman chuckled
and favored Chinaman with a wink. "The truth is, sergeant, the
lady is a tramp. Not a pavement princess, maybe, but still a tramp."

Chinaman smiled. Not, as Hillman supposed, in confirmation of his point of view. But because somewhere inside him, he felt the last barrier break. Whatever it was that he worked so hard at keeping bottled up was out. Poised for action. *Demanding* action. Mr. Hyde was indeed "Poised to wreak havoc. To smite the foe." And it felt good. Almost a sexual ache finding release. He got up and walked to the window. He beckoned to Hillman. "I want to show you something."

As Hillman walked to the window, Chinaman slid it open. Hillman almost pouted. "Jesus, you *are* a fresh air freak. What the hell I gotta see that you need to open the fucking—"

Chinaman made his move before Hillman could finish the sentence. He took a half step backward, reached behind him and grabbed Hillman's left wrist and brought his arm up behind his back. Hard and fast. He placed his right hand on the back of Hillman's thick neck and thrust his head out the window. Chinaman leaned his body weight against Hillman, immobilizing the man's right arm against the windowsill.

Hillman wasn't happy. At first, he had a lot to say. Until Chinaman jerked his bent arm up higher. Then, after one scream, Hillman was still unhappy but quiet.

"Tell me what you see out there, Mr. Hillman."

"See?! Where? For Christ sake—"

"In the river. Over there."

"You mean Liberty Island?"

"What's on Liberty Island?"

"The Statue of Liberty, for Christ sake! I'm freezing! It's snowing! Let me back in. Are you crazy?"

"And what is the Statue of Liberty?"

"What the hell—I don't know what—Ouch!"

"Wouldn't you say the Statue of Liberty is a lady?"

"Yeah, yeah."

"A very fine lady?"

"Yeah, all *right*! Hey, you ain't no cop!"

Chinaman pushed up on the arm. "No, I'm not. And you are not much of a human being. But she is a lady, right?"

"Yeah. Yeah! Yes!"

"And what is Cindy Mae Gardner?"

"What is she? She's...ow! A lady! She's a lady! All right?!"

Chinaman watched the layer of soft white flakes melt onto Hillman's recently washed hair. "And I'll just bet you'd like to send her one hundred red roses and a note of apology for the way you treated her. Isn't that right?"

"Yes! I'll send the roses."

"How many?"

"One hundred!"

"Long-stemmed?"

"Yes! Long-stemmed!"

"And I believe I heard you say you'd pay all medical bills."

"Yes!"

"And the note of apology?"

"Yes! Jesus, I'm freezing to death!" Hillman seemed near tears. Chinaman's right hand felt frozen. He brought the man's head back in, spun him around, then rushed him toward the couch and let him go. Hillman crashed against it on his left side and let out another scream.

It hadn't been easy but Chinaman had been willing to let it go at that. Extracting a mere ounce of flesh — instead of a pound — would eat out his insides for awhile but he could live with it. But when Hillman looked up, something about his expression gave Chinaman reason to hope.

Hillman massaged his left arm with his right hand. "You're not a cop, you son-of-a-bitch, and I know the penalty for impersonating one. But before I turn your ass in I'm going to teach you a lesson so that you'll think twice before defending whores again."

Maybe it was his size, or his youth, or the fact that life had always gone his way. Whatever it was that motivated his move,

Hillman lurched up off the couch, snarling and swinging. Mr. Hyde was almost beside himself with joy.

Chinaman was no martial arts expert. After he'd arrived in the States, he had tried his hand at a number of self-defense systems all boasting exotic names ending in vowels; systems Chinese were supposedly good at. But after a number of false starts and a broken toe from slapping a mat wrong, he found he was actually best at old-fashioned, sweat-drenched, work-your-ass-off, American boxing at Gleason's Gym in Brooklyn. Over the years, his street fighting style absorbed a bit from each discipline he had tried and, though the result was an eclectic and far-from-perfect mix of techniques, he knew he was a difficult man to beat in a fair fight.

From Hillman Chinaman had expected a fast, straight right aimed at his head, but the man drew back and threw everything he had into a roundhouse right. It was the kind of roundhouse right that cowboys swung at each other in early black-and-white Westerns. ("Why, you no-account slippery varmint! Take this!") Even John Wayne knew better than that. Chinaman could have gone out for coffee and still had time to carefully consider which method he would use to counter Hillman's attack. He decided on the one judo move he'd always been good at.

As Hillman lunged, Chinaman did several things simultaneously. He grabbed the man's right hand with his left, dropped into a stoop, threw his own right arm around the man's waist, and while pulling hard with his left hand, thrust his own waist in tight against Hillman's legs. With his own point of balance well below Hillman's, Chinaman executed a by-the-numbers *O goshi*, a major hip throw. It wasn't perfect but over the years he'd found it to be the most unexpected and therefore most effective move he could make against a blow aimed at his head. Hillman landed on his back, his feet striking the fish tank, sending panicked fish searching for shelter.

Hillman got to his feet quickly, anger replacing shock on his face. As he did so, Chinaman moved in and, feigning a right, landed a hard left on Hillman's jaw. He followed it up with a right to the solar plexus, and another left to his nose. Hillman stood with his hands at his sides and stared at Chinaman with an unfocused gaze. Blood trickled from his nostrils, onto his lips and threatened to stain his tennis sweater. Chinaman reached out with his left hand and held the man's right ear. "Ronald, I'd say it's time the referee stopped the fight. Whatdayasay?"

Before Ronald Hillman could express his opinion, Chinaman drew his right fist over to and above his own left shoulder and, with every ounce of fury he could muster, backhanded Hillman across his right cheekbone. Hillman went down again, again striking the aquarium, this time sending waves rippling along the surface of the water.

He lay on his back and wiped blood from his nose with thumb and index finger. He held up his hand. "Enough!"

Chinaman stood over him. "I'm a private detective. One thing we never do is impersonate a police officer, lawyer or federal employee. It's against the law to do so. So I think you misunderstood me when I arrived. I was simply trying to make peace between you and Cindy Mae and I said I was bringing a 'peace offering.' Isn't that right?"

"Yeah, yeah. That was it. 'Peace offering.'"

"And you wouldn't be forgetting about the roses, apology and medical payment."

Hillman spat some blood onto the carpet. A spot of blood landed on one of the panels of his sweater just inside the next. Fifteen — love. He nodded. "Yeah, I'll remember." Chinaman started to step over him to walk to the door. Then he remembered what Cindy Mae had said about the humiliation the man had forced on her. Chinaman lifted one shoe and then the other, wiping the soles along the pleats of Hillman's trousers. "Almost forgot. You told me to wipe my feet." Chinaman walked to the door. "Enjoy your evening."

Chinaman signed out and nodded to the doorman. The man gave him a smile of recognition. "You find Mr. Hillman, all right?"

"Sure did. He's got a great place up there."

"That's the way it is; some got it, some don't."

Chinaman thrust his hands inside his jacket pockets and hunched into the bitter wind rushing in from the Hudson. By the time he reached the subway entrance Chinaman felt a satiated Mr. Hyde once again safely back behind his barricade. Snoring contentedly.

22

CHINAMAN hung up the pay phone and walked toward the RCA Building. The news from Wynne had been good; X-rays showed nothing broken, and the examination revealed that at least all physical damage could be repaired — and without the need of a hospital bed.

The sunlight was brittle but bright, the temperature low but refreshing. Chinaman moved through the bustling, spirited, holiday crowd, past a four-foot tall sidewalk-Santa Claus with a crooked beard, and approached the skating rink at Rockefeller Center. It was not a pleasant walk. His boyhood experiences during Mao's Great Cultural Revolution had left him emotionally scarred and, whenever possible, he preferred to avoid crowds, demonstrations, marches, parades — anything in which human emotion might be manipulated and exploited. He no longer broke out in sweat when walking through densely crowded streets but noisy political demonstrations could still unnerve him to the point where he could almost not function. The only ones he had ever spoken to of his phobia were Scott Sterling, Judy Fisher and his wife. And that was only because they had seen him react to noisy crowds. Scott had told him he would get over it in time. He hadn't. His wife had insisted that he should see a psychiatrist and had chided him for refusing western therapy in favor of meditation. Judy had insisted that great sex could cure anything including traumas induced by the Cultural Revolution and had done her best to prove it. The meditation or, perhaps, the sex, seemed to have lessened his fears, but he knew he was far from being completely cured.

He walked in the direction of the 81-foot-Norway Spruce idly wondering what he would have bought Judy for Christmas had she lived. Last year it had been silver earrings made in Mexico. Now, no doubt, tucked away somewhere inside Cindy Mae's jewelry box. Maybe they brought women bad luck.

He spotted Sam Richards at the eastern end of the skating rink. The slightly fleshy face, closely trimmed mustache, neatly combed black hair and, as always, the immaculate dress. His perfectly fitted Navy blue suit was complemented by a blue-and-red Ivy League tie. The long point collars of his plain white shirt did their best to trim a bit of thickness from the face, and the black plain-toe oxfords emitted a just-out-of-the-box shine.

Chinaman knew that there would be a Rolex "Oyster" under the sleeve and several gold credit cards in a supple and elegant calfskin pocket secretary.

He was a few pounds heavier than he was the last time they'd stood here with Judy. Almost exactly one year ago. And a lot huskier than when they'd been stationed together in C.I.D. Pacific Command, Taipei, Republic of China. Richards looked like an affluent tourist out for a stroll at Christmas time. Or a secret service agent who'd forgotten his sunglasses.

As Chinaman approached, Richards tilted his head and gave him a slight smile. Chinaman had seen that mannerism of his many times before — it was a suggestion that they shared a secret, or that Richards was privy to whatever secret Chinaman might be hiding. Over the years, he had seen it in all-night poker games, from Taipei's Phoenix mountain to New York's East Village. Whenever Chinaman bluffed, Richards always seemed to know.

The men shook hands.

"Been a while, Chinaman."

"Too damn much of a while, Sam." Chinaman withdrew his hand and turned up the collar of his jacket with both hands. "So, what is it exactly you've got for me?"

Richards rubbed his gloved hands together and turned to

him. "What I've got for you is a piece of advice. I want you to stay away from this one."

Chinaman gave him a hard look.

Richards turned back toward the skaters and lowered his voice. "The guy's name — his real name — was Bernard Hoefer. Thirty-one years old. Single. Possibly bi-sexual. Born in Leipzig. Moved to Frankfurt when he turned twenty-five."

"I was right. The good doctor *is* a modern Sherlock Holmes."

"Say again?"

"Nothing. Sorry. Go ahead."

The men began a slow walk through the crowd. Richards kept his voice low. "Hoefer had advanced degrees from the best German universities in aeronautical engineering. A brilliant student. Worked briefly for Lufthansa. At the time of his demise he was working for a German engineering firm in Munich."

Chinaman waited. When no more came, he asked: "And that's it?"

"That's it. Except for his travel plans."

Right. To somewhere that he complained about being "dry." Not as opposed to "wet," but as in 'no alcohol allowed.' As in Muslim countries. As in Libya. "Tripoli," Chinaman said.

Richards turned slightly toward him and raised his eyebrows. "Jesus Christ, you are a fucking detective, aren't you?" Then he lowered his voice still further. "He was about to get on a plane for Libya."

"To render services to Qaddafi in exchange for a big payoff."

"To render services for Qaddafi's air force. An air force which had been in desperate need of expertise in increasing their in-flight refueling capacity. Which just happened to be Herr Hoefer's specialty."

Chinaman stopped to watch a teenage girl in a blue-and-white jacket over a red-and-white chiffon skirt cut perfect figure eight's. It reminded him of an American flag flapping in the breeze. He spoke aloud but mainly to himself. "Israel."

"You got it. Thanks to Herr Hoefer's valuable assistance, Qaddafi's Soviet-supplied Sukhoi-24 bombers can now refuel in mid-air and go on to strike at Israel. Now he was on his way to

Tripoli to provide another service for Qadaffi."

"Such as?"

Richards grinned. "You know better than that, Chinaman. You don't have the need to know."

Chinaman tossed his cigarette onto the ground and stepped on it.

"So you're saying–"

Richards leaned forward and threw his arm around Chinaman's shoulder. His lips were only inches from Chinaman's ear. He smiled to passersby as if he were playing a joke. "What I'm saying is that what went down at the hotel was a Mossad hit. And I'm saying further that I want you to stay away from it. And I mean *far* away from it."

Chinaman gave him a slight smile that came off as a grimace.

Richards sighed and took his arm away. "Look, I know how you feel about Judy. I liked her too. We had some great times together. But she was at the wrong place at the wrong time. With the wrong guy. You can't expect Mossad to leave a witness to a hit. Believe me, they don't like it when somebody threatens Israel's existence. They take it personally."

"And I don't like it when somebody kills a friend of mine. I take that very personally."

Richards pointed to the statue of Prometheus. "This guy made a wrong move and ended up tied to a boulder while a fucking eagle ate his liver. I'd hate to see you end up like that."

Chinaman walked off and Richards caught up. "So are you going to drop this or not?"

"What do you think?"

"I think I'll let you buy lunch. When my turn comes you probably won't be around to accept."

★

23

JOANNE stood at the bottom of the bed holding the towel and making certain Chinaman was paying proper attention. When she was certain, she dramatically whisked the towel away and the coin that had been under it seconds before had disappeared and now reappeared in another spot on the bed. She looked at him with the undisguised pride of an amateur magician whose act was a resounding success. Chinaman looked at her nearly naked body with undisguised lust.

"Well? No applause?"

Chinaman applauded. "Magnifico! Fantastique! You are the next Houdini. Now try your magic in bed."

"Don't you want to know how it's done?"

"Not when I'm horny."

"But you're always horny." Jo Anne picked up the deck of cards and loose coins and put them into a drawer. "The whole art of being a successful magician is to make the audience (that's you)look somewhere else or think something else while the magician's hand moves."

"The whole art of being a successful magician is having scantily-clad young women assistants."

Jo Anne ignored him. "It's all in the set-up. And if the set-up's right, when you think I'm doing one thing, I'm actually doing another. The success is in the diversion. Misdirection is the key."

Chinaman leaned his head back against the bedboard. "I'm looking at your bra and panties and wishing they could be diverted into the laundry basket and you could misdirect yourself under the sheet. Fair enough?"

Jo Anne stretched sexily and gave him a teasing pout. "Humphhh! I thought you were taking me out to dinner to make up for buying me a bracelet under false pretenses."

"If I said it, you can consider it done. A private eye is only as good as his word."

She reached up, removed a green jade pin and shook her head. Her fine black hair cascaded down over her bare shoulders. "Just don't forget I'm performing next Friday in the amateur magician's contest."

"I wouldn't miss it for the world."

Jo Anne moved toward him while running her tongue slowly between her lips. She stared at him while cupping her breasts in her hands, then reached behind her back to undo her bra.

The phone rang. Chinaman reached for it.

"Chinaman don't! You can't leave now!"

"Relax, beautiful. I'm not going anywhere. Wild horses couldn't tear me away when you're dressed like that." He spoke into the phone and blew her a kiss. "Hello."

"Mr. Chinaman?"

Chinaman could hear piano music in the background. "This is Chinaman."

"This is Barney. The bartender at Harry's New York Bar."

Chinaman sat straight up. "Yeah, Barney. What's up?"

"What's up is that the guy that was at the booth with your ladyfriend that night is nursing a beer at the bar."

"You're sure?"

"If it ain't him, it's his twin."

"I'll be right there."

"Better make it fast. I don't know how long he's stayin'."

Chinaman threw back the covers and jumped out of bed. He grabbed his socks and put them on.

"Chinaman!"

Chinaman pulled up his trousers. "Sorry. I gotta go."

"It's another woman, isn't it?"

"No, damn it! It's about Judy's murder!"

"Wild horses, huh?" Jo Anne threw open the closet door and threw a small overnight bag onto the bed. "I may not be here when you get back, Chinaman. Not that you'd notice a small thing like that."

Chinaman grabbed his shirt. "I'll make it—"

"And if you dare say you'll make it up to me again, I'll scream. You haven't been able to make love to me since Judy died, Chinaman. Think about it!"

Chinaman finished dressing and just made it through the front door as the juggler-sized rubber balls slammed after him. He had thought about his inability to make love since Judy died and he would again — but not now.

★

24

CHINAMAN entered Harry's New York Bar and followed the gaze of the bartender. If the bartender's sight was all he said it was, the man who had sat in the booth with Judy shortly before she was murdered now sat at the bar, well apart from other customers, nursing a beer. He might know nothing about the murder; he might know everything.

From the side, he appeared to be in his late thirties, clean shaven, maybe an inch under six feet. Chinaman made a mental note that whatever business the man was in must be prospering — his scarf was silk and his overcoat was blue cashmere.

Chinaman sat at a table facing a mirrored pillar which reflected the door behind him. He ordered a Black Russian and waited. He placed a twenty dollar bill inside a napkin and asked a waitress to give it to the bartender in a discreet manner.

Chinaman was on his second cigarette when the two men entered the bar, passed his table and walked up to the man with the cashmere coat. They quickly moved to a booth close enough so that Chinaman could get a clear view of them but not close enough so that he could hear them. One of the men looked like a professional businessman — wavy white hair over a well-sculpted face. The other was shorter, nearly bald, and lacked the distinguished air of his companion.

The waitress took their drink orders and, when she left, the men began speaking quietly together. Not in anger, not in jest, neither friendly nor unfriendly, just a serious, sometimes intense, discussion. They might have been advertising agency account executives retreating to a bar to rehash their just concluded pitch to an important potential client — what went right; what went wrong; will we get the account. The balding man's chain smoking seemed to irritate the man with wavy white hair. The man continued to smoke. It was when he turned slightly to exhale smoke away from his companion that Chinaman saw the scratches on his cheek. The flesh-colored concealer had helped but they were still visible.

Chinaman thought of the minute amount of skin tissue found underneath Judy's fingernails and he felt as if a surge of electricity had slammed through his whole body. He could feel the rush of adrenaline and the cold sweat breaking out on his forehead. His sudden fury was so intense he held onto his glass with both hands and concentrated on putting the scene of Judy's death out of his mind.

When his breathing had slowed somewhere near normal, he ordered another drink, told the waitress he'd be right back, and quickly climbed the stairs to the phones. He checked his address book and dialed a number in Brooklyn Heights. A man answered on the second ring. "Allo, allo."

"Barry? Chinaman here."

"Well, well, well, if it isn't 'Chinaman here.' I thought you'd call."

"You did?"

"Sure. I've got a pounding headache, my back is killin' me, my ass is draggin' and I was just heading for bed. So I figured some dipshit after some favor was probably going to call with some asinine request that's going to fuck up my night."

"Not a favor. Just your car."

"Damn it, Chinaman, why can't you *buy* a car like everyone else?"

"I did. Thieves burglarized it, meter maids ticketed it, homeless men pissed on it, and there wasn't any place to park. So I sold it. And right now I'm trying to cover three guys in Harry's New York Bar and I have good reason to think they might split up when they leave."

"I get it. You don't just want my car, you want me to spend a night sitting *in* the car staking out some godforsaken apartment house, freezing my ass off and pissing into a bottle. That it?"

"The romance of detective work, Barry."

"Christ! I don't stake out anymore. I'm retired, remember?"

"I was just speaking to Jo Anne the other day about getting you fixed up with that waitress at the bar. The one you said was so beautiful she must have sprung from beer foam like Aphrodite."

"*Sea* foam, Chinaman, not *beer* foam. Some myths are sacred and not to be fucked with."

"Jo Anne says she's about twenty-three and really likes older men. And talk about kinky sex...."

"All right, all right. But these pals of yours may not be there when I get there. You do realize that, right?"

"Then you'll have enjoyed a pleasant winter drive into the city and you can return home to a warm bed knowing that you've got a date with Aphrodite."

"Descriptions?"

"I think a tall one with wavy white hair and his shorter balding friend might be leaving together. Both in suit-and-tie. I'll take the third one. He's in a cashmere coat. They look respectable; but I'll bet dollars to donuts they're all carrying. So watch yourself."

"I'm on my way."

Chinaman returned to his booth and was relieved to see the men calling for a second round of drinks, their coats draped over a chair. For half an hour, while discreetly observing the men, Chinaman acted out the role of a man drinking alone while enjoying the Christmas selections of the pianist. He had noticed nothing changing hands, nothing unusual. At one point the owner of the cashmere coat had passed by his booth on his way to the men's room or to make a call and Chinaman had noticed his face was far less refined than his clothes.

Nearly twenty minutes later, the men stood up and put on their coats. Chinaman cursed Barry Cohn silently and followed the men into the lobby at a distance. Just as they neared the front door, Chinaman spotted Cohn chatting with the woman behind the front desk. She seemed to be enraptured with whatever cock-and-bull story he was telling her and he gave Chinaman and the men only the briefest of glances.

Chinaman remained near the lobby doors while watching the men saying goodbye on the sidewalk near the taxis. Cohn passed beside him and walked out of the hotel away from the men and off into the night. It was then Chinaman saw the man with wavy hair pass a large brown envelope to the man in the cashmere coat. As they walked to the taxi stand, Chinaman walked out onto the sidewalk and moved as if he were walking past them, heading east. Both of the men were bidding "Shalom" to the man in the cashmere coat.

The two men who had arrived together took the first taxi. Chinaman waited for his man to enter the cab, memorized the medallion number, then jumped into the one behind it. Chinaman knew he actually had to utter the words, "follow that cab" and he had hoped for a street-wise, seen-it-all, no-questions-asked, New York cabbie. The man behind the wheel was heavily bearded and wore a turban. He turned toward Chinaman and smiled. "Yes, sir, where did you wish to go this evening?"

Chinaman pointed to the cab pulling out in front of them. "Actually, I'd just like you to follow that cab."

The man turned to observe the cab and then turned back to Chinaman. Lines of confusion spread across his forehead. "Excuse me, sir, you do not have a destination?"

"No. Just follow that cab!"

The man paused uncertainly and gave Chinaman a kind of figure eight nod of the head. "Sir, I must write down where it is I am asked to go."

Chinaman pulled out his badge and flashed it to the man. He raised his voice. "I'm a New York State-licensed investigator! This is an emergency! Just follow that cab! Quickly! Before we lose him!"

The man gave the badge a curious look, then, without a word, turned and gunned the taxi out into the nearly deserted street. The taxi ahead had almost disappeared and Chinaman was certain he would lose it; but the man from the subcontinent proved to be a driver equal to the traffic trials of his urban setting. Within a minute, he had maneuvered his cab through changing lights and angry horns and positioned himself one car behind the cab.

Chinaman leaned forward and read the man's name on the dashboard. "Mr. Singh, you really know how to drive in a city."

He could see the man's proud smile in the mirror. "I drove a taxi in Bombay for many years, sir. I am used to making transit movements by leaps and bounds."

"Transit movements?"

"Yes, sir. At tempo. Bombay is like here, sir. A city at tempo. It is sometimes necessary to make transit movements for gaining dispatch."

Chinaman leaned back in his seat, his attention still riveted on the cab ahead. It was making a right on Second Avenue. A city at tempo — if that didn't sum up New York, Chinaman thought, nothing did.

His quarry's taxi slowed and stopped at the left side of the street. Chinaman had his driver continue ahead to the corner and stop on the right side. He got out but lingered as if discussing the fare. He watched the man in the cashmere coat disappear into the doorway of an office building at number 800 Second Avenue.

Chinaman had his driver ease the cab slowly backward until he could see into the lobby. The man spoke briefly with a security guard and then disappeared into a rear hallway. Chinaman paid the driver and stepped over a frozen, blackened mound of snow. He walked to the 24-hour cash machine lobby of the Chase Manhattan bank on the corner. Before he could insert his card into the slot, an elderly black man in a ragged coat and knitted cap opened the door from inside. The man's wide, angry, eyes locked onto Chinaman's and he held his hand palm up close to

Chinaman's chin. "I'm just tryin' to get somethin' to eat. Some chicken, maybe." The man's bloodshot eyes and whiskey breath suggested otherwise. Apparently, he hadn't agreed with Mayor Guiliani's fiat that all solicitation be carried out a minimum of ten feet distance from a bank door.

Chinaman gave him one dollar and stood by the window facing the street. His shoes squished in something sticky. The floor was littered with yellow deposit receipts — 'Urban autumn leaves,' Judy had once called them. The doorway to 800 Second Avenue was visible and would stay that way unless something larger than a station wagon double-parked.

While Chinaman stood watching the building across the street, the man clutched the dollar bill in his hand with the bill held away from his body as if he feared ill effects from a strange object. He opened his mouth and through broken teeth and rough wine-colored lips gave forth a cross between a series of moans and a few hummed bars of 'The Little Drummer Boy,' then began speaking in response to an internal suggestion.

"Sit down? Sit down?! I ain' gonna sit no down. Thas the firs' thing I learned when I got busted and they lined me up in the reception room. The bench was all full of guys just like me and I started to sit down on the floor but a guy sez, 'Hey, man, don' you be sittin' down on that floor; 'cause when you sit down on that floor, that mean you *stayin'*. An' you don' wanna be stayin; you wanna be *leavin'*. That was one dude that was'n jive-assin' neither, no sir."

Chinaman spotted his man leaving the building and heading north on Second. As he walked to the door, the man's voice rose almost to a shout. "No, sir, a body can give me all the Stagger Lee kind of bullshit in this world, but I know better'n to sit down on that floor."

Chinaman had just reached the spot where his taxi had left him when he spotted the two-tone grey Lincoln town car pull up across the street. The man got in and the car crossed the intersection on a yellow light and sped off into the night. Chinaman cursed inwardly. His assumption was the man had spotted him tailing him and had called for the car. Maybe if there had been more traffic he wouldn't have been spotted so easily; maybe if there hadn't been snow on the license plate, he could have gotten some numbers; maybe if the dog hadn't stopped to take a piss it would have caught the cat.

He was about to wave to another cab to return him to the East Village when he realized he was running short of cash. He approached the Chase Manhattan vestibule again and reached for his ATM card. The door opened and a familiar figure held his hand palm up close to Chinaman's chin. "I'm just tryn' to get somethin' to eat. Some chicken, maybe."

★

25

WHEN Chinaman entered his apartment, he found the lights on and the music loud. His cherished tape of New Orleans's Preservation Hall jazz band was blaring out "When the Saints Go Marching In." So Jo Anne decided to stay after all. Chinaman could handle that. He was cold, tired, wet and angry at his failure. The thought of snuggling-

"You look lousy."

Chinaman turned to see his ex-wife lying on the couch with her shoes off. She smiled at him over a whiskey glass held in her right hand. "I was beginning to wonder if you'd left town."

Chinaman lay his coat across his desk chair and stared at her. She wore a white turtleneck sweater tucked into black leather pants. Light glinted off the glass and coruscated off the pants. "How in God's name did you get in here?"

"Is that any way to greet a lady?" She pointed to a set of lock picks beside her purse on the desk. *You* taught me how to negotiate locks, Chinaman."

Chinaman snapped on the desk lamp and held up the picks. "I wondered where the hell these went."

"I found them in the pocket of an old jacket."

"It happens," Chinaman said. Up yours too, Chinaman thought.

"There's a note on your desk. Of course I respect your privacy too much to read it, but it seems somebody named 'Jo Anne' thinks you're a 'self-centered bastard' who cares more about solving cases than giving himself to a relationship. She must know you pretty well."

Chinaman read the note and walked into the kitchenette to make himself a drink. He heard Mary Anne's nasal voice effortlessly overpower the gravelly toned jazz vocalist. "Nice scarf. Somebody you know has some sense of style. Now all you need is a change of barber."

I changed my marital status, Chinaman thought. That's the change that counts. He weighed that against several other replies, then decided to keep his mouth shut. Concentrate on the drink. Nothing fancy. Just a little Tennessee sour mash whiskey on the rocks. OK. More than a little.

Chinaman carried the glass into the living room and lowered the volume of the tape deck. He sat across the room from his ex-wife in an easy chair, kicked his shoes off and put his feet up on the ottoman. He stared at the woman he had shared four years of his life with: the long, narrow face ending with an angularly shaped chin; the intelligent, knowing eyes with their penetrating stare; the unruly shoulder-length hair brushing against high cheek bones. One face — one thousand memories.

Mary Anne sat up and lit a cigarette. There was always something curt, almost impatient, about the way she did things; even lighting a cigarette. An impatience with the world. As if the world — Chinaman included — was always moving too slowly for her, or was perpetually out of sync with her taste. Like father, like daughter. She spoke through a swirl of blue smoke. "Dad told me about Judy's murder. I am sorry about it, Chinaman." When Chinaman said nothing, she continued. "If it makes you feel any better, my father doesn't think you were involved."

"Not in *that* one, anyway."

"You two really should try to get along. I mean, you're practically in the same business."

"I agree. Try telling that to your father."

"I think deep down he really liked you, Chinaman. That's why he hates you so much after you divorced me."

"*You* divorced *me*."

"I'd say it was a draw, wouldn't you?"

Chinaman took a long drink. "Speaking of which, you're probably wondering about your last alimony check. I could say it was in the mail, but my nose might grow. Then I might look like a Caucasian."

"Chinaman, even in this market, I make enough in real estate so as not to have to worry about your piddly, inevitably tardy, alimony checks."

"I'm relieved to hear it. So that means you just came to offer your sincere condolences about Judy."

Chinaman watched his ex-wife glare at him through narrowed eyes, while blowing streams of smoke through her nose. Chinaman sensed he had hit a nerve.

"One thing you should understand, Chinaman. I know Judy was something special to you. But, you see, from my point of view, Judy was the unconscionable bitch whom I found one night in bed with my husband." Mary Anne stubbed out her cigarette in the ashtray. Forcefully. "But even she didn't deserve what happened to her." Her tone suggested she might have thought otherwise. "I read her essay on her father. Very beautiful."

Chinaman glanced toward his desk. "Where did you get it?"

"It was on your desk."

"It was *in* my desk, damn it!"

Mary Anne shrugged. "Why quibble over prepositions? Anyway, you were right. She was a fine writer."

"It was all a lie."

"What?"

"The essay was a lie. Judy was abused for years by an alcoholic father. He made her life miserable. Whatever she did wasn't enough to please him."

"But...what about the essay?"

"She used to write about him in class. Almost every other essay she turned in was about the kind, loving, understanding, attentive father she'd had. Except the father she wrote about never existed. It was the father she always wished she'd had. And the more she buried the truth the more she hated men."

"Jesus. That's...."

"Pathetic, sad, depressing. Yeah, it is. But now you know: even high-paid hookers have reasons." And, although his ex-wife had never understood, one of the reasons Judy and he were so drawn to each other was that both had been emotionally crippled by past events. Judy had a deep trauma and had understood his. Mary Anne had no traumas and, like her father, seemed uncomfortable in the presence of another's revealed feelings.

Mary Anne raised her voice. A lot. "And that's supposed to excuse what she did? Jumping into bed with my husband? Why couldn't she have punished her father?! Why *me*?"

Chinaman felt their conversation falling into the same deeply grooved pattern. He worked hard at keeping his voice down. "As I told you before, the night you found us in bed she'd come over to tell me that her brother had just called from prison in Louisiana to tell her that her father had died in a bar brawl. What happened...got out of hand."

"And into bed. *Our* bed. Oh, sorry, did you mean the brawl or the ball?"

Chinaman felt his anger rising, warming his forehead. Just like before. "Look, how many times do I have to say it? I'm sorry."

Mary Anne sighed. "Yeah, I'm sorry, too, all right? Sorry for Judy, sorry for us. Sorry about a lot of things. Anyway, I didn't come here to fight." She reached into her large leather tote bag beside the couch and pulled out a Christmas wrapped oblong package. "Actually, I came to give you your Christmas present." She tossed it to him, slipped her feet into her black leather ankle boots and began lacing them up.

Chinaman looked the package over. "That time of year again, is it?"

"It is. But you needn't bother giving me anything in return."

"Better to give than to get?"

"No, just that you can't afford anything I want."

It was just the touch of ex-wife snobbery Chinaman needed. "I know what you mean. Last Christmas your dad and I inadvertently acted out an O'Henry short story. I sold my Colt 9 mm. Elite Nine auto pistol to have enough money to buy your dad specially made mother-of-pearl grips for his Smith & Wesson 10 mm. Model 1006, and he sold his Smith & Wesson 10 mm to have enough money to buy me a DeSantis Side-Winder ambidextrous nylon shoulder holster for my Colt 9 mm."

"That's cute. But the day my father gives *you* a Christmas present...."

"We should both live so long."

Mary Anne stared at the gift. "Actually, I think I made a mistake."

"In coming here? A lot of women say that."

"Very funny. I mean I gave you detective novels for Christmas. I just remember dad saying that the last thing cops want to do after a long day is to read a police procedural. And I suppose the same goes for P.I.'s and P.I. novels."

"I wouldn't know. All my days are short."

"Business still hasn't picked up, huh?"

"In spurts."

"You still editing for Sydney?"

"Yep."

"What was it? *Nymphets and the Nightstalker*?"

"That series ended."

"Oh, no. Literature will never be the same again. What happened?"

"The nightstalker finally got blown away by a 17-year-old nymphet in a satin camisole tucked into mother-of-pearl thigh boots. She used a Glock 9mm. semi-automatic pistol, if memory serves. Unregistered, of course. Now it's 'Amazon Annihilators'."

"You know, Chinaman, there's more than one way to make

money from the detective business. You could write a book about
your cases. I know an agent. She could probably get you a good
advance. You could embellish all you like."

Chinaman shrugged.

"I mean it. Or try a detective novel. Private eyes in fiction
are big these days. A lot of bestsellers are by women. With women
detectives. I supposed you hadn't read any, so those are the ones I
bought you."

"I hate to surprise you but I did read a few books with women
detectives."

"And?"

"You'll only call me a sexist and a chauvinist."

"No, I won't."

"OK. Private eyes who worry about their weight, clip recipes
and shave their legs give me goose bumps."

"Chinaman, you're a sexist, chauvinist asshole with–"

"Thanks for keeping your word. Anyway, blame it on my
Confucian upbringing."

Chinaman walked her to the door and helped her into her
coat. They faced each other in silence. Mary Anne slowly cupped
her hands around the back of his head, pulled his face down to
hers, and kissed him hard on the mouth. When she released him,
she stared hard at him. "Damn it, Chinaman, if it hadn't been for
her, we might have...."

"Hey. I was your husband, not her. If anyone was to
blame...."

"If?!"

Chinaman looked away. Mary Anne sighed. "All right.
Forget it. Water under the dam. Blood under the bridge."

"Venom under the viaduct?"

"Whatever. Listen, I really shouldn't tell you this but, what
the hell. Dad paid me one of his rare visits last night. He got a
little drunk. More than a little. He talked a bit more about the
case than he would have — if it hadn't been her."

"That's something that puzzles me. He only met her at our wedding. And yet he jumps on her case even though he could leave it with the precinct."

"Dad jumps on any case that interests him. You know he hates staying behind a desk. He loves 'the street,' as he puts it. Besides, maybe he *was* hoping you'd done it, who knows? Maybe he figured nailing you for her death would be a nice holiday gift for me."

"Sounds reasonable."

"Ever since Giuliani decided to shake up the police department and dad got shuffled off to One Police Plaza, well, let's just say, if you can keep out of dad's way for a while, do so."

"Good advice on any occasion."

"Anyway, you ever hear of someone named Rocco?"

She had Chinaman's full attention now. He nodded. "Been snitching for your dad for years. Last I saw of him, he was living in Hell's Kitchen. He's a chicken hawk who pushes Lipton Tea." Mary Anne raised her eyebrows. "I mean he has sex with teenage male prostitutes and sells poor quality narcotics."

"I wouldn't know, but dad had an appointment with somebody named Rocco this morning to get some information on Judy's killing."

"Thanks. I mean it."

"All part of the service." She leaned forward and they quickly kissed. "I guess the truth is, I still miss you a bit."

"Too busy with new men in your life to miss me more than a bit?"

"Actually, yeah. The guy I'm dating now is some kind of systems engineer. He's not as eccentric as you and he's not as big as you and he never laughs in bed-"

"Why do I have the feeling that there's going to be a 'but' in this sentence?"

"*But* he makes a lot more money than you, and it's kind of nice having a man around the house who isn't cleaning some goddamn gun all the time."

"Prefers Mace, does he?"

"Don't get bitchy, Chinaman, it's not like you."

Chinaman shrugged an apology.

"At least he doesn't clean a gun with my contact lens solution."

Chinaman had bet himself that she'd bring that one up. "I was *drunk*. And you left the bottle near the cleaning kit. I thought it was my gun conditioner." Chinaman returned her smile. "Anyway, it worked a lot better after that."

Mary Anne opened the door, stared at him, and went quickly into the hallway. He followed her to the stairs and watched her walk down. She spoke without looking back. "Take care, Chinaman."

"You too, lady. And thanks for the gift. Both of them."

Chinaman returned to his apartment and found the door locked. His key was in his coat. The coat lying across the desk chair. He banged his head against the door and fished out his American Express card.

★

26

CHINAMAN interrupted his final proofreading of the next installment of 'Amazon Annihilators' and picked up the ringing phone. "Chinaman Investigations."

"Thanks for the lunch."

"Sam! You're off, are you?"

"D.C. calls."

"So how was Verdi?"

"Puccini. It was great. You should have come. A little opera cleanses the soul; maybe even yours."

"Yeah. I should have. I had an evening I'd like to forget."

"Chinaman. You remember what I said at lunch?"

"You mean about Judy being dead and my not being able to bring her back?"

"No. About you not ending up dead as well."

"Believe me, Sam, I do my best to keep out of harm's way."

"I'm telling you, Mossad does not play by Duchess of Queensbury rules. I want you to drop this one."

"Can't do it, Sam."

"Goddamn it, Chinaman, just once in your life — be sensible. The wrong person gets killed all the time. In IRA bombings. In drive-by-shootings, in police raids, for Christ sake! Walk away from it."

"Sam, I appreciate your information and your concern. I owe you one. Now you'd better hang up or you'll miss your shuttle."

"Chinaman, isn't your life worth more than a dead...hooker's?"

"Take care, Sam." Chinaman broke the connection.

The second call came moments after Chinaman hung up. Two calls within an hour was, for Chinaman Investigations, a better-than-average day. Two within five minutes was a record. "Chinaman Investigations."

"Chinaman. Cohn here."

"Cohn there. How'd you make out? Your derriere frozen?"

"Nah. Your friends made it easy for me. They made a beeline for Kennedy."

"Good work, Barry. You follow them in?"

"Hey, fella, I wasn't fired; I *retired*, remember? Of course, I followed them in."

"Sorry."

"Forget it. Anyway, they just made their 11:40 flight."

"You want me to ask 'to where'?"

"OK."

"To where?"

"El Al flight 8 — as in behind the 8 ball — to Tel Aviv...Hey, you still there?"

"Yeah. I'm here. I think I just remembered something."

"Well, you can start remembering something about lining me up with some of that kinky sex you were baiting me with last night."

"Will do, Barry, I'll get back to you."

"You do that. And try to make it before I'm too old and lose interest in feminine flesh."

Chinaman lifted the phone book from Audrey Lieberman's desk only after agreeing to remember where he "got it from." He opened the yellow pages to "Consulates" and was directed to the section titled, "Government — foreign representatives." And there it was: "Consulate General of Israel 800 2 Av."

★

27

THAT evening Chinaman sat at the desk in his living room cleaning his .38. The only mail had been a reminder from the License Division that it was time to pay one-hundred-and-seventy dollars to renew his gun license. He had decided that for that kind of money he might as well keep it in perfect shape. Over time, he had discovered that the act of cleaning his gun was like hoeing a garden or sailing solo: A meditative experience that allowed him time to think yet gave him a respite from whatever was troubling him at the moment. And it gave his subconscious time to work on a problem. The more absorbed he could become in cleaning the gun, the closer he sometimes found himself to a solution. The trick was to fool the conscious mind by feigning complete indifference to the problem at hand, all the while letting the subconscious mind get to work.

The process always reminded him of the many evenings when he and the professor, his American foster father, had searched wet Long Island lawns for large fat fishbait worms after a rain. If the flashlight were shone directly on them, the worms immediately slithered back into their holes. The trick was to shine the light nearby as if something else were the object of attention; then suddenly pounce, hold on firmly, and pull them ever so gingerly out of their holes. Capturing nightcrawlers or solving problems sometimes required the same circuitous, indirect and devious methods.

Sometimes, it even worked. But, so far, on this case, Chinaman knew that his stream of consciousness remained more of a dry riverbed. And whenever he relaxed his guard, it was easy to remember things best forgotten.

When he got up to replenish his scotch-on-the-rocks the phone rang. He lit a cigarette and picked up. "Chinaman."

"Chinaman...." He spoke again into the silence. "Chinaman here...Hey, look, if this is an obscene phone call, I've made more than a few in my time, so let me tell you you're going about it all wrong. And if you're not a woman you've got the wrong number to begin with...OK. Nice talking with you."

Chinaman was just about to slam down the phone when he heard the heavily accented Arabic voice. "Mr. Chinaman? Please listen to me. The men who killed Judy...."

Chinaman could feel himself sobering up. "I'm listening, friend. The men who killed Judy what?"

"Their address is...Do you have a pen?"

Chinaman opened a drawer and quickly grabbed a pen and turned over an unpaid phone bill. He could feel his mind clear, his heart beat. "Yeah. I've got a pen." And, then, without hesitation, the man gave him a Forest Hills address.

"Do you have it, Mr. Chinaman?"

"Yeah, I got it. Now, who are you, how do you fit in with Judy's death and what's in this for you?"

"Please, no questions. It is in both our interests that these Zionist dogs are eliminated. *Allah Akbar.*"

Chinaman heard the click on the line, waited for several seconds, then hung up the phone. He took his gun case and an ammo pouch from a hall shelf and strapped a cross-draw holster onto his belt. He loaded his .38, slipped it into his holster, butt forward, and snapped it shut. He opened a kitchen drawer, fished out two subway tokens, threw on a jacket and exited the apartment.

★

28

CHINAMAN stood close by the moonlit street in the shadow of a thick oak tree and observed the house across the street. It was not unlike similar half-timbered Tudor houses in the fashionable section of Forest Hills, Queens, known as "the Gardens." An attractive mix of wood, stucco, brick and stone, conferring taste and respectability on anyone wealthy enough to own it.

But there were differences. Besides the obvious one that this house was completely dark. Something about the lawn. First, there was more of it so that the house was, if not secluded, at least separated from its neighbors as well as set farther back from the road. Second, its thin blanket of snow had not been disturbed by footprints. Third, the snow that covered the well-trimmed hedges and flower gardens of other lawns on this lawn covered only grass. The lack of landscaping and the almost somber mood suggested not neglect but a certain lack of interest; as if the owner had better things to do than to plant azaleas and trim bushes.

The light of a street lamp colored the undisturbed layer of snow a pale, desolate, urine yellow. Everything about the house suggested it was deserted. So why did he have the feeling someone had gone to a great deal of trouble to make it look as if the house was deserted?

He crossed the street and silently made his way up the narrow path along the side of the house. When he reached the back, he again stood in shadow and concentrated his powers of observation. Shadows of wind-blown tree branches danced erratically back and forth against a stucco-and-brick facade. A rectangular block of snow fell from a roof hang. Nothing else moved. The only sounds were those of a dog barking somewhere in the direction of Rego Park and barely audible snatches of a television program from the nearest house.

He walked quickly to the back steps and tried the screen door. It wasn't locked. The inner door was. He quickly inserted his lock pick and began maneuvering. In less than a minute he was inside a small hallway and walking silently into a kitchen.

The living room curtains were closed but a small amount of light spilled in from the fan light and sidelights of the front door and from the kitchen windows behind him. As he entered the living room, he fished in his jacket pocket for his penlight. Just as he snapped it on, he heard movement behind him. He released the penlight and somersaulted to his left. A dark figure swished something through the air where his head had been. Chinaman jumped to his feet, drew his revolver and held it on the still moving figure. "Freeze!"

He felt the knife edge of a hand hit his hand holding the gun. His hand opened involuntarily and the gun fell to the floor. So there were at least two. Chinaman kicked out at the second figure and connected with something solid. Whatever parts of his opponent's anatomy he had hit caused the man to exhale air and groan painfully. Chinaman understood that survival meant to keep moving.

He somersaulted again and came up near the first figure. He kicked out, felt his shoe glance off an elbow, and realized too late that his target had his back to him, in the process of completing a spin kick with his right foot aimed at Chinaman's jaw. Chinaman went with the force of the blow and crashed against a shelf, sending objects flying. The second man loomed in front of him and, in the semi-darkness, his fist met Chinaman's in mid-air. As his opponent cried out in agony, Chinaman felt an almost paralyzing pain shoot up his arm into his elbow.

Holding his elbow with his left hand he moved toward the

kitchen. He was tackled at the knees by the same man whose shoe had hit his jaw. Chinaman fell on his side but immediately rolled onto his back. As the man picked himself up and lunged forward, Chinaman worked his feet under his chest and thrust out his legs, sending the man off into the darkness.

Suddenly the ceiling light went on. Chinaman looked toward the other assailant. He stood with his right arm held in an unnatural position and his left hand holding a semi-automatic pistol pointed at Chinaman's head. He motioned Chinaman toward the couch. "Sit."

His companion moved behind Chinaman and shoved him onto the couch. "You son-of-a-bitch."

"Hey! It's *my* arm that's on fire. Let me interrogate the bastard."

His companion gave Chinaman a smirk. "Fair enough. Whoever you are, you're in for a very unique and very painful experience."

Chinaman sat on the couch rubbing the knuckles of his right hand with the palm of his left. Apparently nothing broken. Just excruciating pain. "'Unique' is an absolute adjective. It can't be modified. Something is either unique or it's not."

The man whose grammar was being questioned slapped Chinaman hard across the face. Chinaman sighed. "Don't like your grammar corrected, huh? I know how you feel. I felt the same way in Miss Watson's class in P.S. 23."

"You're a funny man. You could be funny-dead."

The man holding the gun gingerly flexed the fingers of his right hand. His eyes narrowed in pain. "Have the funny man hand over his wallet."

Chinaman handed over his wallet and studied the men. Mid-thirties. Excellent shape. Well built, muscular, but not showy muscles — functional muscles. Professionals. Very pissed off professionals. The man whose grammar had been less than adequate flipped slowly through the plastic. "Chinaman

Investigations."

The other man walked over and picked up Chinaman's revolver. He opened the cylinder, checked to see it was loaded, then tucked it into his own belt. He stood near Chinaman and glared at him. "Stop rubbing your hand and put both of them up in the air."

"I can't raise my arm. I think it's fractured."

The man stepped forward and grabbed Chinaman at the wrist. "That a fact? Well, I'll raise it for you."

Chinaman had counted on that. He'd seen that kind of anger in men before. The kind that can make even a professional incautious. It seemed to Chinaman that the man realized his mistake and was just starting to move his hand toward the revolver. Too late. Chinaman slipped his hand out of the other's grasp, placed it on his chest, and pushed. As the man started backward, Chinaman grabbed the revolver with his left hand. He stood, spun the man around, and stood behind him, holding him as a shield. The first man dropped the wallet and pointed the pistol in Chinaman's direction. Chinaman placed the muzzle of his revolver at his hostage's head. "Thirteen pounds of pressure on this trigger and his brains decorate the wall."

The man held the pistol and said nothing.

"The way it is is that I'm walking out of here. You do anything to stop me and your friend is a dead man. Now kick the wallet over to the kitchen doorway."

The man hesitated. Chinaman cocked the revolver. "Now it takes less than four pounds of pressure."

Chinaman's hostage shouted something to his companion in a foreign language. Chinaman guessed it was Hebrew. The man with the pistol kicked the wallet toward the kitchen. Chinaman pushed the man's hand up a bit farther behind his back, pressed the revolver's muzzle flush against his head, and slowly edged toward the kitchen. If they were going to make a move it would be when he stooped to pick up the wallet. So he'd kick the wallet all the way to the back door and pick it up in the narrow hallway. It wasn't likely the man with the pistol would chance a shot there. Just when Chinaman figured the odds of walking out alive were tilting in his favor, he heard it.

Among the sounds generally acknowledged to present the greatest affront to the human ear are a piece of chalk drawn across a blackboard; a knife across a plate; the wail of a nearby siren; and the roar of a jet engine just overhead. And then there is the very special, singular, inimitable sound of a shotgun being racked. Its action slide being worked. Whether learned behavior or genetically innate, something in the deepest recesses of a human being's psyche is most repulsed by the metallic, grating, jarring, obscenity — the sound of imminent, inescapable and very violent extinction.

Chinaman heard exactly that sound behind him and, tightening his grip on his hostage, turned to face it. A tall, well tanned, clean-shaven man stood in the doorway of the kitchen. He was dressed casually in a V-neck sweater over a checked shirt, tan slacks and loafers. He might have been a college student on vacation about to hit dad up for a loan. Except that this "student" held a "Witness Protection" 870 12-gauge short-barreled shotgun with pistol grips. Chinaman stared into the small dark hole in the barrel pointing toward his heart. The black hole of eternity. He remembered that shotgun loads leave the muzzle of a shotgun at something just over the speed of sound. Its very short trajectory would be supersonic. And he remembered something about how just one buckshot shell has the stopping power of something like eight rounds from the weapon he was holding.

In the few yards separating the barrel of the shotgun and Chinaman's body, the shot column would have no time to spread out. The damage would be concentrated in an area no greater than the gun's bore. The effect of the shotgun blast would to a certain extent depend on its load and other factors; but, in his position as a target, Chinaman felt the distinct possibility that he was about to be cut in half.

He noticed the "student's" hand tightening on the fore grip.
In just a few fleeting seconds Chinaman weighed the odds of
disarming the man with various moves — without being blown
apart. The odds were slim and none. He lowered his revolver and
a second later felt it being roughly jerked from his hand by someone
behind him. He felt a blow to the head, and in a flood of pain
and blood-red darkness, hands dragging him to the couch.

When Chinaman looked up again, he saw the student sitting
at the other end of the couch riffling through his I.D. The shotgun
was on his lap. The man with the damaged arm sat across the
room holding the pistol in his left hand, looking for any excuse to
use it. The third man had disappeared. The student finally finished
looking over his I.D. He spoke with the voice of someone so
completely in authority that he could afford to be polite. "Now,
Mr. Liu Chiang-hsin, if that's your real name, I wonder if you'd be
kind enough to explain why a New York-licensed private detective
is out to kill me."

"I was out to bring you in."

The man smiled uncertainly. "'Bring me in'. To whom may
I ask?"

"The police."

"Any particular reason?"

"The New York Palace Hotel."

"What about it?"

"Room 1204. It was your hit."

"My...'hit'?"

"You're Mossad, aren't you?"

The man exchanged a glance with the man holding the pistol.
Chinaman could see clearly now that the "student" was older than
he had first thought. He had youthful features but he was at least
a decade older than student age. A combat shotgun staring
Chinaman in the face had clouded his judgment.

"And the girl you killed. The potential witness you silenced.
She was...somebody special."

"Mr. Liu, I'm afraid this is a classic case of someone adding two and two and coming up with five. Among many others, I was delighted to read about Herr Schriber's death. In fact, it's not impossible that once back in the Middle East certain...differences of opinion with Herr Schriber might have been brought to the surface; in a conclusive fashion. But it would be very unlike us to settle our differences with someone in a hotel in the middle of New York City. Why unnecessarily endanger our country's already strained relations with your country?"

Chinaman felt the pain at the back of his head dulling to a steady throb. "How'd you know I was coming?"

"I believe in this kind of situation it is I who should be asking the questions. But since you ask I'll tell you. Someone called here a few hours ago and warned us that a hit man working for an Arab country was coming to 'take me out.' Then he hung up. Which means if you are not a hit man working for an Arab country *and* you are who you say you are, that you've been set up."

Chinaman tried to think through the pain. Nothing seemed to make sense. The third man returned to the room and handed Chinaman's interrogator Chinaman's driver license. He gave his boss a nod. The man with the wallet again smiled at him. "You're in luck. Our computer tells us you are most likely who you say you are." He tossed the wallet back to Chinaman. "Now I must ask you how you learned of this address."

Chinaman tucked his wallet into his pocket and began rubbing his right elbow. "Somebody with an Arab accent called and said I'd find the Zionist dogs who killed my ladyfriend at this address."

The man studied Chinaman's face. "And then he hung up?" Chinaman nodded. The man sighed. "If I let you go then this address will be compromised."

"Don't worry. As far as I'm concerned, I've never been here. But it seems to me this safe house — oh, that's right, you people call places like this 'operational apartments,' right? Anyway, whatever you call this address, it seems to me it's already been compromised."

"That's true. And the only hit men I know stalk their prey with silenced semi-automatic pistols or something more exotic; not with 5-shot, Smith & Wesson revolvers." He stared at Chinaman and made his decision. He snapped open the cylinder of the revolver and ejected the five rounds. He slipped the rounds into his pocket, snapped the cylinder shut and tossed the gun to Chinaman. "We are not responsible for what happened in the New York Palace Hotel. I have no idea who is. But I am sorry about your ladyfriend." He stood up. "And now if you will excuse us we have some packing to do."

Chinaman stepped around a broken lamp and over shards of glass. All three men followed him to the front door. Chinaman walked through the door and turned only when he reached the sidewalk. The student gave him a wave. "*Shalom aleichem*, Mr. Liu."

Chinaman returned the wave and began walking. His left knee ached, his head throbbed and his right arm was in agony. Right, he thought, peace be with you, too.

★

29

CHINAMAN lay on the bed staring up at the thin cracks spreading across the white ceiling. Four separate cracks suggested the Chinese character for "heart" and threatened to flood his mind with memories. His parents' death at the hands of Mao's fanatics; his boyhood escape from China; his meeting with the American professor friend of his father in a Hong Kong refugee camp. His growing up in New York. His nightmares. He pushed them out of his mind to concentrate on the business at hand.

His bedroom was filled with the white noise of his environmental sound machine. He had never felt the need to use Jo Anne's early Christmas gift before. Now he did. He had taken a hot shower, swallowed some Advil, drank some Old Granddad, applied ice to his swelling knuckles, rubbed his body's aches with Tiger Balm ointment and then lay back on the bed. Aching. He had passed over the machine's "Surf I" and "Surf II" and "Rainfall" imitations and gone directly to "Waterfall," then turned up the volume and added some bass.

With the electronically synthesized sound of cascading water in the background he allowed the events of the evening to flow through his mind. And then all of the events connected with Judy's death. He seemed to be locked into a trajectory which was taking him farther and farther from her killers. When the phone rang, he turned slowly on his side, careful not to place any weight on his right arm, and picked up with his left. "Chinaman here."

"You'd better not forget amateur night!"

"Jo Anne, where in blazes are you? I–"

"Sure, Chinaman, I know, you've been worried sick about

me, right? Well, I'm staying with Lucinda for a few days while I make up my mind if I want to stay with you or not."

"Of course you should stay with me. Isn't that what Lucinda says?"

"Lucinda says you're the type of man who loves and leaves like a river dandy. She says you even look like one, and that I should check for extra aces hidden up your sleeves."

"Give her my best too, would you? And, by the way, Barry Cohn wants to take her out."

"Barry Cohn!? She thinks he's an aging lecher."

"Everybody has faults."

"So are you going to be there amateur night or not!?"

Chinaman scanned his memory bank, desperately trying to summon up even the faint flicker of a recollection. "Amateur night!" He grabbed his notebook and frantically turned pages. "Of course I haven't forgotten! You're juggling and making like a magician, right?"

"Right. And I don't suppose you remember which night, by any chance?"

He must be almost there. "Don't be silly. Of course I remember which night."

"Well?"

Damn! Where in hell was it? He'd written it–ah! There it was. He squinted and tilted the book in an attempt to read his handwriting. "It's in the West Village. Bleeker near MacDougal. Eight O'clock. Friday night."

"Not bad. But I'll be nervous so when you cheer make it loud, would you?"

"You can count on me. You'll have a one-man cheering section that will sound like thousands."

"I hope you're not the only one cheering."

"You'll knock 'em dead."

"Chinaman?"

"Yes, sweetheart?"

"Do you think you can ever be true to one woman?"

"I tell you what. You come home with me after the show, and we'll talk about it then, OK?"

"OK."

He had barely hung up when the phone rang again.

"Chinaman? Cohn."

"Yeah, Barry. What's up?"

"I just got back from a case upstate. I had an interesting message on my machine when I got back to the house. From Tel Aviv."

"As in Israel?"

"The very same. I've got a few contacts in the business there. So I thought I'd surprise you. Let you know where your two friends went when they got off the plane."

Chinaman remembered Barry Cohn's reputation for thoroughness. He seldom left a case in the middle even if the client ran out of funds or if the client himself lost interest. Another P.I. had compared his method of handling cases with the tenacity of a pit bull shaking a six-month-old child. "Looks like I owe you another one."

"I'm not sure. The fact is they didn't."

"Didn't what?"

"Didn't get off the plane."

Chinaman sat up quickly forgetting the pain sudden movements aroused in his arm and winced when it reminded him.

"Believe me, a damn good man was out there. I gave him the details and the descriptions. The plane landed on schedule at 5 p.m. Next day. But no one like that got off the plane."

"Barry, this case is beginning to stink."

"Chinaman, it has been my experience that each case is like a woman. Some cases flirt with you and make all kinds of early promises, then clam up tight; some start off reticent and heat up; some start off hot and heavy and cool to freezing; a few are cut and dry; and then there's the one that's hiding something ....Of course, some asshole might call that a sexist analogy."

"Some asshole well might."

"Well, then, let me put it another way. In this line of work our problem is that when we hear hoofbeats, we often think zebras, when we should be thinking horses."

"You want to run that by me again?"

"It's something my doctor said he learned in med school. It means consider the simple solution first. The logical choice. Anyway, take it for what it's worth. Hey, Chinaman, is it rainin' there?"

Chinaman glanced at the tiny red light on the white noise machine. "Pouring."

"Not a drop here. Ain't that just like New York?"

"That's it."

"Well, look, give my best to Jo Anne."

"She left."

"No shit...Sorry to hear that, Chinaman...You got her new number?"

"Forget it, Barry. When this case if over, I'm fixing you up with Lucinda — the lust of your life, whom I have good reason to believe is absolutely crazy about you."

"I just hope I can still get an erection by the time you get around to fixing me up."

Chinaman hung up, lit a cigarette and let it burn in the ashtray while he digested Cohn's information. He added more treble to the waterfall, turned down the volume, and picked up the phone. It was time to hit Sterling for one more favor....

★

DAY EIGHT

30

CHINAMAN slipped off his black leather glove and bent over. He brushed the early morning's layer of fine, powdery snow from the surface of Judy Fisher's bronze marker. A simple "In Loving Memory" epitaph, the word "FISHER" and a cross. Above it, a commonplace floral carving; below it, "Judy L 1970 - 2001."

Chinaman stood with his hands in front of him, one resting on the other. His breath was visible in the cold air. The woman who had loved life more than he had thought possible had become a body in a morgue, and now, a corpse in a cemetery. He tried to reconcile the vibrant woman he knew with this desolate spot in a Queen's cemetery. Incongruous. Unfair. Devoid of meaning. Someone's idea of a bad joke. At the sound of voices he looked up.

Across a cemetery path, an Asian family stood assembled about a tombstone. The father seemed to be coaching his small son on what to say to the deceased. Somewhere nearby a bird chirped repeatedly. In the distance, from the direction of Queen's Boulevard, a horn sounded.

Chinaman glanced up at the dirty white sky and turned back to Judy Fisher's final resting place. He said what he had to say silently: All the expressions of sorrow, anger, remorse and, above all, on her behalf, whatever it took, a promise of revenge.

He agonized at not being there when she needed him and apologized for not requesting a graveside service. But other than Cindy Mae and himself, he knew of no one who would have attended. And Judy would have been the first to say that religious rituals are performed for the well-being of the living — not for the dead. The dead don't need catharsis.

Finally, Chinaman said a silent prayer and then immediately apologized for that too. It was cliched, hackneyed and trite. All the devils he had damned in his creative writing classes. He knew she could have composed a better one. He told her so, then he turned and walked off across the snow-covered cemetery.

★

31

COMMUNITY leaders and condo salesmen preferred "Clinton" to "Hell's Kitchen," but anyone stepping inside the Shamrock Bar and Grill on 11th Avenue knew immediately where he was. The bar had acquired its reputation for tumultuous brawls, melodramatic confrontations and blowzy, no-nonsense barmaids long before auto dealerships and their showrooms filled with luxury imports had changed the appearance of the neighborhood around it. Inside, nothing had changed.

Shielded from any form of natural light and isolated from the city's "gorgeous mosaic," the bar provided a rough local neighborhood crowd with a congenial place to congregate, with good quality food and drink, and, at least once a night, with an arena in which to settle real or imagined grievances the old-fashioned way.

Signs of past battles were evident throughout the room. The three-foot high leprechaun near Chinaman's table had lost an arm and part of an ear, but its angry, red-faced stare seemed to challenge all comers. The fan above Chinaman's head had been struck several times with thrown chairs and poorly aimed bottles, and the original shaded bulbs attached to its four blades had, over the years, been reduced to two bulbs shaded, one unshaded, one missing. The fan wobbled erratically as it turned, its bulbs casting a constantly wavering shadow across the "V"-shaped scar on Rocco McGraw's left cheek, a puckered reminder of one of many violent late night encounters at the Shamrock.

Behind the crowded bar, stout, robust, no-nonsense women tirelessly served up Irish draft beneath a blowup of a mock parking sign printed with green letters:

Parking for Irish only;
all others will be towed

The wall nearest Chinaman was covered with a beer-stained oil painting of a young man and a young colleen in the doorway of their idealized Irish hillside cottage complete with thatched roof. Both were naked, their private parts covered only by shamrocks. The painting was titled,

Adam and Eve in Ireland

Rocco held up his pint glass of Guinness draft and spoke with a heavy Irish accent. "Chinaman, me lad, as me old dad used to say in the shebeen, the best of health to your enemies."

Chinaman drank up and put his glass down. Rocco was outpacing him at the rate of two glasses to one. "Cut the act and the accent, Rocco. The only thing genuinely thick about you is your head, not your brogue."

Chinaman noticed just the flicker of anger cross Rocco's gray eyes. Then, just as suddenly, his face broke into an enormous smile. He spoke in his natural voice with just the faint trace of an Irish accent. "Chinaman, you're a man buying me drinks; which is just one reason I like you; and which is also why you're not lyin' bleedin' among the sawdust." Rocco finished his beer and called over the shouts and raucous laughter and loud music for another round. Both of his thick, muscular arms were covered with tattoos, most displaying reclining women in various stages of undress. Chinaman guessed Rocco to be about 40 years old, just over six feet four, and weighing in at least 240 pounds. His close-cropped hair and coarse, broad face reminded Chinaman of the man who'd restrained him while his father had been dragged off to his "trial." Rocco had been inside for everything from criminal possession of a weapon to passing bad checks. Chinaman knew that he'd still be inside if a 16-year-old boy about to testify against him for sodomy hadn't changed his mind.

Chinaman had first heard of Rocco from his father-in-law

when he was still his father-in-law. Chinaman had needed backup during an interview with a hostile witness in the Bronx. Abrams had recommended Rocco. Just the sight of Rocco's 240 pounds of fighting Irish had made Chinaman's job a lot easier and the witness, if not cooperative, at least less antagonistic.

And he knew Rocco had beaten a robbery conviction because Abrams had decided he could make better use of him out on the street. As far as Chinaman knew, Rocco was possibly bisexual, definitely bigoted, and a bodyguard for someone higher up the drug ladder than Rocco himself. He knew Rocco never touched the poor quality stuff he sold; quaffing Irish whiskey and enormous amounts of beer was his old-fashioned way of having a good time; that and his habit of brutally beating anyone who inadvertently insulted his Irish background or his sexual preferences or the New York Mets, or who simply glanced at him in a way he deemed disrespectful.

Chinaman rubbed his elbow where it still ached from his encounter in Forest Hills, then lit a cigarette, adding to the enormous amount of smoke hovering in the room. He wondered how much life he was losing by inhaling the smoke of other cigarettes, not to mention his own. "Well, I'm happy to hear that. I always did prefer foam to sawdust for lying down." He glanced at the wall clock which he knew was always set ten minutes fast to accommodate last call. "Actually, Rocco, this isn't entirely a social call."

Rocco leaned forward on his arms and narrowed his eyes. "'Chinaman'. Say, what kind of name is that, anyway?"

"Italian father, French mother. A combination that every millionth time creates Chinese babies."

"No shit."

"No shit." Chinaman waited for the stern-faced waitress with large red knuckles and a pronounced Irish accent to set the beer down, take her money and leave. "I understand you might have some information about the New York Palace."

"The hotel? Sure. It's up near 50th. Can't miss it. Better

wear a tie, though. They tend to put on a bit of the dog." When Chinaman merely smiled, Rocco stared at him in mock indignation.

So Rocco wanted to play games. Just having fun or attempting to determine what his information might be worth? "I was thinking that the killers of those in room 1204 should be made to pay for their crime. Just think how much pride in the justice system we could have then."

Rocco stared at him then burst out in loud laughter. He banged his fist on the table. "I *like* you, Chinaman. I really do! I like the way you play your cards, you know?"

Chinaman allowed himself a wry smile and said nothing.

"Always digging into the other man's hand but keeping your own cards close to the vest. And doin' it well enough to make a livin'! Now, that's class!" Rocco drained half his glass, wiped his mouth, and nodded. "OK, you're a busy man. You need information and, bein' Irish, I'm only too happy to accommodate you. But, as the Irish like the color green above all others, and as money talks and bullshit walks, let me say one Franklin *and* one question of my own answered. That fair enough?"

One hundred dollars. Whatever Rocco had to say would either be worthless or worth a lot more than one hundred dollars. One way to find out. Chinaman wondered just how many pages of "Amazon Annihilators" he would have to copy edit to get that back. He also knew that if bills he'd sent out to clients weren't paid soon, he'd have to hit someone for a loan. He raised his glass. Light from a wall lamp struck the glass at an angle, turning spots of the dark brew blood red. "Deal."

Rocco rapped Chinaman's glass with his own and drank again. He wiped foam from his mouth. "OK. The question I always wanted to know about you: You were a teacher for years, right? Then you quit teaching to become a P.I. Why?"

Chinaman decided to answer without guile or prevarication. "I was a teacher of Creative Writing, and at some institutions of higher learning, creative writing teachers are somewhat akin to court jesters. Also, I guessed correctly that a lot of the skills are the same."

"Like what?"

"Like writing. More and more a P.I. needs to write reports logically and clearly in order to provide assistance to lawyers who hire them. And what does a writer do? He tries to see a bit deeper into the world than others." Chinaman knew he should stop there but he also knew he was getting drunk. "Tries to see the significance of things. He looks below the surface. He wants to find the meaning in the muddle, you understand? Isn't that also what a P.I. does?"

Rocco stared at him. "'Find the meaning in the muddle.' Damn, Chinaman. That actually makes sense."

Rocco looked off into a middle distance. Suddenly his eyes focused and he pointed to a poker machine near the men's room door. He read aloud the sign written above it. "'For amusement only; no payoff.' Now isn't that just like life itself?"

Chinaman leaned forward to conceal his action of counting out five twenty-dollar bills from his pocket. He folded them and palmed them in his hand. He reached forward to shake hands. "I've been drinking with you before, Rocco, but this is the first time you became a philosopher."

Rocco took the bills and slipped them into his shirt pocket without counting them. "First time for everything. OK. I gave your ex-wife's old man some information that might mean something and might mean nothing."

"Uh, oh."

"OK, wait. A guy I went to school with right here in Hell's Kitchen, a guy I used to make steal hubcaps for me when I needed dough, a go-fer, you know. A guy I haven't seen for years. He shows up and—"

"In the bar here?"

"Yeah. Right here. We used to lie about our age to get beer

in here when we were still punks. Anyway, he was a nerd I had to pound out on occasion, but he always liked to brag a lot; about women, about money, about deals."

"Deals?"

"You know. He was the guy who always knew what was happening; the guy who had an inside track with the 'big boys'. That's how he talked. He used to say he'd been talking with the *big boys* and that's how he knew what was goin' down. Anyway, he shows up a few nights ago."

"When exactly?"

"Friday about ten at night, exactly, OK? We get to talking. I see he hasn't changed. Still the *big man*, still the guy who knows what's goin' down. Only this time the guy, well, this is after a lot of beer, I should mention. Anyway, this time the guy starts dropping hints that he's some kind of hit man for some heavy hitters, you know. He never exactly comes out and uses the word 'hit man,' just somehow gets it across that he's perfected his 'talents,' yeah, kept talking about his 'specialized' talents and 'marketable' skills he's got now. And he talked a lot about guns. Said he was packing two."

"A real Rambo, huh?"

"Yeah. This guy used to brag about scoring a piece of ass off a cheerleader in school — now he's running off his mouth about his weapons collection and his 'talents'." Rocco came close to finishing his beer, then set the glass down, nine-tenths empty. "I can't say as I ever liked this guy. Like I say, I roughed him up a few times after school. Just to keep him straight. Anyway, he says he sure as hell proved himself while he was in New York to some people who weren't sure before."

"Sure about what?"

"Sure about using him." Rocco again wiped foam from his mouth, across the naked woman on his right forearm. "Damn! Best Guinness draft this side of the Atlantic. Did you know the yeast they use to make this head is from the same damn batch as when they first—"

"Rocco."

"Oh, yeah, OK. Well, like you, he was buyin' me drinks, right? So I just listened and nodded and kind of tuned out, thinking what an asshole this guy still is. I began to think, fuck the free beer, time to slug this guy into tomorrow. But just when I'm about to act on my impulse, the guy suddenly looks at his Rolex, says he's gotta go meet some very heavy people, and gets up. I can't stand the guy, right? But then I figure maybe if this guy is not the biggest liar ever born — and he's not, because he's not Irish — then maybe he did do something. Something Abrams might want to hear about. And, what the hell, I can't stand this asshole, anyway, right? So why not?"

Chinaman nodded in agreement. Across the room a beer bottle smashed under a table. Amid scuffling and loud shouts, a bouncer rushed over and screamed for the merrymakers to "knock it off or get the fuck out!" He emphasized his remark by banging the head of one of the group face down on the table. Chinaman suddenly remembered the Shamrock was known for what it didn't have as much as for what it did have. It didn't have a TV because each time there was a brawl something smashed into it. And it didn't have entertainment because even Irish singers didn't want any part of the place.

Rocco glanced at the melee and then smiled at Chinaman and shook his head as if to say, 'What a bunch of pussies.' Two of the brawlers, muscular, barrel-chested men in T-shirts and jeans, were locked together in fierce combat, grunting and swearing. They swayed closer to Chinaman's table, like a cumbersome, two-headed animal performing an exotic dance.

Suddenly, one of the men's elbows accidentally brushed against Rocco's beer glass. Rocco caught it but too late to prevent a quantity of beer from spilling. He looked at Chinaman in amazement. "These assholes spilled my Guinness!"

Rocco stood up and positioned himself as a football lineman

ready for the hike. He then rammed into the two men with enormous force propelling them across the eating area, past the barstools and into the front door. The action had brought the three of them just out of Chinaman's line of vision but, at the sound of the loud crash, Chinaman winced.

Seconds later, to boisterous applause from patrons, Rocco walked back to the table as if returning from an unexceptional visit to the men's room. He sat down, gulped some Guinness, and immediately resumed his monologue. "So, anyway, the guy keeps dropping hints that there might be a place for me in the *organization*, right, that's what he called it. I probably got more of an organization in my pants, but I figured, what the hell, play to the creep's vanity, right? So I try to come on like I was so impressed I was about to cream my jeans, just a wide-eyed, local boy eating it up, like I might actually be interested in joining the asshole in whatever shit he was in, and I ask him how I could get in touch with him. He said he'd be leaving in about a week but he fumbles in one of his jacket pockets and brings out a small pad and writes down a number. I took it, managed to thank him without puking, and off he went; back under whatever rock he crawled out from."

Chinaman took out his notebook and pen. Rocco gave him the number and the name of the man. "What about the notepaper itself? You gave it to Abrams, right?"

"Yep."

"When?"

"The next day. Abrams came here for lunch."

A charming pair you must have made, Chinaman thought. "What's the guy look like?" he asked.

"Medium height, medium build, chain-smoker, chrome dome."

"Chrome dome?"

"Bald. Well, almost. And no mustache, nothin' like that. Flashy suit, silk tie, shoes with, uh, what do you call them faggoty things that flop around?"

"Tassels?"

"Yeah, tassels." Rocco puckered his lips and gave his version of a limp wrist. Chinaman had never quite figured out Rocco's self image or the various shades of homosexuality that seemed to exist. Rocco went to bed with young boys but he considered a man wearing tasseled shoes a "faggot." Rocco chuckled. "Anyway, I hope the guy knows more about weapons than he does about women."

"What do you mean?"

"I mean he had scratches on his cheek. Some bitch must have got him good."

Chinaman felt the trail getting hot again. He decided to get out before the amount of beer he'd consumed took complete control of his ability to function. He knew it might be too late. He stood up. The room swayed a bit, then settled.

Lines of perplexity furrowed Rocco's brow. Even those looked muscular. "The thing is he told me he was staying with a friend in Brooklyn Heights. While he's in town, I mean."

Chinaman waited.

"But the little piece of notepaper he gave me had a crown on top with the name of the New York Palace. A fucking *crown*, if you can believe that! Who the hell elected those assholes?!"

★

32

A N hour after his meeting with Rocco, Chinaman sat back in his living room easy chair sipping Jack Daniels on the rocks while making a second count of the number of cigarette butts overflowing the ashtray. The apartment was filled with the syncopated rhythms of Dixieland jazz. He could feel the whiskey warming him and he knew he was now mildly drunk. It was his favorite state in which to review events, weigh possibilities, and make connections. Nine out of ten times the connections he made were not merely incorrect, but ludicrous. But it was the one out of ten that sometimes led him to hitting the jackpot.

He continued to examine every page of Judy's appointment book, looking for anything he might have overlooked. He had been studying it page by page for nearly an hour when he decided to check the hollow groove of its leather binding. He had given it a cursory look before, but the leather was stretched too tight to see far inside. If Judy had concealed anything he would need to probe for it. He opened a jumbo-sized paper clip from his work desk and straightened it into a single piece of metal just over six inches long. He inserted it into the top of the binding and slowly pushed it through. On the third try, a tiny, folded piece of paper slipped halfway out. Chinaman withdrew the paper and carefully unfolded it. It was a newspaper clipping. Across the top, Judy had written, "December 7th."

COLD SPRING VICTIM IDENTIFIED
Police reported today that the partially dismembered body found buried near the town of Cold Spring late

last month has been identified as Julio Cesar, 35, a Columbian national. According to police, the man's body was discovered by workmen laying water pipes near the railroad tracks just south of Cold Spring. Police said the victim had been shot once through the back of the head by a .357 Magnum.

Police said Mr. Cesar was identified through a fingerprint search. Police have no immediate information on suspects or a motive.

When the phone rang, Chinaman had been staring at the clipping and trying to "connect" for some time. Chinaman drained the whiskey in his glass and reached for the phone. "Chinaman."

"The next favor you ask is gonna cost you."

"Yeah, Larry, what's up?" Chinaman glanced at his watch. "Not s   e office, I hope."

"Nah. Just having a quick one before heading home." Chinaman could hear the music and laughter of a bar background. "Listen, it took some digging, but you were right. El Al did have a case of two men canceling their seats to Tel Aviv that night. At the last minute. Before they got on the plane, but after they'd entered the area restricted to passengers."

"No check-in luggage, I'll bet."

"You bet right. And the tickets were paid for in cash."

"That figures. And they were made out to Bart Simpson and Fred Flintstone."

"Close. You're gonna love this. Their passports were in the names of 'Wesson Smith' and 'Chester Winn'."

"Smith and Wesson and Winchester? Killers with a sense of humor. Maybe they're out-of-work comedians."

"Yeah. Comedians carrying phony passports that must look as genuine as the real thing. You want to tell me what it's about?"

"For sure. Just as soon as I know."

"All right. The airline is supposed to alert me if Wesson and

Chester try to get reimbursed."

"They'll probably decide to forgo the cash on this one."

"Yeah, well, who knows? They might actually need the money, the airline people might actually remember to alert me, and fairytales might come true. That it for now?"

"That's it, Lar. And I owe you another one."

"I'll take it in drinks. And, Chinaman, do an old pal a favor, would you?"

"Name it."

"Stop using words like 'forgo.' You sound like a fucking lawyer."

"Sorry."

"Forget it. See yah."

"Hey! Larry!"

"Yeah?"

"Julio Cesar, 35, Columbian national, found dead in Cold Spring. One .357 round through the head."

"What about him? He owe you money?"

"Paper says a fingerprint search found him."

"Newspapers say a lot of things."

"That means he was most likely a bad boy before, right? If he's in the police computer, I mean."

"Chinaman, you sure all this has something to do with me? 'Cause you might be delivering the right message to the wrong person. It's been known to happen."

"I want his last known address, Larry."

"Chinaman, I think when you applied for your P.I. license somebody misinformed you. They told you that busy metropolitan police departments just love to fall all over themselves to help private detectives solve cases, that right?"

"Larry, look-"

"Hey, I know what, why don't you put a suggestion in a box at One Police Plaza asking the Commissioner to set up a special department specifically assigned to aid private detectives in their work? He's very open to new ideas. Let me know the outcome."

Chinaman knew when silence was his best hope. If the police could use it on suspects, why couldn't he use it on them?

"All *right*! *If* I get the time, I'll see if there is a goddamned last address on Caesar Romero."

"Julio Cesar. J-u-l-i-o-C-e-s-a-r. Thanks a million, Lar."

Chinaman waited until Larry Sterling had completed his stream of epithets before hanging up. It was the courteous thing to do. His glance fell on the books lining the desk. One of Jo Anne's books had been mistakenly shelved with his own. In between Mia Yun's *House of the Winds* and a new translation of the *Tao Te Ching* was a well-thumbed copy of *Magic and Misdirection*. The title locked it all in; the final connection had been made. He remembered Jo Anne's words: "Misdirection is the key to magic. The whole trick is to divert the onlooker's attention from what you're really doing. Even while he's watching." Chinaman knew who killed Judy Fisher; he didn't yet know why.

He reached for the phone. It was just late enough that he might catch Stiggy at home. The voice on the other end succeeded in combining caution and nonchalance in equal measure. "Yeah."

"Stiggy?"

Silence. Very cautious silence.

"This is Chinaman."

The voice grew friendly but defensive. "Hey, Chinaman! My man! I was gonna' call you about Weaverton but—"

"Stiggy. Don't bullshit me. Just be in the bar tomorrow night. Ten o'clock. With the money."

"Tomorrow?" Stiggy pronounced the word in amazement, as if 'tomorrow' were only a few minutes away.

"Tomorrow. That's the day after today. Ten o'clock."

"You talkin' funny, Chinaman. You not shootin' up, are you?"

"Ten o'clock, Stiggy." Chinaman hung up and wondered about a junkie asking him if he's shooting up. People get cancer from other people's cigarette smoke, contact highs from other people's marijuana — could he actually be getting weird by hanging around with weird people? If so, it was just something that comes with the territory. And just how weird was Stiggy? Chinaman often sensed cunning behind his spaced out facade; not unlike television's 'Columbo,' crazy like a fox. He tried not to think of the odds against Stiggy actually having the money.

He reread the clipping and placed it inside his desk drawer. He turned on the local news and learned that a teenager in Harlem had been shot dead for his '8 ball' designer jacket, a teenager in the Bronx had been shot and wounded by someone after his shearling coat, a family in Queens had lost their home to a Christmas tree fire, and the body of a man whose arms and legs had been bound by "duck tape and a string of Christmas tree lights" had washed up in Brooklyn's 'Dead Horse Inlet,' and a major American airline announced that it had taken Sweet 'n Low off its planes after passengers complained that it resembled Anthrax powder.

There it is.

★

33

T HE printer was several hours behind schedule with the latest issue of "Amazon Annihilators." When the resulting sounds of office panic, ringing phones and screamed threats became too obtrusive, Chinaman got up and closed the door of his office cubicle. He returned to his desk and scrutinized *Coles* reverse directory for a third time. The number Rocco had given him wasn't there. Which could mean Rocco had made a mistake. Or more likely that the person assigned that number had asked that it be unpublished. Chinaman would have to call a friend in the phone company for some off-the-record assistance. Or, rather, an ex-girlfriend. An ex-girlfriend for whom news of his death — preferably slow and painful — would be cause for celebration.

He let out a long sigh, lit a cigarette and picked up the phone. He hesitated several seconds while working himself into the right frame of mind, then dialed the number. After being passed along by two people and after waiting nearly a minute, he heard her once familiar voice.

"Linda Davis speaking. How may I help you?"

Chinaman spoke with a bright smile in his voice. "Hi, Linda. Chinaman here."

After several seconds of hyperborean silence, Linda Davis spoke with perfect computer efficiency and corporate politeness. If either could castrate, Chinaman knew he had lost something very important. "Yes, Mr. Chinaman, how may I be of service to you?"

"Linda, believe me, I've been meaning to call you but I was out of–"

"I see. Well, sir, before I could make a determination on that

I would need your account number."

Chinaman hated it when people said "make a determination" instead of "make a decision." No one "decided" anything anymore; they "made a determination." The expression wreaked of bureaucratic self-importance and showed complete contempt for the beauty and economy of language. Chinaman would overlook it. "Linda, look, I got a call from a member of WAD in Miami. World Association of Detectives. And I had to–"

"Well, then, how did you call out just now, sir?...I see. Well, yes, just let me get your account up on our computer and then I'll try the number myself. What is the number there, sir?"

Chinaman gave her his office phone number. "Find yourself some privacy, will you? I'll wait right here."

"All right, sir, I do think this is a job for a repairman, but if you think it will do any good, I'll try the number first. I'll call back shortly."

Chinaman lit another cigarette and waited. He was now on his last cigarette. He picked up the empty pack, folded it, and refolded it. Nearly five minutes passed before the phone rang. He picked up. "Chi–"

"You treacherous, slant-eyed, illegitimate son of a Confucian whore!"

"Linda, that's on the border of being politically incorrect. I only–"

"You son-of-a-bitch! You *want* something, right? Some favor or other that will help some cheating, sleazeball husband client of yours screw his wife out of her alimony. Isn't that it?"

"Linda–"

"Or maybe you just called to say you didn't really drop me like I had the plague; it's just that you were in a coma for six months."

"Linda, I'm sorry. I was on a case that took me out of New York. I just got back. Last week."

"Chinaman, if that's the best you can lie, I feel sorry for you. You shouldn't be in the detective business."

"Linda, listen to me for one minute. I am sorry and you have every right to be furious. But I really have been up to my eyeballs with work. And now I'm investigating a murder. A double homicide. And, yes, I do need a favor. And, all right, I'll take all the abuse you want to throw at me, but I swear to you I'm not protecting any philandering husband from the financial consequences of adultery; I'm trying to fry the killers of a young woman."

"And I'm supposed to believe that?"

"Linda, it is the exact truth; no more, no less!"

"And let's just suppose for a minute I don't believe you. And I don't give you what you want. What would you do then?"

"Well, I'd most likely call up Central Names and Addresses and pretend I'm somebody working within the phone company or call up the number's prefix billing office and pretend the same thing or I'd call the DPAC office and pretend I'm a service rep repairing a phone. And, I suppose, with a bit of luck, somewhere along the line, I'd get what I need. If not, I could try a few overpriced computer programs designed for just such emergencies but I'd need at least a name and a zip which I don't have which means I might actually have to call the number itself and run some kind of scam to get the name and address. But, as you said yourself, I really can't lie well, so I'd probably not be able to-"

"There ought to be laws against people like you, Chinaman."

"There are. But if people like me obey all the laws, and the bad guys don't, then the bad guys don't get caught and the people like me don't get paid."

"It always amazes me that people like you assume you're not one of the bad guys."

"I do what I have to."

"And the end justifies the means?"

"In this business? Absolutely."

Linda laughed. Or at least guffawed. Chinaman took it as a hopeful sign. She was still on the line. Which was far more than he had a right to expect. After a few moments of silence, she gave forth with a long sigh of surrender which suggested that she would have to bear the unbearable; suffer the insufferable. "Give me the name."

"It's not a name, it's a number. Supposed to be in Brooklyn. I've checked *Coles* and the others. On and off-line. It's not listed."

Chinaman gave her the number. She repeated it. Chinaman confirmed it.

"All right. If it's unlisted, I'll see what I can do. If it's unpublished in our internal list as well, you're just out of luck."

"I appreciate this, Linda."

"Sure you do. I'll call you back later. And, Chinaman...."

"Yes, Linda?"

She spaced out the words for emphasis. "You have no idea how absolutely wonderful it makes me feel to hear you squirm."

Chinaman jerked his ear away a split second too late to avoid the loud click. He wondered how many such loud clicks a human ear could take before deafness set in. He closed the door to his office and went to lunch at his favorite Chinese restaurant. The line of customers waiting to get in spilled out into the street. Chinaman settled for a soggy tuna fish sandwich at a nearly deserted coffee shop while cursing the day Westerners "discovered" Chinese cuisine.

When he returned, he found that Audrey had left two messages on his desk: One from American Express concerning an unpaid bill and one from "L" with a man's name and a Brooklyn Heights address.

★

34

"NO justice; no peace! No justice; no peace!"
In an attempt to avoid the demonstration,
Chinaman had pushed through the crowd to the
side of the Harlem street. The marchers were following an ancient
Oldsmobile outfitted with microphones. Placards and banners
denounced police brutality and demanded justice.

Chinaman had watched for just a minute, trying to deny the
rising panic inside him. His stomach churned; his body was
immersed in sweat. He closed his eyes, attempting to think of
pleasant times with Judy, with anyone, but when he opened them
the scene was transformed as he knew it would be and he saw the
same hysterical mob he had seen as a child: The red armbands on
the Red Guards restraining him; the propaganda posters against
enemies of the people lining the ancient city wall; the mind-
numbing shouts in unison — slogans denouncing his parents; the
indignant and unforgiving expressions on each face in the crowd.
His parents stood on a bamboo platform in the center of the mob
with placards hanging from their necks describing their "crimes."
The hands of those he loved were tied behind them, their heads
lowered in shame and despair. Half of his mother's hair had been
shaved and his father's face was swollen and bloody from repeated
beatings. They had refused to "confess."

When Chinaman had briefly slipped from the arms of the
Red Guards and rushed to aid his parents, he had been beaten
himself, and denounced as a child of the people's enemy. While
he lay pinned to the ground, unable to move, someone had spat
on him and shouted Mao's slogan into his face: "The offspring of

a dragon is another dragon; the offspring of a phoenix is another phoenix." Chinaman would be punished for the sin of having been born into the "landlord class."

Chinaman's eyes brimmed with tears and he pushed his way roughly past angry blacks and rushed inside the restaurant.

In the first booth, a fat lady with gold-rimmed spectacles and huge door-knocker earrings sat immersed in a novel. Neither the demonstration outside nor the noisy crowd clustered at the bar waiting for the next jazz set seemed to distract her.

Chinaman slumped into a booth and ordered Jack Daniels on the rocks. The waiter had given him a strange look, no doubt mistaking his sweat-drenched face and wild-eyed look for that of an addict: dumb chinaman too high on drugs to know which way Chinatown is and ended up in Harlem. Chinaman took his drink, ordered another and closed his eyes. By the time he'd finished that one, the demonstration had moved on.

When he'd calmed down enough, Chinaman glanced at his watch. Stiggy was twenty-five minutes late. Men in nearby booths drank themselves into loud talk and louder laughter. While Chinaman had been waiting, more than once, men in other booths had turned to him and then held a whispered conversation with their companions; after which they had all turned to stare at Chinaman. Not without reason Chinaman had begun to feel that something — possibly his yellow skin and almond eyes — set him apart from other customers. Conspicuously.

But Chinaman knew it wasn't just his skin that set him apart. He'd arrived in the States as an eleven-year-old boy already traumatized by his experiences. He could no more identify with a society which worshiped celebrities and sports and babbled about "relationships" and "commitment" than he could with one that worshiped Chairman Mao and denounced "enemies of the people."

He almost envied Chinese born in America, some of whom could self-righteously describe themselves as "disenfranchised victims" without any inkling of how thoroughly American such attitudes really were. Chinaman had stopped attempting to fit in with anyone a long time ago. And Judy had felt his own aloneness and alienation approximate her own and he knew it was one of the reasons she had given herself to him.

Stiggy arrived almost an hour late. His short legs strode quickly across the smoke-filled room while the upper half of his thin body dipped rhythmically, almost mechanically, from the waist with each step; first to the left, then to the right, and back to the left.

Without ever quite looking at anyone or anything his eyes took in everything. His leather jacket had padded shoulders and his shiny trousers were fronted with an enormous diamond-shaped belt buckle. Expensive looking high-top sneakers completed his outfit. He sank into the booth across the table from Chinaman and shook his head. His expression was dour, sullen, cross. "Don' be bitchin' me for bein' late. You not the only jive-ass turkey who needs money."

Chinaman realized Stiggy was crashing from whatever high he had been on. It was a typical Stiggy post-cocaine downer — hard and fast. He managed a smile for Stiggy while signaling to a waiter. "I didn't say a word."

Stiggy lit a cigarette and leaned back in the booth. Chinaman recognized Stiggy's offence as his best defense and knew what was coming.

"Wasn't in."

"Who wasn't in, Stiggy?"

"*Weaverton* wasn't in. I been at it all day."

"Weaverton skipped, Stiggy."

"Weaverton ain't skipped; he just ain't in. Another day or two and I'll fucking have him."

"Another day or two and I go on a forced fast."

Stiggy exhaled long streams of blue ribbons which drifted away from the booth to settle on the fat lady in the booth opposite. She looked over her gold-rimmed spectacles at Stiggy, screwed her face into an indignant scowl, and spoke while vigorously waving smoke away. "Disgusting!"

Chinaman looked at Stiggy's face and saw it coming. "Hey, Stiggy, forget it, she–"

Too late. Stiggy was half out of the booth. "Hey, bitch! This here the smoking section. You don't like cigarette smoke, then don't be sitting in the smoking section. What are you — stupid?"

The fat lady slammed her book shut and took a deep breath. "You better clean up your foul mouth before you open it to address me, nigger."

"Who you calling 'nigger', big mama? You looked in the mirror, lately? 'Cause if you ain't black you been eatin' too much chocolate pie."

The woman was standing now. "Don't you–"

"You cared about your body you wouldn't be feeding your fat face from morning to night!"

An angry waiter, decked out in the bar's uniform of black vest over long-sleeved white shirt and black flared trousers, headed toward Stiggy. The woman's voice bellowed louder. "Junkies like you–"

"You a food junkie. And food junkies like you not goan die from no nicotine poisoning; you goan croak from klestrawl overdose."

As they both lunged toward each other, the waiter — about half the woman's height and weight — jumped between them and shouted. "Knock it off or you both leave."

"No street junkie is gonna–"

The waiter gripped his vest and drew himself up to full height — his pyramid-shaped, high-rise, flat-topped hair was now level with the woman's enormous breasts — and spoke through clenched teeth: "Last chance, mama. I said, 'Knock it off,' and I meant it."

"She not a non-smoker; she a fanatic anti-smoker. No mud duck mama–"

Chinaman placed his hands firmly on Stiggy's bony shoulders

and pushed him down onto his seat. "Stiggy, forget it! We got things to discuss!"

The woman, still complaining, picked up her book and jacket and followed the waiter to the non-smoking section. She sat heavily beneath a posed photograph of Joe Louis in trunks and gloves. Joe wouldn't have lasted a round with her.

Stiggy took a long drink on Chinaman's whiskey. "She as rude as she is ugly. Women fanatics is always the worst."

Chinaman waved to a second waiter and ordered two more whiskeys. "Stiggy, lighten up! I want you to chill out. Now!"

Stiggy's cigarette had been damaged in the fray. Chinaman held out his own pack. Stiggy took one and Chinaman lit it for him. "Now, calm down. You indulged in a little happy dust, right? Right or wrong? So now you've developed an attitude. It comes with the territory. But one thing I can say about you is that whether you're heading up or down, you always maintain well, isn't that a fact?" Chinaman's arm gesture swept the room. "All over Harlem everybody says the same thing: "Whatever he's on, Stiggy Freeman" — and here Chinaman banged the table — "*main - tains!*"

Stiggy exhaled thick streams of blue smoke through his nostrils. It reminded Chinaman of a rocket launch at Cape Canaveral. He relaxed his padded shoulders and leaned forward. "First things first. Whatever shit went down at the hotel, whoever did it, it wasn't a Harlem thing, you know what I'm saying?"

I never thought it was, Chinaman thought. "Go on."

"'Cause I don't always get the whole story on something what's brewing in or from Harlem, but I get at least a *pinch*. This hotel thing — I got nothing." Stiggy's shoulders began twitching and then jumping to whatever imagined tune he was hearing over his imaginary earphones. The state of his health hadn't improved any since the last time Chinaman had met him, but he seemed reasonably coherent.

Chinaman nodded. In his experience, informers often heard

different versions of events — on the street or in their own heads. And like most people who made their living by knowing something worth something to someone else, Stiggy could sometimes be dead accurate and at other times be spinning a tall tale. How much he embellished on what he knew might depend on how wired he was, how intimidated he was, or how much he needed money.

Chinaman knew whenever Stiggy provided him with information it was up to him to separate fact from fiction. He wasn't sure if the skill he relied on to accomplish that stemmed from his detective experience or from his fiction-writing background. But he knew Stiggy wasn't holding out for a higher price on the hotel murders. And the fact that no one local knew anything about it fit in with how he believed it went down.

Stiggy took a drink and grew more thoughtful. Chinaman wasn't certain if his mind was thinking or drifting. "Something else, Stiggy?"

"Them two dudes you ran off last time we was here?"

"What about them?"

"They asked about you."

Chinaman waited.

"They said whether you had a gun or didn't had a gun you definitely did possess a pair of brass balls."

"That right?"

"Yeah. Herman, the big guy, he said you were the blackest Chinaman he ever saw."

"That's swell."

"He said that's why he hopes he don't never run into you again. 'Cause he would take no pleasure in what he would have to do."

"Well, then, I'll try to see Herman before he sees me."

"Yeah." Stiggy knocked back his drink and wiped his mouth. "One thing."

Chinaman waited.

"Herman. The big guy. He's looking for Weaverton, too."

Chinaman waited.

"One of the ladies Weaverton had with him in his apartment. Weaverton roughed her up a bit."

Chinaman waited.

"She was Herman's sister. Herman says if he finds Weaverton, he'll kill him."

And Chinaman remembered yet another saying of his late mentor, Jimmy (the Tiger) Sterling: "Whatever happens, above all else, make certain never to place your client in danger: Dead men don't pay debts."

35

CHINAMAN adjusted the rearview mirror of his rented Hyundai Excel and leaned back in the passenger's seat. He was satisfied that the mirror reflection of the three-story brownstone across the street should give him glimpses of everyone who went in and out. His sitting in the passenger's seat should suggest to passersby that he was waiting for the driver. Unless they came to the conclusion that he was actually on a stakeout sitting in the passenger's seat to fool passersby into thinking he was waiting for the driver.

The mirror didn't give him a glimpse of the two men sitting in the Dodge Shadow nearly half a block back. But he had spotted them as he drove by earlier. No doubt part of Abrams's homicide detail. They blended into the street scene as naturally as mongeese at a snake farm, but it was a free country and Chinaman figured if they wanted to join in a fun game of follow the leader, so be it.

He gulped a last swallow of cold coffee, snapped on the cover, and tossed the Styrofoam cup to the floor of the car. he had bought a new thermos for just such a situation but he had forgotten to buy coffee. Jo Anne used to buy coffee and other necessities. No Jo Anne — no coffee and other necessities. He checked his watch. Ten thirty-five. His stakeout had lasted just over two-and-a-half hours. So far, on a beautiful and clear sky-blue morning in late December, no one had entered or exited the building.

The brownstone was not on one of the Height's best streets but the buildings were well preserved and the area appeared safe. Little old ladies still walked nervous white dogs that resembled their owners and middle class parents still sent red-cheeked children off to school reasonably certain that no drug dealer's stray bullet had their child's name on it.

Chinaman was contemplating dashing into a nearby corner store for another coffee when he saw them. Two men, one tall and distinguished. One of average height and nearly bald. The same men he had seen in Harry's New York Bar; the same men supposedly now enjoying the sights of Tel Aviv. The same men who killed Judy Fisher.

They walked unhurriedly down the steps of the brownstone and out onto the sidewalk, carefully adjusting sunglasses as they walked. They wore conservative sport coats over open white shirts, well pressed trousers and dress shoes. They could have been lawyers heading for an informal meeting or editors dropping by the office on their day off. Chinaman sensed they were professionals in a very different profession.

They crossed the street and got into a car half a block behind him. He lost sight of them but heard the doors slam. By the time their two-tone blue Toyota passed his one-tone white Hyundai, Chinaman had picked his copy of the *New York Post* off the seat, and was deeply engrossed in the sports pages. He reached into the glove compartment, pushed aside the Pentax binoculars and took out a notebook. As he drove at a careful distance behind them, he jotted down the license number, car make, time, date and place.

As the Dodge Shadow passed him, the man in the passenger seat glared at him. Chinaman added the license number of the Dodge to his report. Just possibly he could get the man on a misdemeanor—glaring in the third degree; scowling without a license; first degree frowning. He couldn't see the expression on the driver's face but he was certainly an accessory. He replaced the notebook and followed both cars along Brooklyn's Atlantic Avenue.

Chinaman drove at a leisurely pace; he was more concerned about being spotted by Judy's killers than he was about losing them. He thought of the typical two-hour, made-for-television movie where the detective always seemed to follow his subject to a significant place where said subject met with his illusive contact, Mr. Big, thereby fitting all the missing pieces together and nudging the case well on its way to a quick solution.

In real life, nine out of ten times even bad guys left their dwellings merely to run mundane errands. Chinaman had followed men and sometimes women to barber shops, hairdressers, dentists, cafes, nail salons, bars, gay bars, topless bars, all nude bars, massage parlors, supermarkets, gas stations and movie theaters. Once he had followed a notorious Mafioso to a cemetery where the man had placed long-stemmed red roses on his mother's grave and cried like a baby.

Only once or twice in any ten tries had he actually gained anything crucial to a case by tailing a subject. Still, it was better than sitting in the office listening to psychics warn him off coffee or typing out "Final Notices" for payment to former clients who had no interest in paying the balance once their cases had been concluded.

The one with the wavy white hair was driving and he drove like a man with lots of time to spare. At his first stop, he waited behind the wheel while his companion went into a liquor store and emerged with a brown bag and a newspaper. He got back into the car and they drove off in the direction of South Brooklyn to Carroll Gardens, a pleasant if not-overly-exciting Italian neighborhood where, almost predictably, both men entered a shoe repair store. They emerged with brown shoe bags under their arms. Chinaman reflected that it was reassuring to see professionals take so much pride in their appearance. He pictured their living room wall lined with 'Employee of the Month' awards. He wondered if they had worn color-coordinated ties, shirts and suits the night they murdered Judy Fisher. Maybe they had shined their shoes.

From Carroll Gardens it was a long, slow, tedious drive over the Brooklyn Bridge and into the Chinatown/Little Italy section of Manhattan where the two men eventually parked along a side

street and entered one of the city's few remaining gunshops.
Chinaman wondered if they were buying ammunition — and if
any of that ammunition had his name on it.

The Dodge Shadow managed to back into the only available
parking space. The frowning man now gave Chinaman a superior
smile. Chinaman added "reckless parking" and "smug sneer" to
his list of complaints and double-parked near a phone booth. He
quickly slipped an engraved white plastic sign with red letters from
under his seat. It read:

Picking up emergency blood supply

He placed it on his dashboard against the windshield and
walked quickly to the phone booth. The first phone was missing,
the second had a piece of metal stuck in its slot. He jogged to the
phone on the next corner, dialed and waited.

Audrey answered with a loud "Family Values Publishing" and
a somewhat grudging, barely audible, "Chinaman Investigations."

"Audrey, this is Chinaman."

"Who?"

Chinaman looked at the phone in his hand and tried again.
"Audrey, this is *Chinaman*, of Chinaman Investigations."

"Hi, Chinaman." Lifeless, dispirited. As if afraid he might
have work for her to do.

"Audrey, I'm in a phone booth so I have to be quick. I need
you to do a DMV for me."

A long sigh of intolerable anguish pushed to the breaking
point filled his ear. Where was it Chinaman had read that people
are often eager to help private detectives with their investigations.
He had yet to find one. "All right, what is it?"

Chinaman gave her the number.

"I'll call you back."

"Audrey, I'm in a phone booth. Can't you run it now?"

"Now? You want me to run a motor vehicle *now*?!"
Chinaman's request was not merely a last-straw imposition; he
had clearly asked the impossible. " *'Now'* I've got a million things

on my desk and Sydney is yelling at me to do a million other things. I'm only one person, you know. I can't–"

"Audrey, I'm in a phone booth; I'm tailing someone who may get away if you don't hurry." Chinaman decided to up the ante. "Solving this case could depend on what you find out in the next three minutes."

Silence. Not neutral silence; skeptical silence. "Why don't you have a cell phone?"

"If Sydney gives me the money, I'll get one, Audrey, all right?"

"Why don't you have a car phone?"

"Audrey, I don't have a car phone because I don't have a *car*; this is rented, remember?"

"I never saw a detective on TV take a subway. If you ask me, it's bad for your image."

Chinaman could feel his head starting to pound. Detective shows should not be allowed on TV. Ever. "Audrey, listen to me. I look *forward* to riding the subways. I learn lots of useful things. I can say 'no leaning against the door' in Spanish and, oh, yeah, 'the train tracks are dangerous.' I can say that too. And a few cars still have ads for dentures, warts, hernias, tummy tucks, bunions, hammertoes, phone sex, fortune tellers — Hey, did you know they've got numbers you can call to catch up on the TV soaps if you missed an episode? Any soap you like! If that doesn't prove America has surpassed ancient Greek civilization, what does? And it's all there, Audrey, right on the subway. Only a buck and change for admission. No one but a fool would want to drive a car in New York City with all that below ground. Now could you please *do the DMV*?"

"Hold on." Icy. Very icy.

Chinaman took a deep breath to calm down, tried not to remember the article in the *Times* he had just read about anger affecting the heart, and waited. His car, his subject's car, the scowler's car, and the gun shop itself were now all out of sight but he was gambling the men would spend some time inside; for hit men a gun shop would be like a candy store for a tubby eight-year-old with a sweet tooth. He dropped more coins into the phone and waited.

"...You still holding?"

"With baited breath. What's taking so long?"

"It says, 'No reply from DMV Albany, Retrying'....OK, wait, here it is. You got a pen?"

"Shoot."

"Last name, 'Rudge'. R.U.D.G.E. First name, 'Warren' just like with rabbits. Plate type: commercial. D.O.B. 12/10/41. Sex is male, height is five feet ten inches. Eyes are blue." Chinaman asked her to repeat the address, then asked her to continue. "The license expires 10/11/02. Insurance is United Community."

"That it?"

"Yeah. You want a print out?"

"No, that's all right. I can get it up later."

"Well, I'll tell you, you better get it while you can. It doesn't show much balance left on this screen. You paid your bill lately?"

"All right, print it. And thanks."

"You really should get a car phone, Chinaman. Or a cellular."

"Right. I'll ask Santa to put it on his list."

"And don't forget the office Christmas party is tomorrow night! The writer of 'Amazon Annihilators' will be there. Sydney says even the illustrator may show up."

Chinaman shouted an "OK" into the phone and hung up. He dashed around the corner to where the two-tone blue Toyota had been. The space was now filled with a station wagon. From a rear window a basset hound with large sad eyes looked out at him and tilted its head. The Dodge Shadow was gone. Chinaman walked back to his car. There was a ticket on the windshield.

Obviously, some parking meter maid had seen the "blood supply" routine before. Probably more than once. Chinaman got in the driver's seat and lit a cigarette. Yes, he would ask Santa Claus for a cellular phone this Christmas. Just as soon as he located

him. Also on his wishlist would be a request for information.
Not of the 'Who'd been naughty and who'd been nice' variety —
finding that out was Chinaman's job. What he most wanted to
know now was why a car being driven by two hit men lodging in
Brooklyn Heights sported commercial plates; what was the
company and what was their relationship to it?

Chinaman adjusted his mirror and started the engine. Warren
Rudge fit the DMV description and was most likely the man
driving the car. Knowing what company he worked for might
not be crucial but in investigations every piece of information
often helped to complete the puzzle; and, sometimes, insignificant
pieces of information led to not-so-insignificant pieces of
information.

He thought of the many ways of tracking down the name of
the company. There was the computer route which he had no
access to because of the cost of that type of program; a detective
could go bankrupt signing on to all the specialized computer
programs designed to help him. And Chinaman had yet to find
anyone who didn't want to be found on the general people-finding
programs installed in most computers. That route was out. There
was the credit check route which would almost certainly turn up
the company name. But credit companies often displayed a
noticeable lack of affection for information requests from P.I.'s.
There was the public-official-on-the-phone survey route. But if
that type of gag failed it simply alerted the subject that someone
was investigating him. And there were other ways of obtaining
that kind of information from an open, statistics-starved, records-
happy society. But almost every route would involve unacceptable
expenses, possible exposure or asking someone for a large favor.
Chinaman decided he owed too much money and too many favors
as it was. And he felt too close to something to take a chance of
blowing it now.

He could be wrong but Chinaman decided that whatever
nefarious activities the man was involved in, he might just be one

of the millions of Americans who believe that every vote counts; that his or her vote 'can make a difference'. Anyway, it was worth a chance. He threw his cigarette butt out the window, nosed his Hyundai out into traffic, spun wildly on a patch of ice, regained control, and headed for the Brooklyn office of New York City's Board of Elections. Halfway there he remembered he had no guarantee the man was an American citizen, and, if not, he couldn't vote anyway. He thought about turning around and going home, then decided that, as Gertrude Stein would say, a lead is a lead is a lead.

36

OUTSIDE the window of Chinaman's apartment, a brief flurry of snow had quickly given way to a fine rain. Inside his apartment the living room was filled with the lean melodies and laconic piano style of Thelonious Monk. The last time Chinaman had risen from his desk to check the time it had been a few minutes to midnight. Even without the music and the Scotch he would have been in a meditative mood.

The photocopy of Warren Rudge's voter's registration card was in front of him. Several past and present volumes of business registries were piled beside his butt-filled ashtray: *Thomas register of American Manufacturers* 'Company Profiles Section' and *Standard and Poor's* 'Register of Corporation Directors and Executives.'

Warren Rudge was a registered Democrat, a citizen by birth, and had lived at his Brooklyn Height's address for six years. He had a lousy signature. Too many slanting letters and fancy loops. No sense of proportion. Chinaman wasn't sure but thought that people in the handwriting analysis racket might conclude the guy wasn't wired up properly.

His place of birth was Seaside, California, his date of birth was three days after Germany surrendered, and his alma mater was San Francisco State College — now a university. He was listed as Vice President (Fin. & Admin.) of Security Systems in Flatbush, Brooklyn. He was also listed as a director. Security Systems was a subsidiary of National Security Systems Corporation which specialized in burglar and fire alarm controls. Over a three-year period, National Security Systems Corp. had fallen from over three million dollars in annual sales to under one million in annual sales. Its profits were now probably marginal at best. National Security Systems Corporation was located in Washington, D.C.

Chinaman had never seen the names of the president, vice-president (Sales & Mktg), office manager, or equipment sales manager. Nor were any of the "other directors" listed familiar to him.

He closed the books and took a long thoughtful hit on his Scotch. There were many ways to continue checking on a corporation. The problem was he could spend a lot of time and money chasing through the holding companies and other labyrinths that no doubt protected the real owners and might then find that the information was peripheral to solving the case, anyway. A time-consuming paper chase. An expensive computer search. Or continue to follow the leads of criminals like Rocco and drug addicts like Stiggy. Paper, silicone chips or people. He mentally added up the pros and cons of each and decided that for now people were still his best bet.

He turned on the television and quickly used the remote to switch channels. He managed to catch Mayor Giuliani answering questions about the dangers of Anthrax to postal workers but he had missed the main news. He stopped to watch a few minutes of the black-and-white film of a World War II Nazi prison camp, "Staglag 17." William Holden was exposing a Nazi plant to the other men in the barracks. The Nazi plant had gone on to become the star of television's "Mission Impossible." William Holden, Chinaman's favorite actor, was dead. But something in the scene's tension — a person being denounced and dealt with by a group — was too close to what he had experienced in his childhood. In his mind it was as if Chairman Mao was again raising the question from his grave, or rather, Beijing mausoleum — "Who are our enemies? Who are our friends?" It was the question asked by the comrade in charge when the sentence of death was pronounced on his father.

Chinaman turned off the television, locked the front door,

turned off the light and went to bed. Sometime during the night, the snow began again. Before dawn, he was woken from a series of tenuously connected dreams by the grating sound of a snow shovel scraping concrete.

★

DAY ELEVEN

37

"**M**ANHATTAN Properties." The woman's voice was everything the real estate market wasn't: Upbeat and optimistic.

"Hi. I wonder if I could speak to Mary Anne."

"Certainly. May I know who's calling?"

"Chinaman."

"Just a minute, Mr. Heinemann. I'll see if she's in."

'Heinemann'? Well, why not? Chinaman sat back in his living room desk chair, sipped his jasmine tea and listened to the howling wind thump the window. Something shiny sped by the upper pane. A suicidal pigeon covered with ice? A snowflake on steroids? A slow moving bullet? In New York, one didn't ask.

Mary Anne's voice was crisp and professional. "Hello? This is Mary Anne."

"Hi, Mary Anne. Chinaman here. How are you?"

"Well, this is...a surprise. I thought the receptionist said something about a Mr. *Heinemann*. Sounded like someone with money."

"Unlike me, you might add."

"Whatever you're buying, I have to tell you most banks aren't lending much at all and from you they'd want 110 per cent down."

"Thanks for being upfront and honest."

Mary Anne laughed. "Just kidding. In this market, they might ask for a bit less. Even from you. So what can I do for you?"

"Well, inasmuch as we're being upright and honest, the truth is I find myself running a bit short."

"Short?"

"Short. What in Somerset Maugham's day might have been referred to as 'a state of financial embarrassment.'

"I see. Your wallet's flat so you naturally turned to your ex-wife for a loan."

"Naturally."

"One thing I always admired about you, Chinaman, is that you were a damn good P.I. So may I be so bold as to ask how it came to this?"

"Cash flow."

"What about it?"

"There isn't any. Clients want the job done yesterday; but once it's done, they forget to pay."

"And that's it?"

"Well, I did hang up on a lawyer who was sending me a lot of business."

"Ah, now *that* sounds more like the Chinaman I grew to know so well."

"And, to tell you the truth, I'm putting my other cases on hold while I investigate the New York Palace murders."

Chinaman waited for the ominous silence to end while in the background ringing phones went unanswered at Manhattan Properties. When she spoke again, something new had crept into Mary Anne's voice. Something toxic. "Let me get this straight. You put your other cases on hold to solve the death of the woman who destroyed our marriage and now you have the unmitigated nerve to call *me* and ask for money? You want *me* to loan you money?"

Chinaman reflected that, properly speaking, "lend" was the verb; "loan" the noun. His finely tuned detective's intuition told him this wasn't the best time to point that out. "Mary Anne, I think you can appreciate this isn't an easy phone call to make."

"Chinaman...words fail me."

Chinaman sipped his tea. "Just five hundred or so. You'll

get bank interest. And if I win the Lotto this week I'll give you half."

"Listen, mister. I am too angry, too outraged, too...."

"Incensed?"

"Yes, damn it! Too *incensed* to speak right now. I am going out to show an apartment but I will leave a check in an envelope with the receptionist. Just don't, *don't* call me for anything for at least a week. By then I may have calmed down enough to tell you off."

"Hey, you're all right, you know that?"

"Chinaman, just...don't...just...."

Chinaman listened to the click and the dial tone, amazed at how effortlessly he could vex women. And that was *without* trying.

★

38

A S soon as Chinaman emerged from the subway station, the smell of Korean beef barbecue reached his nostrils and reminded him just how hungry he was. No one outside of a tourist board would ever describe Jackson Heights as a "gorgeous mosaic" or a gorgeous anything else, but the constant influx to the neighborhood of tens of thousands of lower middle-class immigrants had resulted in some of the best Indian, Korean and Latin American restaurants in New York's five boroughs. Not the type pretentious enough to receive a rave review in the *New York Times*; just great cooking at reasonable prices.

Chinaman passed under the elevated number 7 line and, within ten minutes, stood across the street from the "last known address" of Julio Cesar. According to Larry Sterling and to the reverse phone directory, since 1996, the address belonged to one "Rita Cesar," relationship to the deceased unknown.

Rita Cesar, assuming she still lived there, inhabited the top floor of a decrepit two-story wooden building fronting a noisy but poorly lit street. A fat, low-slung gibbous moon the color of tarnished bronze hovered over the house; the type of moon which, when full, served as a backdrop for witches on broomsticks.

A sari shop on the ground floor was closed but pink fluorescent tubes did their best to brighten up the three sari-wrapped mannequins in the show window. The mannequins had been cast to pass as Eastern or Western — Eurasian faces for all occasions.

Their unsmiling faces had unnaturally long eyelashes surrounding tired brown eyes. They held their bent arms out before them, palms out, as if warding off an attack. The fluorescent light

reflected off their elaborate, many-faceted earrings, golden arm
bangles and perfectly painted nails. Each of the mannequins had
a colored dot on its forehead. The dot on the one in the center
was a bright, garish red. Chinaman struggled to shake off the
image of Judy's shattered forehead and began climbing the rickety
stairs to the second floor. Patches of ice over rotted wood made
him choose his steps carefully.

He had decided not to call first, taking the chance that Rita
Cesar might not be home; he'd always had much better luck getting
people to talk to him in person than over the phone. Mary Anne
had once suggested that was because when people saw him, they
felt sorry for him.

He took a deep breath and made an effort to jettison his
emotional baggage of unpleasant memories. As he raised his hand
to knock on the outer door, he reminded himself that he was
alive, in reasonably good health, and could still enjoy many of the
pleasures this particular planet had to offer. That's when the inner
door suddenly opened and he saw the figure behind the screen
door standing in a darkened hallway pointing the gun at his chest.

In what little night light reached the doorway, the gun glinted
like a small caliber, most likely a .22; probably a Beretta. Chinaman
remembered hearing of one private detective taken out of action
for over a month by a teenage girl firing "only" a .22 caliber. At
close range, a well-aimed .22 caliber round was more than sufficient
to take one out of action permanently.

Chinaman did his best to smile. He hoped it was a disarming
one. "Evening, ma'am. I'm here to see Ms. Rita Cesar." Chinaman
had always believed there were two types of people in this world:
Those who have had to make conversation while a gun was
pointing at them and those who haven't. He was certain that
those who had shared the experience would appreciate how little
quaver had crept into his voice. He had smiled his best smile, he
had spoken politely and he had even remembered to use the
liberated form of address for a woman. Yet, despite all that, the

gun still pointed exactly where it had before he'd spoken.

"Who are you and what do you want?"

Chinaman could see the woman's features beginning to emerge from the darkness. A Hispanic woman about five feet, five inches tall, mid-30s, speaking perfect, barely accented English, her hair drawn back into a no-nonsense bun.

"I'm a man who would prefer not to get shot this evening, ma'am. Beyond that, I'm a New York State-licensed private detective investigating the murder of Julio Cesar. I have my identification inside my jacket if you'd care to see it. I'd just like to ask you a few questions."

"I told the police all I know."

Just once in his career, Chinaman wanted to question someone without hearing that he or she had already told the police all he or she knew. Not to mention the fact that if everyone who said he or she had told the police all he or she knew really had told the police everything he or she knew, the police would have a much higher percentage of closed cases than they do. He gave her his best conspiratorial, we're-both-in-this-together, smile. "New York's Finest don't always share what they know with private detectives, ma'am." He thought of adding the line, "especially with minorities," then decided it might sound affected.

The woman raised her voice to be heard over the roar of a passing subway train. "If the police won't talk to you, why should I?"

It was a good question. A damn good question. Chinaman had never been able to come up with a good answer to it. Perhaps there wasn't an answer. He broadened his smile. Too much more of that and his cheeks would start to ache. "If people only talk to the police, private detectives will go out of business and I'll have to get a real job."

The woman's laugh was more than appropriate for his remark. As if it had been a long time since she'd had anything to laugh at. "What's your name?"

"My friends call me Chinaman."

Are you armed, Chinaman?"

"No, ma'am, but if you don't let me in, I'll huff and I'll puff and I'll blow your house down."

She pushed open the screen door and lowered the gun. "You won't need to. Thanks to Julio, I stand a good chance of losing it to the bank."

To catch the screen door, Chinaman first had to lower his arms which he'd barely realized he'd raised. Some of his reactions to guns were more automatic than the guns themselves.

She led him through the hallway and into a living room, snapping on lights as she went. The living room reflected what Chinaman had sensed of its occupant: Neat, clean, sensible, nothing frivolous, nothing out of place, nothing unnecessary. No images of a jolly fat white man in a red suit with an unlimited supply of toys and an inexhaustible supply of optimism would ever appear in Rita Cesar's living room.

The off-white walls had several framed photographs of graduation pictures and studio portraits of family members. A few plants filled in the space between a tape deck with a knob missing and a television set with rabbit ears.

A matching sofa and chair had been positioned in front of a few shelves of books. The books on the top shelf were separated by a pair of porcelain hands placed together in prayer. No exotic pantheon of Hispanic deities need apply.

The coffee table had a bowl of fruit and a stack of magazines with an issue of *People* magazine on top. From the magazine's cover, Burt Reynolds smiled out at Chinaman as if to say, "What, you haven't wrapped this one up yet?" A corner knickknack table held a phone and a vase that, in happier times, might have held flowers. The drapes had been closed but they met imperfectly, and through the opening, Chinaman had a view of elevated subway tracks.

Chinaman moved some pillows and sat on the couch facing Rita Cesar as she sat in the chair. Circular throw rugs covered the dark wooden floor between them like bright stepping stones over a murky pond.

Rita Cesar wore simple teardrop earrings, a peach colored, pleated blouse, a nearly calf-length khaki skirt with a sensible white belt and sensible low-heeled white pumps. Chinaman wondered if she had just come in or was about to go out.

She placed the beretta on the coffee table, but, sensibly, within easy reach. The gun reminded Chinaman of cigarette lighters made to resemble guns except he had the impression Rita Cesar didn't smoke.

With the muzzle of a gun no longer pointed in his direction, his nerves slowly regrouped and he noticed the room was cold. Rita Cesar plucked a shawl from the arm of her chair and wrapped it around her. "Can I get you something to drink, Mr. Chinaman? Seven-up?"

Absolut on the rocks, Chinaman thought. "Nothing, thanks, I'm fine."

"Do people often point guns at you in your line of work?"

"Infrequently."

"May I ask if you ever shot anyone?"

"No one who attended church regularly."

She gave him half a smile. Chinaman returned it. "How about you?" he asked.

"What about me?"

"You ever shot anyone?"

She glanced at the gun as if it were an obscene object. "That's not mine; it belonged to Julio."

"No law says you have to own a gun in order to shoot somebody with it."

She stared at him as if trying to decide if he were being serious, sarcastic, or making a joke. "You're investigating my brother's murder."

Not a question — a statement laced with the cynicism of someone who sometime or other had lost a lot of faith in people.

Chinaman nodded.

"Because you want to see justice done?" Rita Cesar's features were almost equidistant between handsome and plain. Her squared-off chin gave her face a masculine quality but the eyes were soft and the lips were full. When her face became hard — as it was now — she looked fully capable of pulling a trigger. What she had all began with the letter "I": Intelligence, intensity, integrity. Whatever other qualities Chinaman could discern from her face, naivete wasn't one of them. This was not a lady to bullshit.

"Ms. Cesar, I've been in this business a long time, and the number of times I've seen justice done I could count on one hand. We're so proud of our *habeas corpus* and presumed innocence and bill of rights and jury trials, when in fact it's not much different here and now than it was in Imperial China. No physical torture, maybe, but you get caught up in the legal system and you — not the perpetrator — are most likely to get screwed — financially, emotionally, and if his lawyer's smarter than yours, maybe even legally."

He waited for the sudden paroxysm of pounding from the steam radiator to stop — as if defenders of the justice system were vigorously objecting; when they were overruled, he continued. "What I'm investigating is a murder in the New York Palace Hotel. I don't know what the connection is yet to your brother's death, but there may be one. Anything you can tell me about his death-"

"Might help bring him back to life."

"Might help me find who killed him."

The radiator's air vent hissed halfheartedly and then grew silent. For just a moment the expression on Rita Cesar's face reminded him of the mannequins. "Mr. Chinaman, did you ever both love and hate someone at the same time?"

Chinaman hoped the question was rhetorical. It was.

"You see, I'm a paralegal. I worked hard to give myself an education and I studied hard and I even took lessons to 'cure' my accent. And I never stopped trying to find work even when students with white faces and no certificates got the jobs I was interviewed for. Finally, I got a job in a small law firm. At first, they gave me correspondence to type and had me answering the phones. Not even on the level of a legal secretary, just carrying out the duties of a receptionist. But then they began to see what I was worth. And now I don't answer any phones and I don't type correspondence and I help the law school students and the wet-behind-the-ears associates out of college get their feet wet. What I've got now is a position in a large law firm. A good salary and respect for my ability."

The air vent hissing started, stopped, started again and was lost in the rumble of a train. "But a lot of the money I made went to Julio. My baby brother. He was always saying that he was going to make us both a lot of money if I could just give him enough to get his foot in the door. I knew where that door led, Mr. Chinaman. It led to the coca fields in Columbia. Or a warehouse full of illegal weapons in Brooklyn. But I could never say no to Julio. Maybe if I had I would not be in danger of losing my house and Julio wouldn't have lost his life."

"We've all got a lot of 'if onlys' in our lives, Ms. Cesar. If only I had done things differently maybe a woman I once loved wouldn't have been shot dead in the hotel. Maybe if I can get to the killers of that woman and of your brother, then maybe we can cut down on the numbers of 'if onlys' in the world."

The woman stared at Chinaman for nearly half a minute, then made a decision. "My brother got involved in bringing drugs into this country from Columbia. I didn't want to know anything about it, but he always confided in me. He and his friends had a small warehouse in Brooklyn. That's where he put his drugs. In the beginning, when they were dealing in legitimate merchandise, he even took me there. He was...proud. He made money, and then I could tell he made too much money. Drug money. I refused to take one cent...."

Lost in bitter memories, Rita Cesar paused to regain control, then continued. "Then Julio began talking about a drugs for weapons deal with some white men which would make him enough to retire. He was in his warehouse one night when some people — some white men with guns — came and took him away. That is when I took Julio's gun out of the drawer and loaded it."

"Have the police questioned you about the murder?"

"Yes. I told them I knew nothing about it."

"And that was it?"

"Why not? Some spic drug pusher got killed; who cares?"

"Would you happen to know exactly where the warehouse is?"

Rita Cesar glanced at a photograph on the wall of a young Hispanic man with his arm around her. Both were smiling. "I know. And I know when the men who killed him will be there again. To ship out their guns."

"They may have changed the date now."

"No. It was my brother who arranged for the loading. That cannot be changed. But once Judy Fisher learned the date and time and passed it on to her friends, my brother was not necessary to them."

Chinaman understood more than before how other people could feel very differently about Judy Fisher than he did. "But the men on the ship will wait for your brother."

"No. The men on the ship will wait for the guns. They need them badly for their cause and they will pay whoever has them. My brother was expendable."

"Will you tell me where the ship will dock?"

"I know nothing about where the ship will dock. I only know where the warehouse is."

"And will you tell me that?"

She gave Chinaman a hard stare. "I should give information to another man with a gun?"

Chinaman decided to try another tack. "May I ask how Julio met Judy Fisher?"

"Julio said he picked her up one night in a bar. Of course,

my brother was too foolish and too blind to understand that the white bitch picked *him* up. I told him a woman like that doesn't just suddenly appear in a bar in Spanish Harlem. And a woman like that doesn't go with a man like Julio. Of course she was working for the white men in the gun deal but Julio was thinking with *la pinga* instead of his brain, and it cost him his life."

"Judy Fisher is dead. She's paid for what she did. Now I'm asking you to help me make the men who killed your brother pay a price."

There was a knock at the door. Rita Cesar slipped the pistol into a seam pocket of her skirt and stood up. "It's all right. That is my date."

Chinaman listened to the duet of rumbling train and hissing radiator until she returned with a bouquet of roses and a good-looking Hispanic man in his mid-thirties. His colorful paisley tie somewhat overwhelmed his beige tweed sport coat but it lent him the air of Christmas. Chinaman stood up.

"Mr. Chinaman, please meet Ramon Cruz. He is taking me to dinner." The man smiled broadly as Chinaman shook his hand. He seemed to be bubbling over with good will. Even Rita Cesar seemed affected by it. Her smile vastly improved her looks. "Mr. Chinaman was just stopping off from work to ask about a legal matter."

"Yes. And you've been most helpful. But I'd better be on my way."

As her still smiling date picked up the vase and moved it to the table, Rita Cesar unwrapped the roses. When she placed them in the vase, Chinaman noticed that it was already filled with water, suggesting that Ramon Cruz had most likely brought her roses on previous occasions. Chinaman recognized his observation as a classic example of an often employed but seldom mentioned *modus operandi* of all detectives: If you can't solve the big ones, solve the little ones — and feel good about it.

While Ramon Cruz remained standing in the living room, Rita Cesar led Chinaman back into the hallway then stopped to take a pencil and sheet of notepaper from a bureau drawer. She wrote an address, a time, and drew a rough map. Then she folded the paper and handed to him. Obviously, Ramon Cruz was unaware of the full story of her brother's death and her loud cover story was for his benefit: "He is the best litigation lawyer I know. He's so busy I doubt you could reach him on the phone, but you might stop by to see him. He should be in his office at this time. If you can get an appointment, you should be able to work something out. Be sure to send *my* regards."

Chinaman slipped the paper into an inner jacket pocket and stepped out onto the landing. He turned back to look at Rita Cesar. "I'm proud to have met you; and I hope you won't lose your house."

"Not without a fight I won't, Mr. Chinaman. And, Mr. Chinaman. Be careful."

"Thank you. I will be."

As the door closed, Chinaman held tightly to the rail and walked carefully down the icy stairs. Above him, the moon had shed its bronze coat and moved on.

★

DAY TWELVE

39

JUST as he rounded the corner of 11th Street and Avenue B, Chinaman spotted the Chevy. He'd been jogging for nearly half an hour, a small Panasonic player in his right hand, earphones against his head, the sound of U.S. Army cadences in his ears. A sweat shirt with his Taiwan Command insignia, sweat trousers, Avia sneakers. Jogging at night. On a deserted street in the East Village. Someone knew enough about his habits to know when he was the most vulnerable.

From the corner of his eye, he watched the car approach, then keep its distance behind him. When Chinaman slowed to a fast walk, the Chevy quickly pulled up beside him. The man at the wheel was bundled up in a large coat; a fedora pulled down over his forehead. Chinaman turned to face the car while continuing a fast walk backward, ready to dive in any direction.

When he recognized Chief Abrams, he walked to the window. The driver's side was the far side, and Chinaman leaned in on the open passenger window. He turned the volume down but left his earphones against his ears. Abrams would have to guess how much attention Chinaman was giving him. "Evening, Chief. Merry Christmas."

Abrams stared at Chinaman, then glanced away, then stared at him again. He kept both gloved hands on the wheel. His voice was low but forceful. No shouting; just understated anger. "I know she was a real close friend of yours, Chinaman, but I'll tell you again. Get off this case and stay off. This is my homicide and I'll solve it."

"If that's the only message, you could have sent an e-mail."

The expression on Abrams's face was almost hate-filled. "I wanted to make certain you understand exactly what I'm telling you. I'll solve this case. Your P.I. license depends on your staying out of it."

"And your chance of making Chief of Department depends on your solving it before I do," Chinaman said.

"What's that supposed to mean?"

"It means other chiefs can move laterally but not Chief of Detectives. Chief of Personnel, sure, no problem. But you — you move up or you're on your way out. And since you grabbed this case for yourself there's probably more than one pissed-off borough commander hoping to see you fall flat on your face."

Chinaman had never spoken that harshly to Abrams; not even when they were in-laws. He saw Abrams's lips tighten and a look appear in his eyes and he was certain Abrams was about to take a swing at him. Instead, he gunned the motor and sped off, leaving Chinaman a split second to get his head and arms back out the window. Chinaman listened to the hum of the wheels on the newly plowed street and watched the taillights disappear in the darkness.

Chinaman suspected that one of the reasons Chief Abrams hated his guts had nothing to do with Chinaman's ill-fated marriage to his only daughter. Early in his career, fresh out of the Academy, while patrolling his beat, Abrams had rushed into a plush upper East Side apartment responding to a call of a man with a gun. It had turned out to be a false alarm; but Patrolman Abrams had already cocked his gun and couldn't figure out how to uncock it.

Patrolman Abrams excused himself, locked himself in the marbled bathroom, took careful aim, and fired into the toilet bowl. Whatever he thought the toilet water would do to stop the force of the bullet, it didn't; but the .38 did smash its way through porcelain and pipes.

It was the first in a series of incidents and accidents that, after much heated debate, would eventually cause the police department of New York City's five boroughs to issue double action revolvers only — weapons that couldn't be cocked.

The men at Abrams's station house heartily congratulated him on subduing the "Porcelain Bandit," began leaving satirical notes and drawings in his locker and in the mensroom stalls, broke off conversations when he entered a room, snickered loudly as he left a room, and bestowed upon him the nickname "Flusher." The sobriquet was bandied about openly decades into his career until the day he made Chief. After that, as with Cyrano's nose, no one who wished to remain in good health and in line for promotion made any reference to 'toilets,' 'porcelain' or 'flushing.' And that included the city of Flushing in the borough of Queens. Chinaman knew. And worst of all: Abrams knew Chinaman knew.

After he'd showered, he lay back on the bed and tried to catch up on his reading. He lifted a *New York Times'* book review section from a thick stack of old book review sections. Thoughts of Abrams kept his mind unsettled. Over the years, Chinaman felt he had paid very heavy dues for being on the wrong side of Abrams's moods. Like a lot of cops, Abrams had no use for private detectives, and like a lot of fathers, he had no use for any man who hadn't treated his only daughter as a queen.

Chinaman seldom allowed himself to be a punching bag for anyone, but he had felt the guilt of an errant, unfaithful husband and he had taken Abrams's abuse as a matter of course. Now he felt was the time to put an end to the old relationship; out with the old, in with the new.

He threw the book review section back on the pile, turned out the light, and eventually fell asleep. In his dream, he saw himself in a strange bedroom carrying a phone into a hallway. His dream figure was keeping an eye on the extension cord to ensure it was long enough to reach the bathroom. He saw himself dialing a number and when he heard a man's gruff "Hello," Chinaman realized it was Abrams. In his dream, Chinaman flushed the toilet, waited several seconds, then hung up. Chinaman-the-dream-figure assured Chinaman-the-sleeper that "Flusher" would understand. Chinaman was woken up by the sound of his own laughter.

★

DAY THIRTEEN

40

CHINAMAN could remember entering ladies' bedrooms that were larger or more expensively decorated; but it struck him that he had never seen one quite so bizarre. Everywhere he looked, his eye was met with roses. Red roses in vases on tables, pink roses arranged in transparent bowls, red and pink roses bunched together in fruit juice bottles, pickle jars, tall glasses and silver candlesticks. At the foot of the bed was a large wastebasket crammed with red roses.

A brittle streak of late afternoon light enswathed a rose-filled pencil holder on the bedside table. It was as if a practitioner of the occult had attempted to imbue the room with mystical power, and had unintentionally bestowed it with a whimsical beauty.

And considering what Chinaman had expected to see, Cindy Mae didn't look all that bad either. The facial swelling had gone down, the bluish-green bruise had faded to a light brownish-yellow, and the eye wasn't many days away from full recovery. She lay on the bed in fashionably cut red silk pajamas with her blonde hair coiling about her bare shoulders. Beside her, on the quilt, makeup and fashion magazines had been piled beside a tray of toast and coffee. Her lips were once again a bright red, not with blood, but with lipstick. When she smiled she looked more than halfway attractive.

Chinaman decided that a woman once again interested in makeup and fashion was well on her way to recovery. He moved the tray and sat on the bed. When he leaned forward to kiss her cheek, she placed one hand on his chin, one against his ear, and brought his lips down to hers. When she released him Chinaman found her voice strange, then realized it was normal; it simply had no element of tease. "God, I'm glad to see you, Chinaman."

"Dr. Wynne not doing right by you?"

"Frank Wynne is the greatest doctor ever! I mean despite the fact that he talked me into going to a hospital for tests. Except I think he missed his calling. He should have been a stand-up comedian."

"Well, at least he's got you feeling better."

"Lots." She ran her fingers lightly over his cheek then suddenly gave him a mock-serious pout. "I got injured because of you, Chinaman."

"Me?"

She held out her thumb. "Thorns in the roses."

Chinaman kissed her thumb. "Better call a cop."

"Chinaman?"

"I'm here."

"What about the man...."

"The man who sent you these lovely roses? Once he saw the situation in perspective, he was most understanding. He realized the error of his ways and insisted on finding some way to make amends. Oh, yes, don't forget to send all medical bills to him."

"He agreed to that?"

"Agreed? He wouldn't have it any other way."

"He sent a letter of apology. He even apologized that not all the roses are red."

Chinaman plucked a rose from a vase and stuck the stem in her hair. "Very thoughtful. Who says New Yorkers are hard-boiled and uncaring?"

Cindy Mae rearranged her pillow and sat upright, her arms locked around her knees. "Chinaman, can I ask you a question?"

"Sounds fair to me; I recall asking you a few."

"Are you any good as a private detective?"

"Fair to middling. Why do you ask?"

"I was just wondering how come a creative writing teacher

became a private investigator. Aren't they...."

"Opposites?"

"Well, yeah."

"Well, I'll tell you, on the surface it doesn't seem like there's much connection, but the more you dig the more logical it becomes. Of course, there's the obvious fact that both types are extremely observant of people and their habits. But, besides that, detectives interview people and try to separate fact from fiction; writers interview people and then *blend* fact with fiction. But both damn well have to know the difference."

"Hey! That makes sense."

"Good. I'm glad you approve." Chinaman looked at his watch. "But if I'm going to maintain my reputation as a fair to middling detective, I've got to get going." He kissed her cheek.

"Chinaman, please be careful. I don't want anything to happen to you."

"Don't worry. I've got a rain check on something between us and I intend to cash it in one fine day. You'll be all right?"

"Sure. My girlfriend's coming over. She'll be sorry she missed you. I told her all about you."

Chinaman doubted that anyone knowing "all about" him would want to meet him. He got up. His arm and side still ached from his encounter with the Mossad. He had aches and scrapes in places he hadn't realized had been hit. Fights were like that. Once they were over, the memory might fail to remind you of exactly what happened, but, like a nagging spouse, the body makes sure you don't forget a thing.

"Can you hand me the cigarettes before you go?"

"Should you be smoking?"

"Dr. Wynne said people should smoke and drink so that when they're old and near death, they'll have some bad habits to give up. That way they can live a couple more years. He said people who don't have bad habits have nothing to give up, so they die."

DEAN BARRETT

"Next time you see Doc Wynne you tell him Doc Chinaman told him to stop plagiarizing Mark Twain."

Cindy Mae sat up further and reached for the ashtray. "There's a lighter in my handbag."

Chinaman took it out of the bag and held the flame for her. Cindy Mae's eyes widened. "Oh, God, you'll kill me."

"I will?"

"Look at the initials. 'J.F.' That was Judy's lighter."

Chinaman looked it over. "That's all right. It's yours now and she'd want you to have it. Her brother can use matches. Besides–" Chinaman looked at the nearly faded initials on the side of the silver lighter. He held it closer and studied the faint trace of a triangle just beneath the initials. A kind of triangle. An inverted isosceles triangle with a curved top. A nearly faded wedge-shaped symbol, light blue. Whatever figures had been at the center of the area were no longer recognizable. "Cindy Mae, can I keep this?"

"Of course. At least you'll have something to r emember her by."

Chinaman left a pack of matches on the table and walked to the door. "If you need anything, you call."

Cindy Mae attempted a seductive smile. It was too soon in her recovery process to be effective. "I'll call, Chinaman. I'm a callgirl, remember?"

★

41

CHINAMAN sat in the last booth of the 7th Street Bar in the heart of the East Village. Twenty feet away, four greasy-haired teenagers in leather jackets and stone-washed jeans played a dead-serious and silent game of eight ball. A wall light shot through a dozen cue sticks in a wooden rack casting prison bar shadows against Chinaman and his nearly empty bottle of Amstel Light. He read the line beneath the crown on the label: "95 calories." It was 95 too much. He decided then and there to jog more often. As much as he disliked exercise, he hated a paunch and he hated things bottling up inside him even more. He'd gotten the beginnings of a paunch when he'd been married, then lost it when the marriage fell apart. There was a moral in there somewhere but he couldn't quite find it.

A jukebox near the front door began playing Gogi Grant's version of "The Wayward Wind" just as Abrams appeared in the doorway. He passed the usual collection of pension-poor Polish-American regulars at the bar and young blue collar workers in booths and sat down heavily facing Chinaman. He removed his trench coat, folded it and placed it beside him on the seat while Gogi Grant bemoaned the fact that "the sound of the outward bound made him a slave to his wandrin' ways."

Chinaman slid out of the booth and stood up. "No waitress service here. Still Rolling Rock, right?"

Abrams nodded. Chinaman leaned against the bar waiting for his order of two bottles of beer. He turned toward his booth and could see Abrams clearly in profile watching the pool game; no doubt comparing the players' faces with his mug-book memory to see if anyone needed to be arrested.

Chinaman returned to the booth and handed Abrams his beer. Both men drank directly from the bottles. In the time he'd known Abrams, a bottle of beer often seemed to be the only thing that ever even partly relaxed him. Chinaman had shared several six-packs with him in the past — during that short period of time when they'd even held a certain mutual respect for each other. Abrams didn't let people get close to him, not even son-in-laws; but there had been a certain comradery while Chinaman's marriage was good. The occasional Saturday night when the two of them would sit around the solid pine kitchen table of Abrams's riverside apartment drinking beer and being pampered by Mary Anne. A father-in-law, son-in-law and the most important woman in their lives.

The topics of conversation as well as the rhythm of the evening had seldom varied: The Mets chances of a pennant, the pros and cons of the newest handgun, the many ways in which the city was going to hell in a handbasket. And even as they damned the city's problems and declared them insoluble, each knew the other could never conceive of living anywhere else.

Abrams always held his drinks well; he would become more silent and taciturn and introverted even as Chinaman became more talkative and extroverted. Finally, toward the end of the evening, the silences would come. And in those silences Chinaman came to understand that he was being compared to the son-in-law Abrams had wished for. Chinaman never figured out exactly what that was; only that it sure as hell wasn't a private detective.

Their conversations had been superficial, and always bounded by restraint; a reserve that would insure they would never become chummy or intimate. Despite that, Chinaman had found himself almost looking forward to the Saturday night male bonding rituals. The respect between the two men had been real. Then the marriage fell apart and it was just the two of them. Chinaman and his soon-to-be ex-father-in-law. And Chinaman's Saturday night visits grew more infrequent. And more strained. Finally, Chinaman stopped stopping by altogether.

Chinaman offered Abrams a Marlboro, then reached into his inside jacket pocket for a lighter. He watched Abrams's eyes when he lit his cigarette. They held on the lighter. He placed the lighter on the table, moving it slowly back and forth between his fingers. Abrams exhaled a great deal of smoke and spoke quietly but not without bitterness. "You get the reaction you expected?"

Chinaman left the lighter where it was and took another swig of beer. He stared at Abrams, glanced at the still silent pool players, now sharing a joint, then back to Abrams. He thought of how Abrams had observed him when he'd ambushed him with Judy's photos in the morgue; now he had observed Abrams staring at the lighter. One good ambush deserves another. "It took me a while to figure out what bothered me about this. I knew I had seen it before. Cindy Mae said it was Judy's. But I couldn't make out what the faded triangle was. Then I saw that it wasn't 'J.F.' at all. A close-up view under a lamp showed it was a "J" plus an "A" that had lost its right leg. Joseph Abrams. And what I'd taken for an inverted triangle or wedge was actually an almost completely faded police shield."

Abrams took another swig of beer. So did Chinaman. "Then I remembered seeing you use it in your apartment." Chinaman rubbed his chin. He needed a shave. "And not long after that I remembered the description Judy's roommate gave me of how you searched her apartment. It didn't sound like a cop looking for clues. It sounded more like a man tearing a place apart looking for a specific item."

Abrams stared at him for several seconds. Gogi Grant proclaimed that 'the Wayward Wind is a restless wind, and he was born the next of kin, the next of kin to the Wayward Wind." As Gogi finished up, Abrams spoke: "So you figure me for the hit?"

Chinaman rolled the beer bottle between the palms of his hands. "You want to know what I figure you for? I figure you for

becoming infatuated with Judy Fisher. She knew you were a
widower and for whatever reason she decided she wanted to have
an affair with you. I figure Judy came on to you at the wedding;
I wouldn't know, I was busy getting married. Or she called you
after. It would have been easy enough to get your number. If I
were the Freudian type, I'd point out that you even look like the
photograph I saw of her father."

Chinaman felt a bit high. Maybe it was the leverage he had
on his ex-father-in-law. Maybe he was getting a contact high from
the pool players' marijuana. "Whatever, I figure the two of you
got together. If Judy wanted to have an affair with a man, she got
one. And I figure she respected you enough to keep your name
out of any address books. Just in case they ever fell into the wrong
hands. Anyway, you weren't a 'customer.' You were the real thing."

The sharp scent of marijuana wafted over to their table.
Abrams glanced toward the men around the pool table, then back
to Chinaman. "I asked you if you thought I killed her."

Chinaman finished his beer and slid the lighter across the
table to Abrams. "If I thought that, I wouldn't be giving you this.
Besides, I know who killed Judy."

"So you're looking for a deal."

Chinaman took a folded piece of paper out of his jacket
pocket and flicked it over to Abrams. "You call this number at
one a.m. It's a phone booth so don't bother tracing it. The man
on the line will let you know where Judy's killers are. And, if I'm
right, their boss will be with them."

Abrams studied his watch. Nine-thirty-five. "So you want
first crack at them."

"That's the deal."

Chinaman thought of Frank Wynne reluctantly agreeing to
face the frigid cold at one in the morning. Shivering in a phone
booth while awaiting a call from a cop. One more favor Chinaman
owed him. *If* Abrams agreed to the arrangement.

Abrams glanced at the number and pocketed the paper. "I

can't make that kind of deal."

"In that case, I—"

"But I have a duty to follow every lead of a homicide case. I'll call the number. But if you do something stupid, I might just have to take you in too."

"I'll take the chance."

Abrams spoke again as Chinaman stood and zipped up his jacket. "I don't know how I...Judy was...."

"Yeah. I know she was. I loved her too, remember?"

As Chinaman left the bar, Peter, Paul and Mary launched into, "That's What You Get For Loving Me."

★

42

CHINAMAN's headlights swept slowly across a bent and corroded "Truck Route" sign. He made the turn and followed the road along the East River. He glanced across the pitch black water, beyond the silhouettes of Red Hook's loading cranes, transit sheds and canine-guarded warehouses, and focused on a distant area of darkness. Where the tip of the now destroyed World Trade Center's television and radio mast had once emitted its blinking red light there was only an inhuman gloom.

He remembered that Brooklyn's Red Hook area had served such writers as Arthur Miller and Hubert Selby Jr. as a sinister and bleak setting for fiction. One look at the stacks of containers and unlighted warehouses behind chain link fences topped with barbed wire made it clear that little had changed. As he drove slowly along the deserted road, he caught glimpses of a brightly lit Staten Island ferry on its way to the southern tip of Manhattan. He thought of the luxury of a simple ferry ride — and immediately envied the passengers their presumption of safety.

He turned onto Ferris Street, and in just a minute of driving, passed only one car. He slowed gradually as he flicked on a penlight and studied Rita Cesar's map. He pulled off the road into an area littered with rubbish and scrap metal and turned off his headlights. The car was not completely hidden from the road but, to a casual observer, it would look as if it had been abandoned. He got out, picked up his slim leather case containing wire cutters, a crowbar, binoculars and a flashlight and walked along Ferris Street for another ten minutes. He turned down a narrow lane leading in the direction of the East River.

To his right was an open area of weeds and rubbish. In the center, a damaged container appeared to be serving as shelter for the homeless. Piles of old tires had been strategically arranged around the container as a bunker might be protected by sandbags. Still more tires lined both sides of the lane as it wound down to the river. Chinaman kept his flashlight off but kept a tight grip on it. It was a Maylite — long, legal and, if need be, lethal. To his left he could see another chain link fence topped with strands of barbed wire.

He walked silently to the gate and crouched beside the slim trunk of a privet tree. The sign on the gate read:

Prohibida la entrada
no autorizada

Beyond the fence was an open concrete parking lot where several flatbed trucks had been parked for the night. At the edge of the parking area, near the water, was an unlighted brick warehouse. Something about its ominous shape reminded Chinaman of the prisoners' barracks in the film, "Staglag 17." Beyond it, he could see lights of Governor's Island, until recently, the U.S. Coast Guard's private parcel of choice real estate.

Despite the fence, the barbed wire and the "Keep Out" notices, the owners had made no sustained effort to keep anyone from the area. Warning signs were covered with graffiti in Spanish and English, a section of fence was tilted toward the warehouse and a hole large enough for someone to slip through remained unrepaired.

Chinaman studied the opening for any sign of alarm system then squeezed through the fence. He walked across the lot keeping the flatbed trucks between himself and the warehouse. He knelt beside a truck and scanned the warehouse and its surroundings with his binoculars. All was quiet. And dark. He could see pitch black waves rolling in under a pier's loading cranes and, farther along the shore, what looked like a container-loading bridge.

A 'Beware of Dog' sign on the warehouse door included a

drawing of a German Shepard's face emphasizing the canine teeth. Chinaman hoped it was a bluff. As his binoculars searched along the roof of the warehouse, he suddenly caught a glimpse of light. It was so unexpected, he gave a sudden start. A second later, he saw that he had focused on the torch of the Statue of Liberty on Liberty Island. He began to realize Red Hook at night quickly got on a person's nerves and he made a determined effort to relax.

He dragged over a nearby tire and sat on it as comfortably as he could, propping his back against the mud guard of a truck. And waited. He wondered if he chanced lighting a cigarette, then decided against it. The night was still, the warehouse appeared to be deserted. Overhead, clouds tugged at a nearly full moon. A light breeze whipped a can noisily across the parking lot. By the time the minutes added up to nearly an hour, he was ready to trade his flashlight for a thermos full of hot coffee.

He had thought of recruiting Rocco to assist him, then had decided against it. Patience, marking time and enduring lengthy stakeouts were not among Rocco's virtues. Equally important, Chinaman wanted to search the warehouse, not tear it down.

And if that weren't enough of a reason not to use Rocco, there was one other. If Abrams saw that Rocco was aiding Chinaman, Abrams would never forgive his daughter for giving out what had been confidential information; especially for giving it out to her ex-husband. It was the kind of "betrayal" that would damage if not destroy a father-daughter relationship. Chinaman decided against adding to the burden of guilt he already carried regarding his marriage.

Besides, Rocco had done enough. At Chinaman's request he'd called the Brooklyn Height's number his former schoolmate had given him and suggested they meet on Saturday night. The man said he had "something special" on for Saturday night but agreed to meet on Sunday. When Rocco had laughed and replied that "the lady must be really special," the man had gone on to describe his Saturday outing as "business."

"Something special" and "business" didn't exactly confirm Rita Cesar's information but it helped give it credence. Chinaman was reasonably certain that the men who'd killed two people in room 1204 of the New York Palace Hotel definitely wouldn't be sitting home watching Christmas specials with Dolly Parton.

Another ten minutes passed before a car pulled into the lane and rolled silently to a stop near the gate. Its headlights went out and Chinaman found the several-minute period of silence that followed far more intense than the silence before the car's arrival. Finally, the doors opened and four men got out. They unlocked the gate and, leaving it wide open, walked unhurriedly through the parking lot toward the warehouse. The men were nearly swallowed up in the darkness, but one of them stopped no more than thirty feet from Chinaman's position. He cupped his hands around a match and lit his cigarette. The light from the match brought out the now familiar profile of his wavy white hair and craggy face.

Even in the darkness Chinaman could recognize the other three. Two of them he'd seen in Harry's Bar — the man with the cashmere coat and the chain-smoker in the final stages of male pattern baldness. The other was the man who had ordered Judy's murder.

The man rejoined his companions and walked with them to the warehouse. They walked up a short ramp, unlocked the outer door — a rusted iron shutter — and rolled it up, then unlocked and pushed open a set of inner grates and entered the warehouse. Several fluorescent ceiling lights sputtered on, deepening the surrounding darkness. Chinaman scanned what he could see of the interior with his binoculars: a freight elevator, floor-to-ceiling stacks of burlap sacks, thick cement pillars, stacks of double-decked pallets, pallet trucks, an electric cart and a conveyer belt stretching to a mezzanine floor.

He unpacked his crowbar and slid it under his belt, zipped up his case, then jammed it under the wheel of a truck. He had just begun his crouched run toward the entrance of the warehouse when headlights illuminated the parking lot. He dove onto the concrete and rolled frenziedly toward the outer perimeter, away from the glare of the increasing bright light. He felt an excruciating pain in his thigh where the crowbar had dug in during his frantic attempt to escape detection. He lay perfectly still but gritted his teeth and fought a scream down to a muted grunt.

An 18-wheeler drove brashly through the gate into the parking lot, made a tight circle, then backed noisily toward the open warehouse door. The rig's exhaust cover flapped up and down on the cab's vertical exhaust like a bird with a broken wing. The trailer itself was a dull white and its sides were devoid of any lettering. The driver and his assistant opened the cab doors and guided the truck slowly onto the ramp.

Chinaman could see two of the men in the doorway watching. They moved back inside to allow the truck to back into the warehouse. Chinaman knew it was now or never. He stood up and ran to a dumpster near the doorway. He wedged himself into the narrow space between the dumpster and the brick facade of the warehouse and edged himself along until he reached the opening. He crouched at the side of the truck opposite where the men had been standing. Using the truck as a shield, he drew his revolver and crept cautiously into the warehouse.

He made a dash for the nearest stack of burlap sacks knowing that his odds of doing so undetected were less than even. It simply came down to the fourth man. Where was the fourth man who had entered the warehouse? The man who had ordered Judy Fisher's murder. And where was he looking at the time Chinaman made his move.

All around him, burlap sacks were stacked in long rows, some piled to shoulder height, some piled nearly to the ceiling. He felt as if he had entered a movie set about to reenact the trench warfare of World War I. He crouched behind the sacks and waited. No one seemed to be taking a shot at him. He edged his way down a narrow aisle until he reached a wide pillar, then stood up slowly.

To his left, he could see a platform truck, and behind it narrow metal stairs leading up to the mezzanine. He would have to climb the stairs to get a view of the loading. He could hear the voices of the men but not distinguish what was being said. He waited until the gate of the truck was being raised and a forklift being moved into place, then made a dash for the platform truck. He threw himself behind it and froze, alert to any sudden shout or ominous silence. The murmuring of voices continued as before. He moved carefully up several stairs until he could just see over the rows of burlap sacks.

The driver and his assistant wore light jackets and baseball caps with a METS insignia. Both wore mustaches similar to those on the faces of stereotyped Mexican bandits. Both were several inches shorter than the two men they were speaking with. Behind them, Chinaman could see a tall man reach inside his jacket and withdraw a semi-automatic. Apparently, the drivers were of no further use to the smugglers.

As the man took aim at the back of the driver's head, Chinaman sighted on a spot about two feet below the tall man's wavy white hair. He held on to the rail with his left hand and tried to keep the gun steady with his right. At this distance, and in this position, he held out little hope that his shot would actually hit the man. His S&W snubnose Model 36 with its short 1.9 inch barrel had been designed for concealability and compactness, not for accuracy at fifty yards. Still, hit or miss, it had been Chinaman's experience that sending a completely unexpected .38 round into the middle of a gathering at 925-feet-per-second almost always became a topic for discussion. He cocked the hammer, lined up the square notch at the rear with the front serrated ramp, sighted on where he estimated the man's spinal column to be, let out some breath, held it, focused on the front sight for a split second, and pulled the trigger.

He heard his shot ricochet off metal and spotted a brief spark appear on the side of a hydraulic pallet truck no more than three feet from the man. The man dove for cover, his gun spinning across the floor. Chinaman saw the driver and his assistant disappear between rows of burlap sacks and the two remaining men pointing in his direction. Then he realized they were pointing objects in his direction. The objects flashed and bullets ricocheted off the stairs, clanged against the metallic mezzanine floor above his head and slammed into the metal bed of the conveyor belt.

Chinaman released his grip on the rail and dove onto burlap sacks several feet below, then slid and tumbled his way to the floor. He felt a stab of pain where his shoulder had hit the sacks but managed to keep his gun and not break his neck. Spurts of gunfire now resounded throughout the warehouse like peals of thunder.

Chinaman edged his way quickly but cautiously to the end of the row and out into a rectangular space the size of his apartment surrounded on two sides by walls of burlap sacks. In the center were hand trucks, skids, pallets and strapped loads. He passed the area, rounded a pillar and, at the sound of a pallet being moved, turned back. Chinaman and the man with wavy white hair got a round off simultaneously. Chinaman's shot caused the man to double over, and fall to the floor groaning. The shot that had Chinaman's name on it had been deflected by a fire extinguisher affixed to the pillar.

He moved quickly into a narrow space formed by two walls of sacks. In the sudden silence that had fallen over the warehouse, he heard barely audible footsteps approaching his position. He peered around the corner. A glint of fluorescent light reflected off a moving gun. Several shots slammed into burlap sacks above his head. He fired back at a moving target once, twice, three times. He sat on the floor, back against the sacks and began reloading. From each bullet hole in the sacks a stream of small objects rained down on him. He tried to shield his face, then reached out and caught a handful. He found he was holding tiny beans, each a Spanish olive shade of green.

The realization hit him like a punch in the stomach. He looked closely at the sack. There was the familiar peasant and his burro and beneath them the words:

Columbian coffee

The warehouse was crammed from floor to ceiling with sacks of unroasted coffee beans. Chinaman spoke the words in a strained whisper: "Madame Rosha."

He moved quickly to reload. As he swung out the cylinder and ejected his cartridges from the five chambers, he tried to remember the arguments that centered around firefights just like this one: About how automatics carried more rounds in their magazines and how much faster they could be reloaded. Capacity and speed. Then he tried to remember why he had stuck with revolvers. Firepower, yes; but that hadn't been the main consideration. Reliability, that was it. Automatics jam too often. They misfire. And if there was a misfire in one of the chambers of his revolver, he would just pull the trigger and rotate the cylinder to the next chamber. An automatic had only one chamber and if it jammed it had to be cleared manually. Chinaman was still loading and still wondering about the odds of the man's gun jamming when he heard the footsteps behind him.

He turned to see the fourth man pointing a semi-automatic straight at him from a distance of about fifteen yards. Right hand on the gun. Left hand gripping and steadying the right. Right arm nearly straight. Left elbow bent. Shoulders perfectly aligned with the position of the feet. A textbook modified Weaver stance. Suit still perfectly pressed, not a hair out of place. He could have been an affluent businessman surprising a prowler in his study. Chinaman looked down at the open cylinder of his revolver. He had three rounds loaded. He might be able to snap it shut, roll and fire.

Sam Richards took another step forward. "Don't try it, Chinaman. Not even you are that good. Leave it open and just drop it as it is."

Chinaman thought about it another few seconds, then dropped it.

"And kick it away from you."

Chinaman kicked the revolver several feet toward a forklift.

Richards walked cautiously closer. Still gripping the pistol with both hands and holding it out in front. Chinaman put his hands up to about head level. His gaze dropped to the pistol Richards was holding. "SIG-sauer?"

"That's the one."

"Which model?"

"Two-two-eight."

"Oh, yeah, I read about those. They do everything but make coffee and whistle, right?"

"A bit more modern than what you're holding — *were* holding."

Chinaman began to wonder if there was anyone left who shared his preference for revolvers. Maybe he should have been born in a simpler time. Maybe he had been. He could check with Madame Rosha when he got back. *If* he got back. "Thirteen rounds and one in the chamber."

Richards took another step closer. "Right again."

"How many you figure you spent?"

Richards smiled. "Just a few." Then the smile faded. "Don't make me kill you, Chinaman."

"Not here, you mean. You prefer hotel rooms, don't you, Sam? You plan on checking me into the Palace first? Just like you did with Judy?" Chinaman gestured toward the truck. "How'd Judy find out about *this*?"

"She didn't. Not all of it."

"Just enough to be a threat?"

Richards removed his left hand from the right wrist and leisurely gripped his belt. The gun never wavered. "Judy was a floater."

Chinaman frowned. "'Floater'...Refresh my memory, will

you?"

"You know, someone hired to help out occasionally with the Company's operations. Only low level stuff, of course, but she was good; damn good. I hated to lose her."

"Sure you did. But floaters aren't often told the real reason they've been hired."

Richards took another small step. Closer. And another. Chinaman considered making a move for the gun. He tried to decide if a spin kick would get him close enough. Fast enough. The odds on someone successfully kicking a gun out of an opponent's hand were so low that no sane person would consider it as an option. He had seen it work well on TV several times but he knew of no one in real life who had tried it and lived to tell about it. But if he could get in close enough he might be able to try a move which would have a fifty-fifty chance against a pistol. He concentrated on remembering what Jimmy (the Tiger) Sterling had said was essential in such situations: 'Don't be impatient; don't make your opponent nervous; converse; let him close the distance between you.'

Richards shrugged. "Sometimes it's better that way."

"Sure. But Judy was smart. So she probably started putting two and two together."

"Exactly. She learned that Julio had been murdered and rather brutally at that; she learned that none of this was actually Company business. She started asking a lot of questions, making a lot of noise. She was becoming...difficult. Unpleasant."

"So you had her killed."

"We put her on to Julio to find out where the weapons were; I think she fell for him; he wasn't a bad looking kid. Or maybe she saw him as some kind of younger brother she had to protect. But getting the hots for the guy *or* getting protective, whichever — that wasn't professional."

Chinaman saw that the gun had been lowered a fraction of an inch. Still too far away. Still he had no move to make. None that wasn't suicidal.

"We'd been following the German for some time. Mossad already eliminated one just like him right at a Tripoli beach resort. This was to be his replacement. We told them we'd take care of this one for them. Gratis."

"And you made it look like a hit on the German when in fact it was a hit on Judy."

Both men paused as the sound of gunfire grew closer. Chinaman figured the drivers weren't the pushovers Richards's men had expected them to be. When it suddenly stopped, Richards spoke again. "It seemed an excellent opportunity to do a favor for a friendly power's intelligence agency and the perfect way to keep you from investigating. Two birds with one stone. If Judy had simply disappeared, or died in any way which suggested she'd been murdered, as in a suspicious accident, I knew you'd have been on the case. I thought if you believed it had been a Mossad hit on the German, and Judy had simply been in the wrong place at the wrong time, you might let it go."

"You miscalculated."

"Obviously. But what started *you* putting two and two together?"

"A bit of help from a friend who found out your boys didn't get off a plane at Tel Aviv; or on at New York, for that matter. And some serendipitous insight from an amateur magician who mentioned something called 'misdirection.' Oh, shit!"

"Something wrong?"

"Amateur night! It's tonight! I promised to be there. My girlfriend will never speak to me again."

"Given your present situation, old friend, that's quite possible."

Chinaman tried to keep his eyes off the gun. Keep the conversational ball rolling. "Anyway, magicians and spies use almost the same vocabulary sometimes. And I suddenly realized what I was up against. Smoke and mirrors. I forget now —

what's it called when you people fabricate information and plant it so that your opponent finds it? And finds it in a way that he has no reason to doubt that it's genuine?"

Richards allowed himself a smile. The barrel of the gun dipped another fraction of an inch. "False confirmation."

"Right! False confirmation. It can't be obvious, though. The idea is for the opponent to dig out the planted information through his own efforts. So he believes it. And I fell for it."

Several gunshots rang out at the other side of the warehouse. Richards's men and the drivers were engaged in a deadly game of cat and mouse.

Chinaman continued. "I only mentioned the bartender at the hotel to two people. One of them was a cop. He wouldn't know a 'false confirmation' if it bit his backside, so that left you. You brought the killers back for a meeting in the bar, knowing the bartender would call me; then you made some moves to make me suspect they were Israelis. One of your hatchetmen led me to the consulate; the other two led a friend to suspect they went to Tel Aviv. You worked it all out — even down to the farewell 'shaloms' outside the hotel. Cute."

Three shots rang out. Semi-automatics. Then silence. Richards grabbed his right wrist with his left hand but then pointed the gun toward the floor. More relaxed; but at this distance, not careless. Chinaman continued. "But, then, if you thought you'd diverted me, why did you try to get me killed in Forest Hills?"

"Respect."

"Come again?"

"I set up the false confirmation because I didn't want to have to kill you. But then I realized I was letting my personal feelings interfere with the operation. I respected you too much to assume you'd fall for the setup for very long. And, much to my regret, you ignored my phone warning. So I sent you off to one of our safehouses."

"That you did. After you warned the occupants that an

assassin was on his way to kill them. But if that's your safehouse, what's the Mossad doing in it?"

"It was a loan for an operation of theirs. In return for something they did for us recently in the Middle East. *Quid pro quo*. Of course, we had it bugged so we'd know what happened when you arrived. They're good men, by the way. I must congratulate you on managing to survive."

"I'd hate to be in your shoes when Mossad comes around asking why you set them up."

Richards lifted the barrel slightly. "I'd hate to be in your shoes now."

Chinaman looked at his watch. 1:03. "So you heisted the weapons from Julio and his friends and killed them. You really need money that badly, Sam, or are you donating your share to a favorite charity?"

Several more shots rang out. And then silence. Chinaman thought the last two shots had been from a revolver. A cat and mouse game had ended. One way or the other.

Richards took two quick steps to the left. Chinaman figured he did it not so much to circle him but to keep a better lookout on the passageway in the direction of the shooting. Chinaman reminded himself that Sam Richards had been one of the best competitive shooters on Taiwan. Richards glanced toward the passageway then back to Chinaman. "You know I like comfort, Chinaman. Comfort and style. My salary doesn't buy that. My investments did once. But things went wrong. So I had to find a way to continue my lifestyle in the manner to which I'd become accustomed."

"National Security Systems took a big fall, did it? It stopped being profitable but it can still launder your money for you, that it?"

Richards gave him a nod of admiration. The gun never moved. "You *have* been doing your homework, haven't you?"

"Sure. But my homework hasn't told me to what extent the CIA is officially involved in this."

"*This?* Not at all, old friend. Just two working stiffs inside the Agency who saw an opportunity to use our positions to enhance our abysmal official income. Myself and the man you followed from Harry's Bar to the Israeli consulate."

Chinaman gestured in the direction of where the last shots had been fired. "What about those two? The men who killed Judy?"

Richards gave Chinaman a look of distaste. "People who provide services for a fee."

Chinaman nodded toward the sacks of coffee. "Heavy weapons?"

"Skorpion Model 61s, Heckler and Koch MP5s, Uzis. And maybe a little plastic explosive. But, don't worry. It's all been professionally packed inside coffee and straw. The best buffer there is."

Chinaman tried to keep his eyes from focusing on the muzzle of the gun. He remembered the ad in the mail for Kevlar material in the form of bullet-resistant vests, side-panels and kiddy clothes. He'd thought they were far too expensive. He was in the process of revising his opinion. "Funny thing. Judy used to say she thought you were a cold fish. That you gave her the creeps. I was pretty sure she meant it."

"I'm sure she did. Rest assured, there was nothing personal between Judy and me. She was just a lady who couldn't resist testing her sexual prowess on men. Getting information and getting paid for it. I think she saw it as the ultimate challenge for her acting ability. She knew you wouldn't have approved of what she was doing, but she loved it; so I wasn't too worried you'd find out. In any case, no one was forcing her to do anything against her will."

Chinaman thought he heard footsteps somewhere behind him. Then, from another direction, he heard one shot fired from a revolver. A man screamed. First, loudly, then softly, then silence.

Richards allowed himself a long, satisfied sigh at the demise of the men in the van. "I am sorry about this, Chinaman. But I don't suppose you'd agree to go home and forget about everything."

"At least you got that right."

Richards took half a step forward. "Chinaman, listen to me. It doesn't have to end like this. Nothing is worth dying for."

"I wish I could believe that, Sam. Then I *could* just walk away."

Chinaman was about to make his leap; he figured his odds at about 80-20 against him. He'd faced worse. Richards saw it coming. He raised the barrel and pointed it at Chinaman's chest. "Chinaman — don't."

In his experience, a gun pointed in his direction was always more than enough to ensure that Chinaman would think of little else until it was either lowered or fired. But, suddenly, he had an intense split second image of the real estate broker in Little Rock, Arkansas, pointing the gun at his own chest and pulling the trigger; and Chinaman suddenly realized what he had overlooked: An overwhelming majority of suicides by firearms result from a shot to the head; what had prompted the salesman to aim at his chest? Had he regarded the heart as the center? Was the shot fired in moonlight (or in bright sunlight?) meant to extinguish the organ most associated with unbearable pain?

The image faded as abruptly as it appeared. Chinaman now knew he was definitely going to make his move and would almost certainly be killed. As he understood that, time slowed, texture transformed. Richards now appeared to be standing in a tunnel at the center of a vortex, an almost surrealistic, Daliesque landscape submerged in a viscous liquid. Two figures emerged from the blurred periphery. They seemed to move with infinite slowness as men walking underwater, then at last entered the tunnel behind Richards. As they did so, time and texture immediately returned to normal, as if the world were once again viewed through a perfectly focused lens.

Chinaman took a deep breath and relaxed. "Sam, don't turn

around, but there are two men behind you pointing guns in your direction. And I suspect they know how to use them."

Richards smiled broadly. "Chinaman, remember our poker games? How I always knew when you were bluffing? You always gave yourself away. You tried too hard to look relaxed. Like now."

At the sound of two revolver hammers being cocked into single action positions, his smile faded. One of the men behind him spoke. "Don't turn around. Just drop it."

Chinaman lowered his hands. "Do it, Sam. They mean business."

Richards turned his head without moving the gun. He saw the driver and his assistant holding their guns on him. "Don't be stupid! I'll give you half the shipment!"

Now it was the driver who assumed a modified Weaver stance. "I'll only tell you one more time. Drop the gun."

Richards hesitated, then lowered the gun, then dropped it. Chinaman moved quickly to him, kicked the gun away, and began frisking him. He removed a small frame Ruger five-shot from an ankle holster. The driver holstered his gun and walked to Chinaman. You OK?"

"I'm fine. Thanks to you two. Everything secured out there?"

"All secured." The driver bent to pick up Richard's SIG-Sauer. A streak of blood appeared between his knuckles.

"You hit?"

"Just a scratch."

"How about them?"

"Two wounded. One tied up. Sorry about the firefight. They were getting suspicious about why we'd replaced their regular drivers."

"So I noticed."

Richards looked from the man holding his gun to Chinaman and back to the man. "Why do I get the impression I'm missing something?"

Chinaman picked up his revolver and placed it alongside the

Ruger on a sack of coffee. He leaned forward and whisked off the driver's mustache and cap. Fluorescent light reflected off the man's high forehead. "Sam, meet Barry Cohn, private eye. And Larry Sterling of One Police Plaza. They persuaded your usual drivers to let them take over for one night."

Richards shook his head and smiled ruefully. "You really should have been a magician."

Chinaman took off his jacket as he spoke. "Naw, I'm just a run-of-the-mill detective is what I am, Sam. That's all I'll ever be."

Chinaman checked his watch as Abrams and his men entered the area with guns drawn. Abrams glanced first at Chinaman and then at Richards. He held the gun midway between them. Chinaman wondered if that were his way of saying there wasn't much to choose between the two of them. "Drop your weapons...Now what the hell is going on here?"

"Not much, Chief. This is Sam Richards. CIA. He ordered Judy Fisher killed so he could cover up his corruption and other murders. Now he's going to prison. But, first, he and I are about to have one last session; then he's all yours. Take off your coat, Sam."

"What?"

"Take your coat off."

"Are you serious?"

"Very serious. I don't think Judy would want you starting your 25 years to life looking as fit as you do now."

Abrams holstered his weapon. "I can't allow that, Chinaman."

Chinaman glared at him. "Yes, you can, Chief. Because you owe me one. After this, we're even. Barry will take you to the others. And I think you'll find enough guns and ammunition inside the coffee sacks to start a fair-sized revolution. Just be careful with the plastic explosive."

Abrams glanced at Barry Cohn, then glared at Larry Sterling. A glare that suggested that any friend of Chinaman's wasn't a friend of his — cop or no cop. He looked back at Chinaman then glanced at his watch. "You got ten minutes; then he goes with us." He waved to his men. "All right. Let's secure the building. Sterling, keep them *both* covered."

Sam Richards grinned and removed his coat. "You know the problem with you, Chinaman? You overestimate yourself."

"Maybe. But I've got some anger burning inside. That gives me an edge."

Ten minutes later, as two police officers helped a bloody, disheveled and nearly unconscious Sam Richards into the rear of a police car, Abrams looked him over and shook his head. "If you'd like to file a complaint for assault I'll be happy to get you a form."

Sam Richards managed a grin. "No, thank you."

"Then don't bleed all over my seat."

"I'll try not to."

Chinaman walked up rubbing his scraped knuckles and stood beside Abrams. "Problem, Chief?"

Abrams looked at his cut lip and seemed disappointed that there was so little damage. He walked to the passenger side front seat of the police car and got in. Just before he motioned for the driver to pull out he looked out at Chinaman. "Stop by for a beer some time. If you like."

Chinaman gave him a nod and watched the car speed off. It was the first open sign of approval his ex-father-in-law had ever favored him with. Chinaman couldn't believe how good it felt.

★

43

WHEN his watch sounded, he'd been jogging for nearly half an hour. Chinaman slowed to a brisk walk. He headed back through the East Village to his apartment; past a young hooker with bare, shapely legs and the rubbery face of an old woman, past a man with matted hair and a half empty gin bottle screaming at invisible enemies, past a used-up teenager selling soiled books on a table fashioned from a snowbank.

He felt good. He had made love for the first time since Judy died. He hadn't exactly set the bed on fire but, after a few false starts, it was Jo Anne he had made love to — not Judy. The smooth thighs and jutting breasts had belonged to Jo Anne — not Judy. The passionate woman in his arms had been Jo Anne — not Judy. Once he had found Judy's killers, she had released her grip on him.

If only he hadn't introduced her to Sam Richards. If only she hadn't been so willing to test her sexual prowess in trapping men. If only she had realized the game could turn deadly. If only. It was a cadence he could run to. Remorse. If only. Guilt. If only. Anger. If only.

He hadn't taken any key with him as Jo Anne would still be in. He felt good enough to get in bed with her again. If she had time before work. He hadn't locked the door but when he tried to open it he found the chain was on. "Jo Anne, it's me. Open up...Jo Anne!"

The door opened and Jo Anne appeared — fully dressed

with her now familiar overnight bag in one hand and a large crumpled paper in the other. Tears smudged her makeup but her main emotion was not sadness but anger. With the hand holding the paper she slapped his face. "You bastard!"

Chinaman blinked. "I thought you forgave me for missing amateur night."

"I'm not talking about amateur night!"

"Oh, Jesus. *Now* what did I do?"

She tried to slap him again but he caught her wrist and moved her inside and shut the door. "What has gotten into you?"

She thrust the paper at him and retreated a few steps. "*This* is what has gotten into me."

Chinaman unfolded the paper. It was a 'bad guy' target from the pistol range. Chinaman had seen this particular target before. The 'bad guy' had nine holes through the crotch area forming the shape of a heart. In the center of the holes someone had pressed their lipstick-smeared lips against it. A dainty red-and-white Santa cap, massive white beard and tiny spectacles transformed the "bad guy" into a grotesque, menacing Santa Claus. Across "Santa's" chest was a message in blue ink.

THOUGHT YOU MIGHT LIKE TO
KEEP THIS UNDER YOUR PILLOW OR
IN YOUR STOCKING AS A SOUVENIR.
HO, HO, HO! UNTIL NEXT TIME.

LOTS OF LOVE
CATHY

Chinaman turned to face Jo Anne. "Where the hell did this come from?"

Jo Anne moved to the door. "In the mail!"

"Jo Anne, don't be ridiculous. I can explain this. This is just some idiot woman at the pistol range who— well, she keeps coming on to me and–"

As she flung open the door, Chinaman followed her into the hallway. She stopped at the stairs, reached into her coat pocket and pulled out three rubber balls. Juggler's balls. She took careful aim and threw them at him, one after the other. Hard. Chinaman ducked two and caught one. Just before it would have hit his head.

He stood watching her descend the stairs, then walked back to the door. It had closed. He started to check the pockets of his warmup suit for his keys. His warmup suit had no pockets. And he had no credit card. He'd left home without it.

★ THE END ★

NEXT IN THE CHINAMAN SERIES:
MURDER IN DOMINATRIX BLACK

Praise for *Memoirs of a Bangkok Warrior*

"*Memoirs of a Bangkok Warrior* is a marvelous novel, yes-novel, about the Vietnam era. So marvelous that upon finishing it, I promptly handed it over to my brother, the Nam vet, and told him, read this - you'll love it. So, read it. You'll love it. I promise." Stars 5+
- *Buzz Review News*

"Funny from the first page to the last. A fine and funny book, ribald and occasionally touching. One of the better Asian reads of the past few years."
- *The Bangkok Post*

"Succeeds nicely in the creation of a time and place that transcends mere setting."
- West Coast Review of Books

"This is a funny and human book which can describe sex without descending into sheer nastiness."
- *South China Morning Post*

"This is M*A*S*H, taken from behind the Korean lines, set down in the rear-echelon of steamy Bangkok–titillated with the tinkle of Thai laughter and temple bells. And it is an even funnier triumph of man over military madness."
- Derek Maitland, author, *The only War we've Got*

"An Awesome read! Way out, Far out, Groovy....I can smell the smell and see the green and feel the magic of Thailand!"
- Terry Ryan, TCLB (*Thailand, Laos, Cambodian Brotherhood*)

"*Memoirs of a Bangkok Warrior* is recommended reading for anyone who ever donned a uniform and found themselves far from home."
- Midwest Book Review

"*Memoirs of a Bangkok Warrior* remains one of my favorite books about Thailand. Excellent characters and dialogue. It would make a great movie."
- Dave Walker, author, *Hello My Big, Big Honey*!

Praise for *Kingdom of Make-Believe*

"*Kingdom of Make-Believe* is an exciting thriller that paints a picture of
Thailand much different from that of *The King and I*.
The story line is filled with non-stop action, graphic details of the country,
and an intriguing allure that will hook readers of exotic thrillers.
Very highly recommended."
- BookBrowser.com

"A tantalizing taste of a culture, worlds apart from our own.
Dean Barrett paints a sharp, clear picture of the reality of life.
An excellent account of one man's struggle to find the truth in his existence.
Very highly recommended."
- Under the Covers Book Review

"An absolutely astounding novel.
Its depth and layers of perception will have
you fascinated from start to finish.
Highly entertaining!"
- Buzz Review News

"Barrett spins a tightly packed tale that is part murder mystery, part midlife
crisis love story and part travelogue, with vibrant and seductive Thailand in a
leading role. This mystery keeps the reader guessing at the next plot twist."
- Today's Librarian

"A gripping mystery documenting Dean Barrett as a writer in
full possession of his craft."
- Midwest Book Review

"Sharp, often poetic, and pleasantly twisted, *Kingdom of Make-Believe* is a
tautly written fictional tour of Thailand. Author Dean Barrett has woven a
compelling and believable tale about a country he knows well.
Barrett's prose is spare but his images are rich: a winning combination.
His obvious intimate knowledge of Thailand combined with a very
considerable writing talent make *Kingdom of Make-Believe*
a tough book to put down."
- January Magazine

Praise for *Hangman's Point*

"Setting is more than a backdrop in this fast-paced adventure story of mid-nineteenth-century British colonial Hong Kong....A riveting, action-packed narrative....Chinese scholar, linguist, and author of two previous books, Barrett draws on his vast knowledge of southern China during a time of enormous change and conflict, providing richly fascinating detail of the customs, fashions, ships, and weapons of the times."
- ALA Booklist

"An expert on Hong Kong and the turbulent time period portrayed, Dean Barrett has fashioned a swashbuckling adventure which will have both history buffs and thriller readers enthralled from the very first page. An outstanding historical novel."
-Writers Write Reviews

"If Patrick O'Brian's Aubrey and Maturin ever got as far as Hong Kong in 1857 on their world travels, the aged sea dogs would feel right at home in China expert Dean Barrett's totally convincing novel of high adventure."
-Dick Adler, *Amazon.com Reviews*

"A great epic of a historical mystery."
-Bookbrowser Reviews

"The adventures of this latter-day Indiana Jones will leave him fleeing for his life through the town of Victoria (Hong Kong), bring him face to face with the perils of the pirate-infested waters of the Pearl River, and finally fix him a date with death at *Hangman's Point*....The novel is peppered with well-defined characters from all walks of life....It would be just another potboiler a la James Clavell, but Barrett's extensive research sets this novel apart: as well as a ripping adventure story, it is an intimately drawn historical portrait."
-South China Morning Post

"There is adventure and mystery in every corner of this well-researched and well-written historical."
-1BookStreet.com

"Rich in historical perspective and characters, Barrett's debut is good news for those who love grand scale adventure."
-*The Poisoned Pen Booknews*

"*Hangman's Point* is vastly entertaining, informative and thought-provoking....Dean Barrett weaves an intricate and many-layered tale. Barrett clearly has in-depth knowledge of his field, more so than most Western novelists can command....Barrett offers more than an exciting story. He provides an understanding view of China and the Chinese, guiding readers toward a fuller appreciation of that complex culture."
- *Stuart News*

"*Hangman's Point* is a great historical fiction that, if there is any justice, will enable Dean Barrett to become a household name. Highly Recommended."
-*Under The Covers Book Review*

"Excellently written and steeped in details of the times, all obviously very well researched and accurate."
-*The Midwest Book Review*

"Adams's adventurers take him on a thrilling chase, almost an odyssey....*Hangman's Point* is a page-turner that is guaranteed to keep both male and female readers enthralled to the very end. Romance and high adventure."
Romantic Times

Dean Barrett first arrived in Asia as a Chinese linguist with the American Army Security Agency. He has lived and traveled in Asia for over 20 years. His novels on Thailand are *Kingdom of Make-Believe* and *Memoirs of a Bangkok Warrior*. His novels set in China are *Hangman's Point* and *Mistress of the East*. Several of his plays have been staged in the United States and his musical set in 1857 Hong Kong, *Fragrant Harbour*, was selected by the National Alliance for Musical Theater to be presented on 42nd Street, NYC. Mr. Barrett is a member of Mystery Writers of America.

Sample chapters and covers of his books can be found on-line at http://www.angelfire.com/de/YumCha/Novels.html.